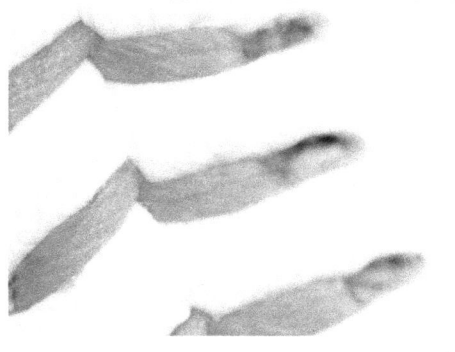

VARSITY
Rulebreaker

GINGER SCOTT

VARSITY RULEBREAKER

VARSITY SERIES BOOK 3

GINGER SCOTT

Cover Design by Ginger Scott, Little Miss Write LLC

Cover photo by Michelle Lancaster

Cover model Andy Murray

Print ISBN: 978-1-952778-05-6

For Ruthie.
I could not have done this without you.

1

CANNON JENNINGS

I'm perfectly content ringing in the new year with a sparkler and leftover pizza. Unfortunately, my cousin Zack is an extrovert. He *needs* to feed off the energy of others. I prefer to eliminate distractions.

"It's one party, Can. You need to pull the stick out of your ass and enjoy one night. One party will not derail your future."

Zack has been on me about loosening up for weeks. Deep down, he's probably right . . . to an extent. If I keep grinding like this through my entire senior year, I'll burn out before I even land at summer camp wherever I get signed. But when you've dreamed of pitching for Vandy since you were six years old and it's legit within your reach, it's hard to let up off the gas, even just a little.

"Come on, man. It's New Year's Eve." Zack's head falls to one side and his lip juts out.

"Are you gonna fuckin' cry?" I toss my glove to the

corner of the sofa and get to my feet. Zack rubs his hands together while shuffling his feet in this weird-ass jig.

"I'm not going if you're going to do that," I say, pointing at his lower half. He freezes and instantly stands tall, rolling his shoulders and clearing his throat.

"Sorry. Must have been overcome with shock that Cannon Jennings is actually going to do something social," he says.

"*Pfft*," I huff at him. I grab my keys and my lucky hat and we both head out to my car.

Zack is overexaggerating. I've been social. I went to a party a week ago, and I've made some decent friends. I've done pretty well for being the new guy at school. I moved in with my cousin over the summer as part of the grand plan my dad and my uncle, Zack's dad, devised to maximize the attention we both could get for offers to play college ball. Zack has caught for as long as I have pitched, and we used to play together when we were younger. But Zack's family moved to Indiana for work right after junior high, and it broke up our dream duo. We've both done all right without the other, but we've got one more year to really show our stuff, and Allensville Public High just hired a new coach—with Division One coaching experience. It means I'm sleeping on the futon in the spare room at Zack's while my parents sell our place in New Mexico. Once they do, we'll move into a rental together—and I'll have a bed that doesn't fold up during the day.

"I don't know June very well," I mention as we pull up to the Mabee house. We only live two blocks from them, so the drive was easy.

"Yeah, but you know Lucas, so it's all good," Zack reassures me.

He gets out of the car with an actual skip in his step, still cradling the six-pack of micro brew he snuck from his dad.

I let myself enjoy the quiet of the car for one more breath. He's right. I've gotten to know Lucas pretty well, and the D'Angelo twins. They're all pretty decent athletes, and it's nice to mess around and do things with a group of guys who aren't all about baseball. I gel with Tory D'Angelo the most. He's got plans to play basketball in college, so he gets my constant focus. I swear, as much as my cousin Zack *says* he wants to play college ball, he doesn't seem to have the obsessive passion that I think it takes.

My cousin raps on the window, tired of waiting on me, so I get out and put on my best *happy-to-be-here* face.

It's a strange collection of people inside. Someone who clearly is someone's father opens the door for us, and he eyes the beer in Zack's hand as we enter.

"Maybe we shouldn't have brought beer," I whisper to my cousin, but he ignores me, weaving through the house and into the garage, where an extra refrigerator is stuffed with drinks. He pulls a beer out and hands it to me, taking one for himself, too. I arch a brow, not sure this is allowed.

"It's fine. June said as long as we don't make it obvious around the adults, we're good to go." Zack pops the cap off and takes a swig, gesturing for me to do the same. I do, but only because drinking half this beer might settle the knots in my chest. I'm not so great at social things.

We weave through the house to the back yard where I recognize more faces. My shoulders relax when I spot

3

Lucas sitting near the fire pit with space next to him. I nod in his direction, letting Zack know where he can find me, and head toward the flames. Lucas's girlfriend, June, beats me to the open seat by two seconds, and I'm about to bail when an absolute goddess steps in behind them.

I don't know a lot of people in town or at school, but how I've missed this face, I have no idea. She's tall, maybe only an inch or two shorter than my six-foot-three, and her long blonde hair looks like molten gold as she stands near the fire. I can't tell if her eyes are gray or blue, but I need to get closer to settle the debate in my head. She's supermodel hot, but playing it down in a pair of baggy jeans and an old baseball jersey worn over a hoodie to keep her warm. I bet her dressed-down look keeps her under the radar. Most of the fucking douchebags at this school only want to keep score and see who can date the hot girl first. Lucky for me, she showed up tonight dressed for the part of *exactly my type*.

"Jeter fan, huh?" I say, stepping up next to her and tugging on her jersey sleeve.

A short laugh puffs from her naturally pink lips while she takes a small sip from her cup. I suspect she's actually drinking soda, so I casually set my beer on a small patio table behind me.

"Yankee fan. Jeter's all right," she says, a wry smile on her mouth. I hold her stare for a full breath, partly to challenge her and also to get a good handle on the color of her eyes. Blue, and maybe a little green too.

I match her smirk with one of my own, letting it crawl up into my cheeks before glancing down at the small patch emblazoned on the right sleeve of the jersey. This thing came from a game.

"Bullshit," I say, nodding toward it.

She twists her head to the side and tucks her chin, noting the authentication patch with a slight breath and a smile.

"You got me," she says, her eyes flitting up to mine. I again hold them for a long second, this time because I like the way it feels when I challenge her to return my stare. She's a worthy opponent, and I'm the first to break.

"You a fan?" she asks.

"Of the Yankees? Fuck no. But Jeter's special; he's like a level above the Yankees. He's folklore," I say.

Our baseball banter must annoy Lucas and June because they make a lame excuse to leave us alone. We take over their seats, propping our feet on the lip of the firepit and settling in so we can glance at one another.

"I have another one of these . . . signed," she says, pulling down the front of the jersey to even out the Yankees logo.

I lift my brows, impressed. Also, I catch a hint of her accent, which I'm pretty sure is from the heart of New York, possibly one of the boroughs.

"Super fan, I take it?"

She wobbles her head side to side, playfully, and her eyes dance with this proud kind of joy you only get when you have a childhood full of memories at the ballpark. I know because I've got them, too. Between spring nights at New Mexico State and spring breaks spent in Arizona hunting autographs from my favorite MLB stars at training camps, I've got a pretty full childhood of baseball fairy tales of my own. I can't wait to write my name into those stories.

"I'm Cannon. I'm new here," I say, holding out my hand.

She blinks at it, her lips parted for a few seconds before speaking. She finally takes my palm in hers, her grip impressive.

"I'm Hollis, and I'm new here too."

Definitely from New York.

"Long Island?" I question.

She quirks a brow and blows out from her lips.

"Heck no. Staten Island, baby." She's teasing me, and it's cute as hell. I should have known; Long Islanders are Mets fans.

"Ah, right. Well, nice to meet you, Hollis. I'm from New Mexico. Not nearly as exciting as your big city," I say with a shrug.

"I don't know," she says, leaning her head back and looking up at the sky. I follow her gaze to the stars and the embers popping in the air above us. "You probably have some pretty epic views where you're from."

She's right. We do. Or, at least, we did. I guess these are my views now. Lots of . . . trees.

"We're both from Allensville now, don't you think?" I put that idea out there while we stare up at the black sky, speckled with salt diamonds and masked by smoke.

She sighs.

"Yeah, I guess we are." She drops her chin to her chest and I do the same. "We came from both ends and met in the middle."

She has a way of letting this faint smile linger on her

lips after she finishes talking, and I'm having a hard time looking away. Normally, I'd be embarrassed by my overt infatuation with a girl. I'm shitty at flirting. But Hollis, she makes this pretty easy.

"So, what brought you here? To the middle?" I ask.

Her brow pulls in with thought, but that faint smile is still there. She's calculating something. Maybe it's how much to tell a guy she just met.

"Family . . . er, work. My dad moved here for work." I sense that she's conflicted by something, so I don't pry. She probably misses a lot of things from home. I get that. I miss my parents, but at least they'll be here eventually. Can't really move New York to the middle of Indiana.

"We moved here for family too, sorta. I came to play ball with my cousin. He's here, somewhere." I glance over my shoulder, only to find that everyone in the back yard has disappeared. We're completely alone out here.

"I'd introduce you, but . . ." I hold out open palms when I look back to her, and she giggles. The sound she makes pushes my half smile up high into my cheeks, and I quickly realize I'm grinning like a fool. I don't stop, though. I let the ache remain on my foolish face because maybe I've just met my soulmate in pinstripes.

"We must have missed the memo," she says, looking beyond me and into the house.

It was after eleven when Zack and I left the house, so the countdown is probably on for the new year.

"You wanna go in?" I ask her, moving my gaze back to her eyes. This time, she dares me, studying my face intently as if waiting to call my bluff. I don't have one. I'll literally go wherever she tells me to. I'm hoping—

"I don't like crowds. You cool ringing in the new year out here with some girl from Staten Island?"

Foolish grin makes its second appearance on my face, so I lick my lips to tame it just a little.

"For sure," I say, leaning forward with my feet on the ground and elbows on my knees. "Though, you're an Allensville girl now, aren't you?"

She breathes out a laugh and stands, stretching her arms to the sky. It lifts her jersey and sweatshirt just enough that I get a glimpse of her cream-colored skin and the silver stud in her belly button. I never thought that would be my thing, but it's totally my thing. Maybe it's only my thing on beautiful blondes from Staten Island.

"Let me get used to being an Indiana girl for a while, then we can move on to the local titles, yeah?" She sounds so tough when she talks, and the contrast with her angelic face would be almost comical if it weren't so goddamn mesmerizing.

I stand so I can match her height, and maybe get a better read on whether it's okay to kiss a girl I just met at a party I didn't want to go to. I kinda think maybe it is, but only because she didn't want to be here either. And because she's wearing a Jeter jersey. And because I'm pretty sure her eyes have put a spell on me.

With a foot of space between us, I measure how close we come in height while she glances around me to the house filled with people who have started counting down from ten. I was right to guess we're only two or three inches apart. She licks the corner of her lips and smiles, her cheeks suddenly red, and not from the heat of the fire.

"Happy New Year, Hollis from Indiana," I say, my lips

in a closed-lip smile to stem off the hungry vibrations urging my body to lunge at her and taste her tongue.

"Happy New Year, Cannon from Indiana," she returns, biting her lower lip but only briefly. She's trying to keep up the act that she's tougher than I am. Maybe she is.

I step toward her, my movement slow and cautious while I read her body language. She doesn't move away, and her hands don't nervously fidget at her sides. They're tucked in the pocket of her hoodie, the front of the jersey lifted so she can slip them inside the warmth underneath. She's so calm I'd almost think she's sleeping with her eyes open, but I know she's not. She's staring at me with a dare—a welcoming dare.

I take another small step, lifting my hand to her chin and touching the pad of my thumb to the soft skin just below her pouting lip. I brush away her hair and bring my other hand up to cup her face.

"Happy New Year," I whisper one last time, mostly to test the waters and see if she flinches. She merely breathes the words back and closes the remaining inches between our mouths until we're locked in an electrifying kiss that feels like fucking home. I lift her chin, coaxing her mouth open just enough for me to slip my tongue inside to taste her sweet mouth. Her lips move with me, and her hands come up to grab at the front of my own hoodie, tugging on the strings as she slips away slowly with a giggle.

My face is numb in the wake of our kiss. It was ten seconds of my life, but quickly rockets up on my top-five moments list.

"Thanks for the New Year's kiss, Cannon. I have to get home, but . . . maybe we can hang out sometime?" She lets go of the strings, her finger drawing a line down the center of my chest as she backs away.

"Most definitely," I say, a bit stupefied that I've been so quickly whipped by a girl I barely know. Maybe it's the haze of New Year's Eve, or maybe I really have been over-working myself and I'm exhausted. Whatever it is, I'm grinning like an idiot again and it doesn't go away for the rest of the night.

I've never had a coach want to hold a meeting with his potential players on January second, but that's what makes coming here an even better decision. Coach Taylor has a reputation for being stern. His last job was at some private school in New York, and they took state twice, back-to-back. He sent us all texts on New Year's Day telling us he wanted to get started with workouts before tryouts come up. There was a subtle overtone that the serious players would be here, so Zack and I arrived before anyone else just to prove we're a cut above dedicated.

It's cold as hell outside, so Coach invited us all to the small clubhouse behind the dugout. This might be a great program I'm walking into, but the facility is shit. Back home, we had brand new everything. My school was barely eight years old, which in terms of a high school lifespan is infant-like. This place was built in fifty-seven. The club-house has a plate on the door that says DEDICATED IN 1965. I'm not sure we aren't breathing in lead and asbestos.

"Gentlemen," Coach says, clearing his throat and getting our attention. There's another cough from the back, but I can't quite see who it's from. From the way it sounded, it came off a little bit snarky, like someone making fun of the new coach's style. Coach seems to have picked up on the same nuance because he's staring back there with a scowl on his face.

Bad idea, dude, whoever you are.

"First, thank you all for coming in today. The bad news is this isn't just a meeting. We'll be running two miles too. I'd like to see you all come in under ten minutes by the time season starts."

The collective groan is comical. Me and Zack, though, we keep our mouths shut. Some of the guys showed up in slip-ons, and I have a sneaking suspicion Coach is not going to care. They'll be running either in those or barefoot. Zack and I always dress. In fact, we have our gear and cleats in the car just in case.

Coach spends the next few minutes going over basics, like I had to do at my old school. I've already taken care of the things on the list like my physical and the waiver forms. I zone out through most of his talk, but perk up when he mentions competing for roster spots. Zack doesn't flinch, probably because he's been the starting catcher since freshman year. He's solid. I am too. Hell, from what Zack told me, I will probably be the ace this year; but still, it's never good to assume. There's always someone busting their ass out there. I have to work harder.

"I'll be pairing you guys for head-to-heads and training. Competition fosters greatness, and I don't believe positions are guaranteed; they are earned. You understand me?"

"Yes, sir," we all say. Funny how we know we're supposed to.

"Okay, so listen for your names to be called. This will be your group until we move into official tryouts next month and I have our final roster. I'm keeping fifteen, and other than pitchers, some of you might not get to play. If you're okay with that, stick around. If not, well, thanks for coming in today."

Nobody leaves, but I can tell a few of the guys sitting in front of Zack and me want to. I glance sideways at Zack and he lifts his brows.

"This guy isn't fucking around," he says.

I breathe out a laugh and shake my head.

"Jennings," Coach says.

Zack and I both answer.

"Oh, right. I meant Cannon first. Pitcher only, right?" Coach peers at me, his finger pushing up the brim of his hat just enough to bring his eyes out of the shadow. They're crystal blue and a bit like lasers, wrinkled at the corners from squinting in the sun for years, I imagine.

"Yes, sir," I respond.

He nods and makes a note on his clipboard.

"Jennings, Zack," he says, reading my cousin's name as it's probably written. "You'll be working with Hollis."

Hollis? I casually glance around the room, not seeing the girl of my dreams. Maybe I didn't hear it right.

The first thing I notice on Zack is the way his forehead creases, a dent between his brows. His mouth is parked in an O shape, so I slide my right foot into his to jostle him from this sudden trance.

"Hollis, uhm, okay. Sure." He heard the same name I did. He also did not say *yes, sir,* and given the way Coach narrowed his eyes on him, it was not the right move.

Coach holds his clipboard against his chest, folding his arms over it and leaning his head to the side. I think if he could give Zack a detention for that answer, he would.

"Is there a problem with that?" Coach's brows are lifted in expectation. I tap my foot against Zack again, willing him to respond.

"No, sir. No," he sputters out.

"Good," Coach says. "You might learn a thing or two from her."

From her. Oh . . . fuck.

"You mind working out with a girl, Jennings?" Her voice is as rich with her Staten Island roots as it was when I kissed her two nights ago. Puzzle pieces fly together: her accent, Coach's accent. His eyes, her eyes. New to town, her dad moved for work.

I turn just enough to catch her pulling her catcher's helmet and mask from her head, her blonde hair tied up in a knot at the base of her neck.

"Gear's a little tight, but it should do," she says, handing it to her dad.

Fuck me, that's her dad.

"Thanks for taking it for a ride," he says, nodding to his daughter.

Fuck me, that's his daughter.

"Sure, but next time remember . . . it's *ladies* and gentlemen when you're talking to us, 'kay?" she says, reaching forward and playfully punching his arm. Guess I know where the laugh came from when he started his speech. Pretty sure he's not going to punish her for it, either, on account of her being right and all. Oh, and being his freaking spawn.

"Hey, Cannon from Indiana," she says, the same mischievous bend to her lips that made me feel absolutely drunk on her mouth forty-eight hours ago.

I don't dare respond with the same flirtatious tone I used last time, instead opting to nod as she backs away with a wink. I think I just got played.

"Your partner is leaving without you, son," Coach says to Zack. My cousin is still a bit stiff from the shock of having to fight for his position against his new coach's daughter. Talk about delicate.

"Oh, yeah. Thank you. I'll catch up," Zack says, his words all jumbled and hesitant. His confidence literally just crawled away and sank through the cracks of the club-house's concrete floor.

Not wanting the same fate, I grab my bag from under the bench so I can escape without taking more blows to my ego. I'm nearly out, too, when Coach stops me by hollering my name. I turn with my back flat on the door, my mouth suddenly dry with the mystery of the unknown.

"I see you know my daughter."

There's a pregnant pause that's thick enough to choke our football team's offensive line. I keep expecting him to say more, to ask a question or shoot me some warning to stay away from her, which of course I will absolutely obey. He doesn't. Just that one statement, along with his laser stare from his weathered death eyes.

"A little. We just met," I say, finally, my delayed response clearly exposing my nerves.

"Hmm," he says with a nod.

I pull my lips in tight, mostly to keep from saying anything else.

"Go on," he says, after another painful pause.

Yes, sir. I only think it this time.

I round the clubhouse and look out on the track, where Hollis is about to lap someone. Zack hasn't even finished tying his laces. My cousin is in trouble, but not as much as I am. If I want to make it to Vanderbilt, or anywhere *like* Vandy, I need to be at the top of my game. One midnight kiss, though, and my season is cursed. So help me if that vixen ends up calling my pitches.

2

HOLLIS TAYLOR

For a bedroom filled with so much crap, it's weird how I can't seem to find anything. We've been moved in for a month. That's thirty days I've had to dump my clothes out of trash bags and put them into actual drawers. I miss my gym, though, and I found a place to lift and work out that I want to try. The only thing stopping me is locating my Nikes. I'm probably compounding things by the piles I'm making in the center of my floor while I search.

"Mom!" She's going to rip me a new one the second she walks in, but her lecture is worth the use of her location superpowers. My mom can find anything. My dad reported a credit card missing last Christmas, before consulting her. The moment she found out he lost it, she walked straight out of the house and to the driveway where she began surveying the bushes. She plucked it from some branches in seconds and held it up proudly. He'd been holding it in his teeth while wheeling in the trash receptacles the night before and must have spit it out and forgot. She remembered; she *always* remembers.

"Jesus H. Ch—"

"I know. I'm working on it," I lie, cutting off my mom's assessment of my room mid-blaspheme.

She digs her fingertips into her forehead with both hands as she steps over the pile in the entryway and into the center of my room. Chin down and jaw tight, she holds back all the little comments I know she'd like to make about *how could she have raised such a slob.*

"Nikes," I say. It's best to give her a task.

She breathes out through her nose loud enough that I fully understand how irritated she is. She makes a slow quarter-turn while she scans the perimeter of my room and stops abruptly, letting out another huff that indicates I would have seen them myself if I only got my shit together.

"They are on your PlayStation, for whatever reason," she says through a grimace.

"That's right!" I leap over the new pile I made and grab my shoes before leaping toward my mom and kissing her on the cheek. "You're the best."

"*Mmm hmm,*" she hums.

"Keys?" I know, it's a big ask considering the state of my room. My parents are suckers, though. With her tongue over her front teeth, she sucks in and reluctantly hands me the keys to the van.

"Tonight, this gets taken care of, okay?" She doesn't bother to look me in the eyes, and it's probably because she knows I'll fail at her ultimatum. I'll try to unpack, though. I truly will.

"Deal," I say, catching the short laugh that leaves her chest, showing her doubt.

I dart from my room, shoes in one hand and keys in the other while my mom lingers in my room and opens my drawers. I bet most of my things are put away by the time I get back.

"Off to try that workout place. I'll let you know," I shout at my dad as I hit the driveway. He gives me a quick wave while playing street hockey with my little brother, Ben. He's taking shots at my brother with whiffle balls. Ben is eight, and he wants to be a goalie. My dad tried to talk him into catching instead, but Ben is obsessed with the ice. He's going to outgrow my dad's hockey-coaching skills soon, but until then, Coach Travis Taylor will be splitting time between the ice and the grass.

I slip my feet into my untied shoes before backing the van out, my dad moving my brother's goal out of the way while I pull into the road. It's going to take me a while to line up the view I'm used to seeing with the one I will for the rest of my senior year. Both my old street and this one are tree-lined, and both houses have a certain nineteen-seventies charm about them with banged up vinyl siding and pretend shutters glued on either side of the windows. But where a two-minute jaunt down a Staten Island road took me to Sal's Meats and Cheese, Al's Liquors, Rose's Deli, and Rick Manning's Boxing Elite—the gym I grew up on—the only thing two minutes down this street is more trees. They're nothing but winter sticks now, but I bet when spring rolls around, it's pretty.

Having a real yard is nice too. And Dad promised Mom a pool in the ground. The above-grounder we had back home—our *old* home—leaked twice a season. Even when I take off for college, my family will stay put. That's what this deal is about, finding a good place to settle in and raise Ben. While I loved being so close to the city, it made my parents nervous. They said Ben isn't tough like I am, which I guess I can kinda see. He doesn't get bullied or nothin', but he's quiet. Whatever their logic is or was, it ended up with us living here.

At least I get to be part of a better team during my senior year. Xavier Prep back home was competitive, but only against other small schools. We won state in a tiny division that means nothing to colleges because our school was more about academics. We didn't exactly have the largest pool of ball players to choose from, either. And the parents on the board were not keen on the idea of me playing on a team with boys. It didn't seem to bother them enough to fund a softball team—not that I wanted to switch sports—but the topic sure dominated the conversation at parent meetings.

"What's she gonna do, play football next?"

"I suppose Coach Grady will bring his daughter in to QB?"

"She's going to get hurt."

My dad and I heard that last argument time and time again, and it irks me the most. Nobody knows how much I can endure, not even my father. Some trials in life are survived and meant to be kept close to the chest, used to build armor and grow strength. I'm strong on my own, but the battles I've come through on my journey to do something I love have definitely shaped my fortitude. They're my stories to either tell or keep tucked inside, and I see no reason to share them with anyone.

After ten minutes of weaving through streets and stop-sign intersections, I spot A&P Fitness. It's promising, especially because the building doesn't look like some slick treadmill factory. Rick's was a boxing gym, so I'm used to working with free weights and jump ropes. The occasional speed bag is fun too. I pull into a spot near the door, between two sedans. I should probably back out and move somewhere else; the fit is tight. But before I shift into reverse, a jacked-up pickup slides into the spot behind me. I won't be here long; this is only an exploratory visit.

I grab my dad's ear pods from the center console and head inside. I'm greeted by a heavy boom that echoes around the brick walls, and I flinch a little.

"It's just the tire," says an older man from behind a desk. I'd guess he's in his late sixties, but maybe he's just a smoker. His skin is pretty tan and wrinkled. Straw-like blond hair pokes through the sides and back of his trucker cap, and his arms fill the sleeves of his Notre Dame T-shirt. He's fit for a senior. I have a good idea this place belongs to him.

"Ah," I say, glancing around the gym again until I find a familiar body squatting to lift the side of a monster tire. His body was the first thing I noticed about Cannon at the New Year's party. Tacky and predictable, maybe, but he's not built like the guys back home. He's taller. And pretty stacked for a pitcher. I see why now that I watch him pushing up what must weigh 400 pounds with ease. His gaze hits mine briefly across the tire's tread.

"Hi," I mouth, holding up a hand. His cheeks sink in,

his jaw clenching as he grunts and hoists the tire over again. The boom doesn't startle me this time. Cannon looks away, tearing tape from his hands with his teeth.

"You know the Jennings boys?"

"Huh?" I jerk back to the muscle-man behind the counter. "Oh. A little. I'm new here, like Cannon. From Indiana."

I giggle lightly to myself, but he just looks at me like I'm nuts.

"You're from Indiana?" The man quirks a brow, and I realize how stupid that sounded.

"No, it's just a nickname. Sorry, inside joke," I mumble.

"Ah," he grunts. He centers himself at his register and I spot the half-empty pack of cigarettes left on the chair he was sitting in. My assessment is spot on so far.

"You wanna a day pass, sugar?"

I roll my shoulders from habit. Some men have always talked to women that way, but it still makes me want to vomit and punch them when they do it to me. That's what you get when your mom teaches women's studies for an online university. I hear the same lessons every semester, and the one about the cycle of labeling hits home.

"Sure, pumpkin," I shoot back. His eyes dart up, away from his register drawer, probably not sure he heard me right. I wink to let him know he did, and he laughs through one side of his mouth—the one with a well-chewed tooth-pick hanging out.

"Alright, then," he says. I hand over my card and he rings me up for a five-dollar pass while I scan the board behind him for the monthly rates. There's an old black-

and-white photo tacked on a corkboard, and even though I don't quite see the similarities, I take a gamble.

"That you?" I motion to it.

He glances behind him and pulls the pin from the board, bringing the photo closer.

"In my prime," he says, fond memories tugging up the corners of his mouth, toothpick and all. He leans forward on both elbows, studying the photo closely.

"You know, I could have put those Jennings punks in their place back in my day. Joker flips that tire like he's something, but I'd like to see him move the whole goddamn tractor!" His joke echoes loud enough that Cannon turns his head and grimaces. I can tell this banter must be normal between them.

"Well, I'll try and put him in his place for ya. What do you say?" I expect more of a laugh than I get, but there's a slight smirk and hint of a nod. He's daring me to try, or at least, I decide that's what that gesture means.

I move over to the area near Cannon, dropping my things on the metal chair in the corner and pulling one of the jump ropes from a hook on the concrete wall. He paces around the tire with his hands threaded behind his neck, a good deal of sweat discoloring his gray T-shirt, his hair slick and floppy and super sexy. His hands fall to the bottom of his shirt as he turns to face me, and he lifts the front to wipe the moisture from his face, giving me a good view of his perfectly sculpted abs and widening chest. He's disciplined, and that is sexier than the damp waves of hair falling into his eyes, but just barely.

"This is a cool place," I say, swinging the rope out to untangle it as I hold on to either end.

"I guess," Cannon laughs out, a bit abruptly for someone whose tongue was in my mouth a couple of days ago. My gaze ices over as he turns away.

"Oh, I get it," I say, lining the rope up with the front of my feet. I glance up to briefly catch his eyes on mine.

"What?" he grunts, grabbing a water bottle from the floor near my things. He twists the top and guzzles down every last drop.

"Nothing. Just that you're one of those," I say with a shrug. Swinging the rope out, I wait for it to come back at my feet and I jump, a methodical double bounce to my feet as I whirl the heavy rubber rope in circles around my body to get my heart rate up.

"One of what?" He doesn't make the *pfft* sound after his words, but it's implied in the sour look he wears. Standing, he grabs a rope and moves about ten feet away, turning to face me as he jumps rope a little faster than me.

I wobble my head side-to-side and glance up, catching sight of the loose blonde hairs that have crept out from my head band and hair tie. I blow at them, maintaining my jumping speed. I'm not winded in the least. Back home, we lived on a hill. Dad made me sprint up it ten times in a row before I was allowed to sit at the dinner table. This rope, it's nothing.

"One of those guys who kisses girls for fun, then acts like a total prick the next time he sees them." The *thwap* of my rope against the concrete floor picks up its pace as I take away the double bounce and jump fast enough to hear the wind caused by my rope whirling through the air.

Cannon's rope stops completely.

"Okay, now, hey," he says, a defensive shake to his head. "That's not fair."

He runs the side of his fist over his brow to blot away sweat, his rope clutched against his hip in his other hand.

"Okay, how?" I continue to swing and jump, my heart rate picking up. Like hell am I gonna let my breathing pattern reflect that, though. I'll pass out first.

"How? *Pfft!*" Aannd there it is. His forehead dents and he puffs out a heavy laugh. I can't wait for the excuse he's trying to form. I see his brain working in overdrive behind his scrunched-up eyes. He's still pretty, just a little less so because I don't like boys who act like assholes to make themselves feel cool or whatever.

"You didn't tell me you were Coach's daughter!" He points at me with the same hand that holds the rope, and it swings harshly as he gesticulates. I can't help but laugh, which only pushes more of his buttons. Irritated, he grabs my rope mid-air and tangles it around his palm, ripping the ends from my grasp.

"I'm sorry, was I supposed to offer up my resume?" I giggle at the thought and imagine that scenario playing out.

Hi, I'm Hollis Taylor. I'm almost eighteen, and my favorite foods are fried zucchini and every kind of cheese. My parents are Dina and Travis Taylor, and they're forty-two and forty-three, respectively. Oh, and my father, he's a coach. Oh, you play baseball? Me, too! No, not for fun. Like you! No, I don't think I should play softball. Why? Because I like baseball. Oh, but it's for boys? Huh, I didn't know that. Is there a sign somewhere that says NO GIRLS ALLOWED?

"You don't understand," he grunts out, interrupting the

argument going down in my head. Cannon continues to pace with both of our ropes tangled in one hand.

"Spot me?" I say, moving on to the squat rack. I shuffle the plates around, pulling out the forty-fives while he fusses with the mess he made with the ropes.

I've got my bar ready to lift by the time he's done, but he stops about ten feet short of the rack, his hands on his hips, shirt soaked with sweat and his black joggers pushed up on his calves in that super cute way.

"No, I'm not going to spot you. I can't . . . I mean, you're—"

"Coach's daughter," I say with a roll of the eyes. I step under the bar and find the right fit along my shoulders. I wait a beat to see if he gives in, and when he doesn't budge I step forward with the bar balanced along my back and shoulders and steady my feet. I get through two whole squats before he mutters, *"Fuck"* to himself and steps in to assist me.

We don't talk through my first set, and he shakes his head when I offer to trade off and on with him. I tend to step side to side when my muscles recover, keeping the burn at bay and making the most of the tingles as blood rushes to the skin. I catch Cannon's eyes on my feet, though, so I abruptly stop to get his attention. I tap a toe until he looks me in the eyes. God, his face is beautiful. His eyes are this deep ocean blue, and his hair is the kind that I'm sure looks good right out of bed. I smile at him with tight lips, silently urging him to spill it, whatever his unexplainable issue seems to be. His expression tightens, his eyes pinch, and his gaze dips to my neck for a full breath.

"My cousin Zack, he's our catcher. Our *starting* catcher."

"Well, I mean, that's not really decided yet, so . . ." I know where this is going. I'm used to it. It's partly the reason we're *in* Indiana.

"No, you don't get it. Zack and me, we're family, and we've had this plan for years, to do this together. Our dads have had this plan. Zack, he gets the best out of me. Throwing to him is basically the entire reason I'm out here. And, I mean, just because your dad is the coach . . ." His eyes droop with this desperate plea for me to bend to his will, without forcing him to finish that sentence—*that incredibly offensive, full-of-false-assumptions sentence*. If I were another guy, he wouldn't say these things. He'd tell Zack to suck it up and compete. Double standards are so obvious to the one getting stung by them; meanwhile, the perpetrators are ignorant to their own biases.

I guess I'm glad I got the sweet kiss before this conversation. It was a nice kiss, and I choose to keep it separate from this display before me. Maybe I'll pretend they are two completely different people—the New Year's Cannon and this sexist one who doesn't want a girl in his boys' club. Nodding silently to myself, I glance to the floor as I close the distance between us until I'm close enough to flatten my palm on the cold wet cotton clinging to his chest. He's rock hard beneath my touch. Damn if both Cannons aren't built to perfection.

With hooded eyes, I lift my chin just as he tucks his, the feel of his heartbeat strong underneath my hand. I tap out its rhythm a few times and his gaze flits briefly to my fingertips, then back to my eyes. The slight tick up on the right side of his lips probably means he thinks things are going his way. They're not. Not even close.

"Cannon Jennings from Indiana by way of New Mexico, you have no idea what I'm capable of, so I wouldn't rush to judge. Maybe I'm the catcher who makes you great. Or maybe I make someone else great, and you, you ride pine a lot more than you're prepared to."

My lips close with the satisfied curve that comes along with saying the perfect thing at the perfect time in the perfect way. I let the smile linger as I back away until my shoulders run into the cool metal of the bar and I situate myself, ready for a second set. I lift an eyebrow. In the face of my challenge to pick a side, he does, leaning forward to spit on the concrete, just beyond his shoes.

"This is bullshit," he says, shaking his head as if I've actually broken some sort of law by being good at a game. He tosses his empty water bottle in a nearby recycle bin with a flick and picks up his keys and a towel from the wall on the other side of the gym. He holds up a hand to wave at the old man behind the counter; he grunts in return. Bright light spills into the gym as Cannon pushes through the heavy metal door without bothering to give me a final glance. It slams closed behind him, and I move with the weight on my shoulders to begin my second set alone.

It's the same every time. Every team. And I'll prove him, Zack, the whole fucking roster, wrong, the way I always do. It's a shame I had to kiss him first. And that he had to be so damn good at it.

3

CANNON

I didn't tell Zack about my little run-in with Hollis. Pete doesn't exactly make newcomers feel welcome at the gym, so I'm thinking she won't be back anyway. Hell, the only reason Pete can stand me is that Zack's been coming here for three years.

I noticed he charged Hollis for a day pass. I've never seen him do that once. *Ha!* He certainly never charged me before my parents were able to get automatic payments set up for him. That's probably half the reason he likes me, honestly. My mom works in programming and she built him a website. Until last month, Pete just collected cash and stuffed it into a zipper bag to take to the bank every Friday.

Practice and workouts start for real today. Not that the impromptu January second practice wasn't real. Two miles is a lot longer than I thought it was; I was pretty gassed and still several seconds over. It's going to take some work to pull off two miles in under ten minutes, but not nearly as much work as it'll take Zack.

Where my body is long, he's squatty. His legs are built for catching, power pedestals digging into the ground, ready to stop everything and pounce for a throw to second —not necessarily the kind of legs that hustle around bases. He's always been a great hitter, though, so his lack of speed shouldn't hold him back. The whole situation is stressing him the fuck out, though. He hasn't stopped badgering me with questions I don't have the answers to since the team meeting and running drill three days ago.

"You don't think she's actually on the team, do you?"

"Isn't there some sort of rule against this?"

"What happens if she gets hit with a bat?"

"Can she really handle your slider? I mean, come on."

I feel another question coming on, perched on the tip of his tongue, waiting to plunge out of his mouth while we sit here in the school parking lot. It's our first day back after winter break, too early for him to start in on this shit. I have a statistics class I need to get my head ready for; I can't be all jacked up with my cousin's anxiety.

"You think she was the starter at her old school?" He's asked me this one already, twice. He already confirmed Hollis didn't play softball at her last school by scouring her social media, going back years. It's always been baseball for her. She's always been special it seems, racing through the doors that "daddy ball" opened for her—all-star teams, batting cleanup, MVP. It's bullshit is what it is, and I get why Zack's pissed. But I wish he'd start doing something about it rather than just *talking*—er, *whining*.

"Who?" I answer my cousin finally, mostly to be a dick.

He punches my arm with the side of his fist.

"Come on, man."

I scowl at the throb left in the wake of his hit.

"Piss off. You're lucky I'm left-handed." I rub the spot and breathe out, overexaggerating the exhale so maybe Zack will finally get it. I don't have the answers to his questions, and I have my own questions.

"I don't know. Why don't you look up their season," I suggest.

"Smart, yeah." He's already got his phone in his palm, his thumbs typing in the search bar.

Eventually, I step out of the car and toss the keys to my cousin at the curb. Zack's not great at getting up early, so he eats breakfast during our car rides to school. I don't like how other people drive, and prefer being behind the wheel anyhow.

I miss my truck. Dad's driving it out here in two or three weeks with a bunch of our stuff, so I'll have my own wheels soon enough. How we're all going to fit in Uncle Joel and Aunt Meg's house until our rental is ready, I have no clue. It'll be a chaotic two months, and these few weeks before tryouts are going to be painful.

"Can, hey, look at this," Zack says, slapping at my arm and shoving his phone in my face. He can't seem to quit swatting me.

I shirk away from him but take his phone and speed read the story he pulled up from some news site.

XAVIER PREP BOARD OF DIRECTORS VOTES 7-1 TO ACCEPT RESIGNATION FROM COACH CREDITED WITH TURNING SCHOOL'S BASE-BALL PROGRAM AROUND

I skim through the first few paragraphs, losing interest as it goes into detail about private-school politics and unhappy parents. I wouldn't call this *breaking news*. I scroll down to the end to see the comments, noting maybe a dozen, mostly from players' parents praising the board for making the decision.

"So, he's a winning coach who doesn't do politics. He resigned and they told him not to let the door hit him on the way out. Not sure what you want me to take away from this," I say, handing the phone back to my cousin. I don't want to entertain his trip down this rabbit hole, but I admit to myself that it is a little odd that a school would be so okay losing a coach like him, especially one with college experience.

It doesn't matter whether I indulge or not; Zack is going to kick this can around with or without me.

"It means something's up with him, that's what it means. Think about it—a coach goes, what, thirty-six and four, two state titles, and he gets shit-canned? Nah, bruh. Something's off with that, and I bet it has to do with daddy's little girl."

Our friends Hayden, Tory and Lucas are sitting on the brick wall by the front office, so I kick my leg over to sit on the end and turn my back to my conspiracy-theory-spinning cousin.

"Who's daddy's girl?" Tory nods, lifting a curious brow. He's taking this in a *whole different* direction.

"You talkin' about Abby?" Lucas sticks his tongue out and nudges Tory, who only slaps his friend's arm away. It gets uncomfortably quiet after Lucas's ill-timed joke. I haven't been hanging out with these guys for long, but from the bits I've seen the last few weeks, I'm pretty sure Abby moved on to the D'Angelo twins after she and I tried hooking up.

Let's just say Abby Cortez and I were a bit like oil and water. From what I heard, it was basically one huge love triangle bomb with the twins, too. That girl is all drama. She took off for some acting gig, and all I know is nobody talks about her dating either of them. I have a feeling Tory isn't telling the whole story, though. He was pretty into her, but his brother is *here,* and Abby is long gone. Brotherly loyalty and shit, I guess.

I'm glad the bell rings before Zack can bring the conversation back to Hollis. As far as I know, nobody's aware of the New Year's kiss. I'm not up on bragging, and now that Hollis is the enemy, I'd prefer not to throw a meaningless kiss into the mix, especially if I'm supposed to throw ninety-mile-per-hour fastballs at her face.

I hold out a fist and pound my knuckles against Zack's then the other guys' before heading to the far west end of campus. It took me a while to learn my way around this place. My old school was all inside, three stories with glass windows and stairwells, super modern and spotless. Allensville Public is laid out like a prison, complete with graffiti. The windows don't even open anymore thanks to years of paint layers. And the brick buildings are scattered so far apart it's impossible to get to class on time when you have to motor from one end to the other. I quit trying last semester, and other than a few scowls from a very picky biology teacher, nobody cares if you wander in during attendance.

I slip into statistics as the door closes. Nobody notices.

The teacher doesn't even look up. His glasses are pulled down on the tip of his nose and he's scratching at the back of his neck while struggling to read his tablet.

"Sherman *Poo . . . scooter?*" There are snickers at his attempt because even though most of us in here are seniors, we also possess third-grade senses of humor. Dude said poo. It's funny.

"Uh, it's Sharmaine? And my last name is Poscotier —*puh-sca-tee-ay.*" The voice comes from a girl in the front row. From the back, all I can see is the irritated head waggle that shakes her long, blonde ponytail. Her tone is enough to inspire me to take a seat in the very back, though. No way I want to be paired with that—*ever.* Pooscooter.

"Right." The teacher nods. There's a smirk peeking out from his overgrown beard and mustache that makes me wonder if he's making a mental note to mess her name up for the rest of the year. If he does, he will win the spot of favorite teacher ever on my list.

"Alright, and Jennings? Did Jennings finally make it?"

I must have missed his first trip through the roster.

"Present," I say, lifting my palm slightly from the desktop. The girl in front of me tucks her head into her shoulder while she twirls a lock of her red hair around a pen. I lean forward enough to catch her eyes and make her blush at getting caught peeking.

"Hi," I whisper. She whispers *Hi* back and hunches down in her chair. She shouldn't be embarrassed. It's cute when girls check me out; the ultimate compliment, really. I could spend a few more seconds silently flirting with her, but that plan is cut short the moment the teacher attempts another name.

"And Taylor. Or is it Hollis?"

A whirlwind hits me, both mentally and physically, as Hollis flings open the closed door behind me, announcing her arrival in a hurried, disheveled, and chaotic scene. You'd think a hurricane was brewing on the other side of the door, her hair wild and her plaid flannel shirt falling off one arm almost completely.

"Hollis, yeah. That's me. I'm . . . Hollis." She's panting, and her eyes land on the open seat next to me. A look of relief colors her face and she takes it, dropping her heavy backpack at her feet and immediately twisting her hair up in a bun on top of her head. She pokes a pencil in to hold it in place.

"Phew, that was rough. How's it goin'?" She blows up at the loose hairs on her forehead, her cheeks red.

I lean forward and grip the front of my desk, keeping my eyes on the wood grain and my periphery as closed off from her as I can. It takes her about three seconds to tap my shoulder with the eraser end of her pencil.

"Hey!" she whisper shouts.

I sigh heavily and slowly turn my head to the right, forcing a smile and quick nod to respond. She leans to her side to cut the distance between us.

"What'd I miss?" She's already got a notebook out, her hands opening the cover while she stares at me.

"We took a quiz," I joke, shrugging. For a flash, she believes me. I can see it in the way her eyebrows lift and her pupils bleed into the blue of her eyes.

"Ass," she bites back after a few seconds, moving back

into her own space and writing the date at the top of her paper. She must be a good student. That's a *very good student* kinda move.

There are seven open seats in this class. An entire row on the far right. Of all the seats, she took this one, but it doesn't mean I have to stay here. While our teacher flips on a digital screen at the front of the room, I grab the strap on my backpack and twist to the side, ready to make my break for the farthest desk from Pooscooter and Hollis. Before I can make my escape, though, the teacher flashes a layout on the screen that already has us labeled in our seats.

"Welcome to statistics, brought to you by the Allensville School District's latest technology grant. I'm Dr. Vanetta, but you can call me Dr. V for short. If you could all be cool and do me the solid of staying in your seats, I won't have to butcher your names ever again, *unless I want to.*"

Most of the class chuckles at his introduction, and maybe later, when I'm not pissed off at getting stuck next to *daddy's girl,* I'll laugh about it, too. Right now, I'm focused on making myself as closed off as possible, to the point that the guy to my left is sliding his seat from me inches at a time as I encroach on his space.

"This is my first year here, and last semester was my first as a high school teacher. I'm used to college kids, so my expectations are kinda high. Prepare yourselves to work," he says, switching the screen over to the syllabus. I note the label at the top—PAGE 1 of 12. *Jeeeezusss!*

I take my phone out and click to the class listing on my school app, pulling up the documents Dr. V is flying through on the screen. The guy is pretty funny, but he wasn't kidding about expectations. He's quickly losing his bid to become my favorite teacher. To my right, Hollis is feverishly scribbling, and I could probably clue her in on how to use the app, but she said it herself—I'm an ass.

It takes almost the entire class period for Dr. V to get through his expectations for this semester. I decided somewhere around the fourth assignment that I would be fine taking a C in this class. It won't affect where I go; I'll be signed long before that final grade locks in.

While Hollis squeezes her hand and flexes her fingers from writing cramps, I lean back and zone out, mentally preparing for the next month of conditioning before tryouts. It's almost impossible to ignore my biggest hurdle, though, especially since she's constantly moving right next to me. I don't know whether she's jacked up on caffeine or ADHD or nervous or *WTF!* Her knee has not stopped bopping since she started taking notes, almost as if her hand's in a race with her leg to burn calories. If this is what she's like on the field, I'm screwed. I'm used to a focused catcher. At my old school, I threw to a guy who was almost three hundred pounds. He wasn't great at running down balls but he somehow blocked everything, and he could lock me in when I was getting wild. Zack's got that gift, with the scrappiness to make fucking amazing plays behind the plate. I don't know why he's so freaked out about losing the starting position to Hollis. He's made the all-region team the last two years and he's proven himself. He'll do it again.

"Pshh." My scoff slips out as I laugh silently to myself and lean forward on my elbows. Hollis's knee stops gyrating, so I quirk a brow and give her a glance.

"What's funny?" she whispers.

My mouth begins its slow curve because suddenly, so many things amuse me. My tongue pokes out over my bottom lip and I lock it down with my teeth, nodding.

"Just ready for today." My grin is lopsided and arrogant, and Hollis's brow dips as she studies me, as if looking for the loophole.

"Better be," she says, her knee returning to its constant tapping out of Morse code.

We must have made enough noise to catch Dr. V's attention because he abruptly stops talking. His posture is pretty ready for conflict with his hands clasped in front of his body and his shoulders rolled back, chest puffed and chin high. He's looking at us through his lenses now—they've moved from the tip of his nose to the bridge.

"Mister . . ." He muses for a moment, leaning to the right to check my name on the tablet that shows the seating chart. "Jennings. Right. I made a note by your name. Athlete, I see. You'll be needing to stay eligible for the season. Let me guess, do you two play doubles tennis?"

He waggles his finger between Hollis and me. I shift in my desk, feeling the rush of blood travel down my neck and spine. I don't like being made an example of, and Mr. V is officially out of the running for favorite teacher.

"We play baseball, sir." Hollis speaks up. I wince because of the way she says it, so sure of herself. Her knee has stopped moving again, and her hands are clasped on top of her notebook, mimicking Mr. V's in a way. A confident smile plays at her lips, and while she seems to grow taller in her seat, I find I'm shrinking in mine.

"Oh, that's . . . progressive. I didn't know we had a girl

on the team," he says, engaging and leaning one elbow on his podium.

"We don't, yet," I blurt out. It's my temper—a knee-jerk reaction when I'm embarrassed.

"We will," Hollis pipes in, turning to face me with the smug mask tightly pressed to her face. She blinks slowly and I shift again in my seat as I make eye contact with her. I hate that I don't fit in these things, my legs too long to completely bend my knees under the tabletop, and my body too tall to rest my arms comfortably on the desk. I look like a monster breaking out of a cage. I'm not sure how Hollis fits so easily. Girls are just flexible I guess.

"Interesting," Mr. V says, actually running his palm over his beard while evil ideas appear to swirl in his head. "You two are perfect for my first statistics question. Let's give it a try, shall we?"

His question lingers in our silent classroom while nobody steps in. I finally shake my head and say, "Sure."

"Great. Here's the data set."

He quickly pushes the screen to the side, exposing a whiteboard underneath. He takes a red marker to the board to write with the same fervor Hollis just did, explaining the details as he writes. Hollis doesn't seem to be taking notes, and I wonder if the attention is chipping away at her brave face.

"First, we have you, Mr. Jennings," he says, drawing the male symbol on the board. "And over here, we have Miss—"

"Just call me Hollis," she interjects.

Her boldness earns a smile that barely breaks through the beard.

"Hollis it is," he says, drawing the female symbol on the other side. He next writes the number fifty on the board between our names, tapping his marker against the number a few times to punctuate it before turning to face us.

"There is one spot open on the baseball team, and both Hollis and Mr. Jennings are trying to take it."

He takes out a coin.

"Let's assign heads to you Hollis, and Mr. Jennings, you're tails." He dips his head, peering over his glasses, waiting for us to agree. We both nod. I have no idea where this is going.

Flipping the coin in the air, he waits with an open mouth, eyes eager to see how it lands in his hand before flipping it against his forearm.

"One of you will make the team, and one of you will not. Based on this coin, would you say there is a fifty-percent chance it will be you?"

I shrug and nod as Hollis does the same. Mr. V peels back his fingers to expose the coin, walking through the desks to stand between us so we can verify the coin. It's tails. I smile as if I actually did something to earn the win.

"Congratulations, you've made the team. Hollis, I am sorry," he says, leaning to her side. Taking this entire scene in stride, Hollis snaps her fingers in front of her, a gesture that says, "Darn." One side of his mouth lifts with his short laugh.

"Ah, but wait. You know what? Let's do this again. And for fun, let's put some theory behind it. What are the chances I will land on tails again?" Pinching the coin between his thumb and finger, he twists it around in front of us so we can see both sides. "Mr. Jennings, what are your chances now? Can I land this on tails again?"

I stare in thought at the coin, not sure how to wrap my mind around his question. "Maybe," I eventually say.

"But what are the chances? More? Less?"

His eyes bore into me waiting for my answer. I let my mouth hang open, mentally playing out the game and testing the odds in my own mind.

"Fifty percent. It's exactly the same," Hollis answers.

Mr. V's smile gets bigger this time as he strolls backward, flipping the coin in the air again and catching it, finishing with a swift slap against his arm. He cups it in place, waiting until he returns to the front of the class, and before looking, grills me one more time.

"Is it the same? Or is it harder for you because now you're trying to win a second time?"

I swallow, but his question makes sense, and that's what I was thinking.

"Yeah, it is. I've already done it once, so the odds of doing it again, twice in a row, are smaller," I say.

His smile lingers, but becomes stale. I sense that I'm not right.

Bringing his arm up in front of his eyes, he slowly uncups the coin and shifts his focus to the emblem that landed on top.

"Tails again," he says, smirking.

I breathe out and relax in my seat, suddenly aware of how tense my muscles were in anticipation.

"Looks like you were lucky," he says, and I chuckle in agreement, completely hooked into his trap. "Or was it luck? I wonder."

He tosses the coin in the air and it lands in his palm once again. He holds it out in his fist, staring at me.

"What are the odds?" His face is devoid of emotion, zero expectation. He looks at me as if he doesn't know the exact answer. I take a guess, doing my own form of math by taking the three tosses and dividing them into thirds.

"Thirty-three percent," I throw out with a shrug.

"You don't seem certain." His mouth is a flat line, and he maintains eye contact with me as he flops the coin on his arm once again. His gaze shifts to Hollis.

"It's the same as the first time. It's always the same. Every time you toss it there is a fifty-fifty shot that it will land on heads," she says.

I sit forward wearing a grin that stretches into my cheeks because I think she's wrong. But with the coin still covered under his palm, Dr. V stretches out a finger to point at her and winks.

"Exactly," he says, uncovering the coin. Once again, it's tails.

"Seems this experiment proves my point." I fold my arms over my chest and lean back, one foot braced on the chair leg in front of me. Dr. V dips his chin and pulls in his brow.

"The sample size is too small," Hollis says, again calling his attention to her.

"I could do this a thousand times. Every time, there is a fifty-fifty chance that the coin will land in Mr. Jennings's favor. And to spare you all the pain of watching me do this nine hundred and ninety-seven more times . . ." He slides the digital screen back, switching to a slide that details some famous coin-flipping experiment. The chart shows dozens of trials with samples of thousands. The red color bars are nearly dead even with all of the blue ones. Fifty-fifty, I'm guessing.

"Okay, but baseball isn't like that," I argue. I can feel Hollis's eyes on me to my right, but I ignore them, pushing ahead to dispute this experiment.

"How so?" Dr. V questions.

"Well, we aren't coins. I'm not going out there and flipping to see which end I land on. I'm going out there to work," I explain.

"Hollis? Do you go out there to work?" he queries her. I get the point he's trying to make, but still, he has to see mine.

"Of course. Some might say I go out there and work harder." Her snide tone draws my glare, and when our eyes meet she sneers at me, her feminist claws ready to take out my eyeballs.

I sigh.

"That's not what I'm saying. I'm saying there are variables that don't work with the fifty-fifty method. You have my speed versus her speed. You have my weight and height, and then the natural differences between male and female athletes. I'm going to be stronger. It's a fact."

Anticipating Dr. V's counterpoint, I hold up my palm.

"And yes, not all male athletes are going to be stronger than all female athletes, or faster or whatever. But on the average, those are the facts." I finish my point with a slight head shake, my chest pounding with adrenaline. I've gotten worked up over statistics, and I have to give it to the guy—he made this interesting. Maybe he's not my *least* favorite teacher.

The bell rings, but nobody leaves their seats. All eyes are on me and Hollis, waiting for more arguing, more coin flips, more . . . something. I swing my backpack around from between my knees and stand, initiating everyone else, but before the clamor becomes too distracting, Dr. V throws out one more morsel for me to chew on.

"Mr. Jennings, given everything you just learned, and your points in response, care to give me your best guess on the odds that you will have a female on the Allensville Public baseball team this season?"

He's baiting me, not even looking at me after his question, instead turning his focus on erasing the whiteboard and prepping the room for his next class. There are variables I haven't mentioned, namely that Hollis's dad is the coach, which sort of takes odds right off the table. I'm pretty sure that argument won't be popular with him, though, and I know how Hollis will feel about it. I'm pretty sure she regrets kissing me as much as I regret kissing her.

"It's not fifty-fifty," I say, tugging my bag up my shoulder.

"You sure about that?" he asks, glancing at me over his shoulder.

My eyes meet Hollis's waiting gaze as I turn to my right, a steady tremor of anger brewing behind her sky-blue eyes. Her mouth is a tight line. She pulls the pencil from her hair, letting the twisted blonde waves fall around her face. Her nostrils flare.

Daddy's girl.

"Yeah, pretty sure."

Hollis's eyes haze as her lips curve ever so slightly to meet my challenge. I'm sure to Dr. V my answer sounds like another cocky chauvinist pig out to tell girls what they can't do. But the faint smile Hollis flashes me just before her eyes blink rapidly in disgust says she gets my real point, that this whole thing is rigged, and she's a guarantee, no matter what the other variables are.

I'm going to have to get Zack in shape enough to force a fifty-fifty toss-up for playing time.

4

HOLLIS

I knew today would be hard. I didn't think it'd actually suck. Cannon Jennings is an asshole. I'm sick and tired of assholes. We left a bunch behind in New York, and I hoped we wouldn't get a new crop here. Worse yet, Cannon isn't even a local. He's an outsider too, he just doesn't have tits. Such hypocrisy.

I'm used to being independent. Growing up in New York does that to a girl. You learn to ride trains young. Biking around city blocks to meet up with friends when you're nine or ten is a basic rite of passage. And hanging out in front of the 7-11 until three in the morning with a bunch of teenagers is totally normal. Walking into a middle-America high school cafeteria without knowing a soul, though? Nothing normal about this.

I managed to kill seven minutes standing on line for a slice of pizza and an apple juice. I'm half-tempted to find a corner to lean against and eat on the run. The only person in this entire room I sorta know is June, and that's only because my mom reached out to the school's parent group to find me friends before we moved. June emailed me a few times before I got here, and insisted I show up for her New Year's party.

The New Year's party, scene of my first mistake with Cannon Jennings. He dropped a clue when we first met, told me he moved out here to play ball with his cousin. I was so charmed by his unbelievably handsome face that I didn't put the facts together that playing ball was what I was here for, too. That we'd be playing ball together. *Teammates.*

I'm about to go for the wall-leaning option when my gaze lands on a waving hand. June's smile is like a light-house in a really foggy sea. I don't know why I feel so intimidated by the students here. I think it's because the culture is so different. Back home, my friends were loud. And new people were rare. We all grew up together, and everybody knew everybody else. The only time things got sticky was when I started high school at Xavier. There was a sense of privilege there, a thread of extremely conservative traditions—that's not how the Taylor household runs. We're not hippies, but we're definitely progressive. Hell, my dad sees no reason I can't play D1 baseball. I know the realities, though, so I'm aiming for a two-year school, to keep baseball in my heart a little longer. If I have to give in and switch to softball for a full ride somewhere, then so be it.

June kicks a chair out to make room for me when I get close to her table. She's chewing a bite from her sandwich, so she cups her mouth to talk.

"This is Lola." She points above the head of a really pretty blonde girl with magazine-style beach waves.

"Hi," she squeaks before puckering her lips around the straw of her soda. She smiles around it. She seems sweet.

"Hi, I'm Hollis. I like your hair," I say, pointing at it.

"Oh, thanks," she says with a giggle, pulling a few of the strands out to the side and glancing at her periphery. Her eyes are more white than blue at this point. She's funny. "I have one of those curling irons that basically does all the work for you. I just hold my hand in the air while I eat breakfast, and voila!"

"Cool," I say, unscrewing the cap from my juice. I turn it over to read the words on the inside, a weird habit I've been doing ever since I had my first Snapple. I like it when companies leave you with little positive messages. There's nothing on this cap but an inspection number, though. Guess I'm glad it was inspected.

"I can do your hair sometime, if you want," Lola says, bringing my attention back to her. I laugh out some of my juice and catch the dribble at my chin with my long sleeve.

"Sorry," I say, coughing out the last of the choke. "I'm just, well, I'm a lot of work."

I pull my hair down from the makeshift bun I made while waiting on the pizza line. Jagged curls flop in various directions, and several strands jut straight out from my shoulder. Lola reaches toward me with a fork and combs out the wildest pieces. I'm left stunned, eyes wide and brows high.

"Nah, my magic curling iron can do anything. We'll try it sometime." She tosses the fork-turned-comb onto June's tray and sits back in her chair, seeming satisfied, and once again wraps her lips around her straw, drawing in a long sip.

"Okay," I relent, running my fingers through my hair a few more times to get the wild strays away from my face.

"So, how's your first day?" June asks. Once again I laugh, this time mid-bite. I cover my mouth with a napkin and finish chewing.

"Oh, it's been epic," I say, sparking their intrigue. Both lean in, eyebrows drown into Vs.

"Well, let's see. I'm taking an English class that is the exact same curriculum I *just* finished in New York, and because of my late transfer, the only credited elective I could get into was culinary. I hate cooking, and I hate cleaning dirty dishes more."

They both scrunch their faces to echo my disappointment.

"Sorry. That sucks," June empathizes. They both lean back, I think a little disappointed in my definition of epic, but I draw them back in with my last bullet point.

"Oh! And do you guys know Cannon Jennings?"

The flat-lined mouths and blinking eyes staring back at me tell me they do, and that their impression matches mine.

"Right, well, so . . . he's an ass." I sum him up neatly, not going into all the details. I don't need to bore my new friends—my *only* friends—with baseball politics and details of a sexist sports culture. My assertion seems to be on point, because within a blink they're sharing their experiences with him.

"He literally patted me on the head once when I was sitting next to him at a basketball game. I was trying to get to know him and asked a question about the game. He turned to me with an open palm and patted me like a puppy." Lola's innocent features are suddenly fierce, a bit of a snarl to her lips; I like her even more.

"He led my friend Abby on for weeks, but then she got tired of his games," June says. "It all worked out because now she's filming a movie in Toronto, and thinks she's totally meant to be with someone else."

"You said games," I echo, picking up on that word especially. "What do you mean, games?"

June shrugs and takes a bite of her sandwich, glancing up in search of an example.

"Okay, so like, when he's at a party or hanging out with the guys, he acts one way, but then when you get him on his own, he's totally a different person. He held my friend's hand and cuddled up to her at parties then ignored her existence the next day. Abby says he's moody, and I think that's the best description. Maybe he's only chill when he's buzzed at a kegger. I don't know."

Her examples fit the mold I've made for Cannon in my head. Our kiss was a caught-in-the-moment thing, but still, the switch he flipped between attitudes is unreal. Maybe his behavior isn't all driven by the fact I'm encroaching on his turf. Maybe he's just a douchebag.

By the time our lunch hour ends, I feel relaxed and a little more accepted. When I look around at the other girls, I still feel as though I stick out in this place, but that's not going to change. I like high-top shoes without laces and baggy sweatpants, and shirts stolen from my dad's college collection. I don't wear bras, unless they are sports bras, opting for camisoles or nothing at all. I want to feel I can breathe under my clothes, and I don't want to wake up early just to change the girl I am. The only rule I might break is letting Lola curl my hair, and mostly on a dare because I don't think it can be done. Plus, her hair is pretty freakin' bomb.

The end of my day is pretty easy. I opted for study hall instead of taking an early release. I did it to be able to take weight training at the end of the day. It was the only way I could avoid spending two full hours hanging out in my dad's office. It's bad enough being his daughter, I didn't need to add to the optics by being glued to his side. I'm riding the high of decent lunch company and the comfort of knowing that tomorrow I will have a place to sit, when the warm fuzzies turn into blistering acid. Cannon is sitting in the back of the study hall room, hat brim tipped down over his forehead to shade his eyes, probably so he can sleep. I recognize a guy from the New Year's party sitting next to him, one of the twins I've heard about. I'm about to slip by unnoticed when the guy's eyes land on mine, causing him to sit up straight and slap Cannon's hat from his head.

"Dude!" The few people already here turn to look as Cannon chastises him, and I take advantage of his attention on his friend, darting to the other side of the room and making my way up front. I slip into a desk, pulling out my phone to double check my schedule that I have the right room. My hope is dashed quickly, though it was a longshot that there were two study hall locations at the same time. Tucking my chin into my shoulder, I peer behind me to see if Cannon has gone back to hibernating. His eyes are glued to mine the moment I glance in his direction. His mouth a hard line, and he gives a slow shake of his head as if he's disappointed in me.

It's the other way around, buddy.

Not wanting to let him in my head, or give him the satisfaction of feeling he matters, I shrug and shift my gaze to his friend. I nod a silent hello that makes his friend chuckle and nod back. I'm pretty sure he's gotten the full story from Cannon, only neither of them have seen me play. Today is important, and I knew it would be. I've been in this position before, the one who has to prove herself to an overly skeptical crowd. The hardest part is that no matter how hard I work and how good I am, there are some who will still wear their blinders and refuse to acknowledge they maybe had me pegged all wrong.

Renewed, and amped with the familiar sense of drive, I turn back into my seat and pull my notebook from my bag, flipping to the middle to write my goals for the next five days. I got this habit from my dad. He's always done it in his scorebooks and on lineup sheets. He doesn't write down criticisms for his players, but instead takes the things he thinks they're failing at and makes notes for himself, for the work *he* needs to do to make them better. It's one of the things that makes him great at his job, and that's not simply my opinion as his daughter. He won a few awards from the university he coached at for his player-driven dedication. It's his approach, always looking for the things he can do rather than blaming someone else for failing on their end. It doesn't mean he doesn't expect his players to pull their weight. In fact, most of his players end up making their own notes, taking ownership of their weaknesses and goals. It's a proven method that has made his winning record one of the best in East Coast baseball. It'll work here, if the people in this program embrace it. The guy napping under his hat about twenty feet behind me gives me doubts.

The teacher for our study hall kicks out the door stop to shut the door before he beelines to the desk at the front of the room, laptop in hand. After a quick run through roll call, he ignores us completely, immersed in whatever he's working on. If he weren't typing constantly, I'd think the guy was watching porn. His eyebrows keep flickering in reaction to whatever he's reading, and I'm distracted by it for longer than I'd ever admit. I find my focus again before the hour is done, sketching out five goals for today's work-outs. The physical stuff I'll knock out without a problem, but that last item—*make Cannon see me as his equal*—will be ongoing, I fear.

I wouldn't care so much if it weren't for the fact Cannon is our ace. I haven't even seen him throw in person yet, just the videos my dad watched from the scouting sites. I know his numbers and what he throws; I memorized all that before we got here so I'd be ready to catch him. I would never admit this to my dad, but I'm a little worried about Zack. The pitcher-catcher relationship is special, and they've had a childhood of playing catch to gel. They have blood ties. The only thing I have going for me is my hunch that I might be able to amp up Cannon's adrenaline, pissing him off enough to gain a mile or two per hour on his fastball. I note that in the margin before the class ends, packing up and breaking between Cannon and his friend before they reach the door. My shoulders brush their arms as I pass, something I make sure of and do not acknowledge. I grin over it, childish as the move was, and I maintain the high all the way to the girls' locker room.

It would be easy to dump my things in my dad's office, but again, I need that separation. It has to be noticeable for this to work. It's one of the things I learned from Xavier; one of the things we did wrong, though I don't know if that would have mattered. There was hostility brewing there for some people that ran deeper than the appearance of nepotism. I'm encouraged to see three other girls dress out with me. I'd braced myself to be the only girl in the weight room. It's nice to have sisters. I don't know them yet, so I rush to catch up to the last one in the locker room after I finish getting dressed. I reach her just as she hits the door with her palm.

"Hey, wait up!" I yell.

She pauses at the door, spinning to show me a bright smile that makes me feel as though she needs a friend in this class, too.

"Hey! Oh, my God, I'm so glad I'm not the only girl." She holds the door open wide and I slip by her, noting her slender arms and legs as I pass. I don't think she's done this sort of thing before, but I don't know that for certain, and I would be a hypocrite if I assumed.

"I feel that. I'm Hollis." I hold out my hand as I walk backward along the short sidewalk between the locker rooms and weight room. She's amused by my formality, another habit I got from my dad, I guess, but she takes my hand and gives me a fish-like shake. I bury the creeped-out expression I want to make and commit myself to taking this girl under my wing in here. Goal one, learn how to shake with authority.

"I'm Maddy. And I have *no idea* what I'm doing." She laughs through her words.

"Okay." I nod, still walking backward.

I sense the building is getting close, so I shift to turn and my chin slams into a ¡thick bicep. An arm curls around me from the other side, catching me mid-collision. The smell is familiar, and it takes the same amount of time for me to place it as it does for him to speak.

"You gotta be fucking kidding me." Cannon's hand instantly lets go of my midriff, as if repulsed at the realization that I'm the body he caught. I jump back, equally repulsed to be caught by him, and angry with my hormones for fluttering at his touch.

"I don't have to do anything to you," I respond. Checkmate for having the right comeback, but boo for making my goal even harder to achieve.

The three of us stand in an awkward triangle, Maddy caught in the middle of Cannon and my silent showdown. She's tugging nervously at the bottom of her T-shirt. I see the movement in my periphery because I refuse to fully look away from Cannon.

"Hi—ey," Maddy interjects, thrusting her palm between the two of us. *Oh, God . . . she's going to shake his hand.*

Cannon's gaze drops to the pale, spindly fingers quivering in front of him, and I flash my attention to my new friend, warning her to retreat with a buzzing shake of my head. She must be young. I think she's a freshman. I never should have put the handshake idea in her head.

"Hi," Cannon says, his head cocked and eyes now on Maddy. I can't tell whether he thinks this is a joke or not, but he tentatively takes her hand, his eyes flinching when he experiences the same thing I did.

Oh, man. I squeeze my eyes shut and pinch the bridge of my nose.

"I'm Maddy," I hear her say.

"Cannon," he responds. I open my eyes in time to see their hands fall away, and I'm not sure who I'm more glad for that it's over.

"You should get better friends, Maddy," he adds, before flinging open the weight room door and letting it slam in my face.

Maddy. I'm more glad for Maddy.

"He is beautiful," she hums, her eyes entranced in the space he left behind.

"He's a pig," I say without pause. I hold the door open for my infatuated friend, and as she passes me, a flash of jealousy hits my gut. I want to ignore it, but I've got a lifetime of experience acknowledging my feelings, and there's no mistaking that's what I felt. It was brief, and it was irrational. But it was there. And it's because even as awful as Cannon is behaving, Maddy is right. He is beautiful.

On the outside.

5

CANNON

W hat are the odds that Hollis Taylor is in fifty percent of my classes? Scratch that; I'm tired of dwelling on odds of fifty percent. From now on, I avoid fifty-fifty like the plague! But seriously, do I have to start *and* end my day with her?

Hollis is basically a hot but disheveled mess. By the time we had weight lifting together, she'd essentially tied her hair up in an actual knot. I'm pretty sure I saw a binder clip holding that shit up. And yeah, I was staring when she turned her back. That's the problem with the *hot* mess part. She was wearing black leggings and a gray T-shirt that was about two sizes too big, and it shouldn't have been sexy, but on her it just . . . was. There was something about the way she rolled the sleeves up tight over her toned shoulders that I couldn't ignore. She's tan, which is a rarity for this town, especially in the winter. Back home in New Mexico, everyone is always outside. Sun-kissed skin is a year-round feature. Everyone here looks pale. Hollis defies the gray, though, which means she must thrive outside. I guess New York tempers you for freezing cold weather.

It's blustery today, maybe forty-five degrees out. My arm hurts just thinking about throwing a bullpen, but Zack and my uncle keep telling me I'll get used to it. I guess if I could get acclimated to regularly playing in ninety-degrees back home, then forty shouldn't be a problem. By late April when playoffs hit, it should be about perfect. I just need to stay healthy.

Zack's waiting for me outside the clubhouse, already dressed out and ready for workouts. I nod and grin, holding up my fist to pound as I pass.

"First one dressed and ready, nice job," I say before spotting Hollis already hitting the track beyond his shoulder.

"Second," he says with an eyeroll. Everything about him is closed off, already defeated.

"Hey, you're the starting catcher. Go show him why," I encourage. My cousin fakes a smile that lasts for a fraction, then hoists his gear bag over his shoulder and trails backward toward the track.

"Your stuff's in the corner," he says. His last class is near the front of the building, and he did me a major solid by hauling my things across campus.

"See you out there," I say.

He merely nods and takes off in a rhythmic jog, the weight of his catching equipment smacking against his side with every step.

There are only a handful of guys in the clubhouse when I enter, so my cousin is still a shining example of being on time by being early. Hollis and I came from the same spot on campus, so I'm not sure how she beat me here.

For the most part, I know most of the guys doing the workouts. It's the same team as last year, minus one senior who wasn't very good. We should be tight this year, contenders, as long as we put the right people on the field. I can't imagine Coach Taylor going the *everyone gets to play* route just so his daughter gets a turn, but my cousin's worry is messing with my head. Today should put a lot of that to bed, though. We're gonna be on the field, and I'm throwing to both of them. Weaknesses will show themselves.

I pull on my compression pants and shirt and slip my shorts on over the top. Then I grab my cleats and push my feet into my turf shoes for the time being. There are only two other guys who are just pitchers like me. The rest of the rotation is made up of position players who throw decently. I like having a small squad to work with. It means I get more attention from our pitching coach, more work in, and better looks from the schools I'm targeting.

I wait by the door for Jay and Roland, the other two in my group. When they grab their gloves and jog my way, I push through the door, the bright sun making me squint, and the steady wind drying out what's exposed of my eyes. *Goddamn, I miss the Southwest.*

We jog in sync down to the track and dump our gloves and cleats in a pile before starting our first lap. Our pace is steady but slow. By the time we round the curve, Hollis and my cousin are at the field, throwing.

Atta boy.

My gaze once again drawn forward, my eyes land smack on Coach's. Arms crossed over his chest, he squints against the sun, his face hard. I'd say expressionless if it weren't for the obvious ire slightly pulling down the corners of his mouth. I'm not sure what makes me speak up. Maybe I still feel the curse of my day and schedule, or maybe Zack is in my head. I stretch my hands out at my sides, palms up, and my lips move with the word just as my brain shoots a warning to my vocal chords. *Noooo! Don't . . . do . . . it!*

"What?" The simple question spills from my mouth, loud enough that it's distinguishable, undeniable that it came from me, hostile and oppositional—all qualities that get you cut before you even make it to tryouts if you don't throw like I do.

My feet keep going, though my partners pick up the pace, distancing themselves from me. I don't blame them. I manage to pull my stare from Coach as I round the corner and kick it in a little faster through the straightaway. When I pass Jay and Roland, they up their pace to match me, and by the time we round the next curve and hit the final straightaway, we're near a sprint, a shotgun race to see who crosses the finish line first. Roland edges me out by a foot, and I beat Jay by a full two strides.

Chests pounding, the three of us rest our folded hands over our heads, slowing from a jog to a walk as we make our way back to our pile of gloves and shoes, cheeks red and mouths panting.

"Jennings!"

The guys don't even spare me a glance. It was a long shot that he'd let this pass. Things always seem to start off this way with me. By the end of the season, I'm coach's favorite, but for whatever reason, I always go into relationships adversarial. It's a flaw. I'm aware. I hate it. Still, *every fucking time!*

This one, it's on Zack. And Hollis. I wish none of it concerned me, only Zack is the entire reason I'm here. Me and Zack, that's how it was always meant to go down. Our fathers have this shared dream, and yeah, maybe there is some vicarious living happening, but regardless, it's had years of hope invested in it. That's too much importance to be ruined by some chick out to prove a point, and her pissed-off, protective father.

"I'll see you guys in the bullpen." I nod. Jay lifts his hand up, but neither of them glances over their shoulders. They're safe. My fuck up, my punishment.

"Coach?" I say as I jog to where he stands at the edge of the track. Assistant Coach Dixon gives me a short nod, a hint of a smirk buried under his mustache. At least he's amused by my hot head. I won't have to do the make-up work with him.

"Ten percent of the population is left-handed. You know that?" Coach Taylor's jaw rolls as he chews at a piece of gum. His eyes are trained on the track, his focus on the clump of fielders making their way around it at different paces.

"Something like that, yeah. I read that somewhere maybe," I answer, even though I haven't. It's just a fact that seems about right.

"I bet you think that makes you special," he spits out, and my mouth pops open in awe. I close it quickly, disciplined enough to know that anything I say next will surely be incriminating. He snaps his gum once as his head swivels my direction, his eyes full of years of experience dealing with players like me.

"No, sir," I decide on. It's the right response, and I can tell by the way he draws his mouth into a tight, satisfied smile. Despite this little spat, I know that I am, in fact, special. I know that throwing the way I do is rare, and I know he is aware of how rare it is. I know in my gut that this is simply him showboating to get the upper hand. But he's tugging this little thread that leaves me unsure whether he means what he says. I get the insinuation—he's not afraid to cut me. Right now, I'm not sure he is.

"Run it again."

I blink, still out of breath from my two-hundred meter sprint. He pops his gum and gnashes his back teeth, flashing his canines.

"Now?"

Damn it, Cannon. Of course, now.

Coach shifts his stance, his shoulders squaring up with me, his arms still crossed over the taught coaching shirt stretched over his chest. He's in shape, not a has-been.

"Right, now. Okay." I exhale, letting my lips flap with the air. I'm probably going to throw up, but I get the sense he would be impressed by that.

Dropping my things at his feet, I jog over to the curve where I started last time. Just before I kick into a run, Coach calls out, "Two and a half minutes will put you on pace!"

I crane my neck back and stumble a little. That's what a ten-minute-two-miler breaks down to over two laps. I planned to work up to that, maybe by next week. Mouth agape, I manage to stop myself from questioning this time, nod, and hope he's too far away to see the *WTF* written all over my face.

"I'll tell you when," he says, lifting his arm and tapping on his digital watch. He's actually going to time this.

I nod and kick out my legs, already tightening from cooling down. I get the idea that this—sprints—running in general—gets the blood moving, makes stretching more effective, and preps the heart rate. What I'm doing right now, though, is purely to satisfy his ego. It's bullshit, but I'm gonna do it anyway.

He shouts *Go* as the largest group of fielders passes me for their second lap. I use their pace to kick me into overdrive, burning past them until I leave them well behind by mid-straightaway. My cheeks puffing in and out on a steady count, I mentally coach myself into the first turn, feeling the burn threaten my chest and numbness tickle my calves and thighs.

"A quarter through. Do this. A quarter through," I grunt out, nobody around to hear me.

Beads of sweat slide down my forehead as Coach comes into view at the end of the track. He holds up his arm when I hit the curve again, tapping on his watch.

"Two seconds slow," he shouts.

Fuck me all to hell.

My brain tells my legs to move faster, but I don't know if they are. I pump my elbows back, hoping for slingshot, and lengthen my stride, thankful for my long legs. If I had to do this with more steps, I think I'd die.

I'm completely gassed by the time I get to the next curve, and now I'm basically falling my way through the rest of the run. I lean my weight forward, using it, grasping at every advantage, my breath coming out in heavy grunts and pants. I sound like a woman birthing a forty-pound baby. My arms begin to flail at fifty meters, my balance threatening at thirty, but I hold on through the finish line, giving in to gravity and tucking my shoulders as I fall into an awkward double summersault that gashes up my knee and leaves my forearm with one hell of a raspberry.

Finally stopped, I let my arms flop to my sides, my legs out like a scarecrow, my chest rising and falling like a giant, blood-filled heart. That's what I am right now, and I'm not sure whether I'm going to pass out, vomit, or burst open.

Coach's shadow shades my eyes, and I run my forearm over my matted, sweaty hair and forehead as he drops my ball cap on my chest. I clutch it, too tired to put it on my head, too exhausted to sit up. I shield my eyes from the sun with a chopped hand at my brow, my eyes wanting to close, my body begging me to sleep, right here, just for a minute or two.

"Eight-fifty-eight," he says, followed by a snap of his gum. He gives it another chew and spits it out into the dead grass near the long jump pit.

"What?" I breathe out, not sure what he means. Afraid he'll mistake my question for more attitude, I force myself to sit up, palms flat behind me, legs lifeless and stretched out before me. I shake my head and widen my eyes.

"Sorry. I mean, I don't understand."

He's smirking. *Smug prick.*

"You ran an eight-fifty-eight two-mile pace. I lied about your first lap."

He reaches down to help me to my feet. I puff out a sharp laugh, my chest giving out a breath it's been working hard to find. I stare at his outstretched palm for a few seconds, working my way up to a full sit, my elbows propped on my knees. A drop of sweat falls from my brow into my eye, and I squint before taking the bottom of my soaking T-shirt to my face. Then I grip his hand and haul myself to my feet.

I slide my hat over my damp hair, tucking the sides in as we slowly cross the space between the track and the ball fields.

"You sure it was eight-fifty-eight?" I quirk a brow as I look at him sideways.

He lifts his watch to show me the time.

I have to stop walking to get a good look at it, and after a full two seconds of staring, I laugh out loud enough that the guys stop throwing and look at me.

"Hot damn! Woo!"

"Personal best, I'm guessing?" Coach questions.

I continue to laugh silently, a little in disbelief, and I nod.

"Uh, yeah. You might say that. My dad is going to think it's an honest to God miracle," I confess. My response pulls a laugh from him, a genuine one that's raspy and accompanied by a smile that reaches his eyes.

I bend down and grab my glove and cleats, my body suddenly full of a zest, as though I could do that again if I really had to. I'm not going to offer, but I do feel that little additive pride gives my steps, and I'm not completely empty.

"Cannon," he says as we near the bullpens. It's the first

time he's said my first name, and the significance is not lost on me.

I nod and straighten my hat, pulling down on the sides to offer more shade and curve to the brim.

"Tomorrow when you come out here to run, know what you're capable of, and don't sell yourself short. Every workout and drill and warmup and stretch is an opportunity to be better. Don't waste your own time on mediocre."

I let my eyes meet his directly, feeling the burn of the uncomfortable stare, letting him look behind mine to see that I hear him, that I'm sorry, and that I'm about to prove to him that I am indeed special.

"Yes, sir," I say, a little stunned at how damn good this guy is. It took two and a half minutes for me to buy in completely. And I'm in—one-hundred percent—when it comes to this team and this coach. What I'm *not* in for just yet is the catcher waiting in the bullpen with her helmet and mask balanced on her head, her hip jutted out, shin guards covering her legs, and chest protector layered over her Yankees practice shirt.

Coach lingers behind me, waiting to see what I do. My cousin is already catching Jay, and I know that's on purpose. I can tell he's pissed, based on the extra zip he gives to every ball he throws.

"You about ready, champ?" Hollis shouts. It's both infuriating and sexy, and my brain is doped up on serotonin from just pulling off a miracle.

"Lemme get on my cleats," I shout back, a neutral response that doesn't raise Coach's eyebrow or tick off Zack.

It's going to be weird throwing to someone else right

next to him. I'm already mentally preparing myself to pretend he isn't there, that this is just some camp or a different team entirely. It's a game of catch, with a girl who swears she can handle my heat. If I can run two laps like my life depended on it—and I think maybe it did, just a little—then I can do this.

She jerks her mask down and crouches behind the plate while I slip out of one set of shoes and into my cleats. Pounding her glove a few times, she stretches her legs out to the side one at a time, clearly showing off how flexible she is. I catch Zack trying to do the same, and it's not smooth. He stops trying after losing his balance on his left.

Relax, buddy. You don't have to do everything she does. You're good at doing it your way.

Dropping my turf shoes on the bench, I step up on the bullpen mound and dig in at the rubber. Grass overgrows much of it. This field needs some love. I roll my shoulders and hold the ball up for Hollis to see, making sure she's ready for a warm-up toss. I throw it at half speed, not surprised when it pops in her glove above her head. She stands and rolls the ball in her hand a few times, and I hold my glove out for her to toss it back. We're going to be here all day at this rate.

I knew she could play. I didn't expect her to come out here and be weak or not at least hang. I expected Zack to blow her away, but I figured she would be able to handle a little bit of catch. This game is nothing like softball. It's fragile and dangerous, and tiny mistakes in calculation result in disasters, in a blink. What I expected from Hollis was a gamble, a risky move for the sake of proving a point. My assumptions topple the second she sends the ball right back to my glove, hitting me square in the chest, the pop on my end as loud as it was on hers.

The sound is resounding enough that Zack stops mid-throw, distracted by the game of catch happening next to him. He eventually tosses the ball back to Jay, but I can tell he isn't invested. I also see right through his lame attempt at tightening his mask so he can watch Hollis and me throw for a full minute. He's crouched, fumbling with his gear, eyes lasered on the ball zinging between Hollis and me with increasing speed. Either seeing enough or realizing how obvious he is, he puts his helmet back on and drops to his squat, returning to Jay who was as lost in Hollis as the rest of us.

"Damn, girl," he says. A second later my cousin pounds his mitt, forcing his partner's attention back to him. Hollis just keeps doing her job, pretending not to notice any of it. She has to, though. Her mask hides most of her features, so underneath there must live a bit of arrogance. Not that it isn't warranted. *Damn.*

I shake out my arm after our last toss and situate myself on the mound, ready to really throw, motioning that I'm starting with a four-seam. She lowers and pats her glove, flashing it open and closed where she wants it. She seems ready. Every little nuance is as it should be. This is the true test, and I'm glad Zack isn't watching. No matter what happens, I'll have to make him believe he has nothing to worry about, that she can't handle this. To be honest, I'm not sure what I'm hoping for right now. If she can't handle it, she's going to get hurt.

I raise my leg and draw my hands in to my chest, then extend my arms with my stride as I push off and let it fly.

It's an inside pitch for a lefty, and meets her target right at the corner of the plate. A strike if they don't swing, a probable double if they do. It's exactly what she called for, exactly where she wanted it. And she handled it like it was nothing.

These odds are not fifty-fifty.

6

HOLLIS

I t's not like my dad to take Fridays off from workouts. He believes in using every inch given, and there are no rules against holding "optional" workouts seven days a week. Of course, everyone knows the unwritten rule of workout attendance—it's *silently* mandatory. Not today. Today, my dad sent out a text blast around lunch hour letting everyone know they were on their own.

Apparently, for most of the team, this means bypassing the field completely after the last bell of the day and heading home, or to this hill everyone keeps talking about. I thought for a while I would be the only person to show up, but about five minutes into my run, Cannon arrives. I went a full mile today, to make sure I could still do it, and I'm about to hit my final stretch, my legs pleading with me to give them the rest I've been promising them for the last seven-eighths of a mile.

I slow to a steady jog and eventually a fast walk, my hands folded atop my head to give my lungs a good stretch.

The sky is blanketed with a deep gray, the clouds thick and threatening to dump rain or snow, or a little of both. You can really see the weather out here. Back home, it was more of a surprise. The news told you the storm was coming, but the height of the borough's buildings made it easier to ignore the oncoming threat. More times than I can count, I got caught blocks away with nothing but my bike to get me home. Something tells me rain and snowfall are a little different out here.

Cannon nods to acknowledge me. It's . . . strange. We spent the week barely exchanging words. We talk more to one another in statistics than on the field, but that's basically a proximity thing. I did the mental measurements and we're less than two feet apart in stats. Out here, it's sixty feet, six inches.

"Those clouds gonna do anything?" I force the question out because I want this to be pleasant. I don't want him to finish his run and just go home. I'd actually like to practice, and that's damn near impossible on my own. Not that I haven't done it.

Finishing the laces on his shoes, Cannon rolls his compression pants into his socks and tugs down the pant legs of the joggers he's wearing on top. He glances up as he stands, squinting from the reflection thrown off the clouds.

"Fifty-fifty," he says.

His gaze is on me for a solid five seconds before I get his joke.

"Oh," I breathe out with a laugh. "Right."

He grants me a short laugh of his own, accompanied by the slightest tick up on one side of his mouth. It pushes a dimple into his cheek and for a flash, I get a glimpse of the boy I kissed to ring in this year. It's gone before he turns toward the straightaway of the track for his run.

I let him get about fifty meters into it before my legs relent and let me take on another two laps. I've already cooled down, so the tightness in my hips keeps me from sprinting to catch up for the first half-lap, but I'm loose by the time I hit the curve and we round it together, crossing in front of the home stands with our strides in sync.

We both glance to our sides, making eye contact for a stride or two.

"You already ran," he pants out. He's breathing harder than I am. I gloat internally.

"Didn't want you to run alone. It's good to have someone push you." My pulse is picking up again, partly from the cardio, but mostly from this awkward conversation. I decide to let the rest of this run finish in silence, and Cannon seems all right with that, picking up his pace for the second lap. I have to double my steps to keep up. He's only an inch or two taller, but it feels as though his stride is twice the length of mine now that we're really running.

We cross the finish line and I'm a solid ten meters behind. I expect to see him turn and gloat, but instead, he lifts his arms up to match mine and utters "Good run" through pants.

I nod. It was.

We walk in large circles until our heart rates find their way back to normal, and pick up our gear. I didn't come out here expecting a bullpen, and he's probably on his day off from throwing, but I'm both tense and pleased that he makes his way into the dugout with me.

"Think you can manage to throw strikes?" He jerks his

head toward the batting cages as he drops his bag on the bench.

I set my gear on the opposite end and unzip the pouch with my batting gloves inside, pulling them on while I study the nearby netting. I twist my mouth as if I'm really giving his question thought.

"Guess I can throw 'bout as accurate as you can," I respond, looking back at him with a shrug. He laughs, a genuine one, but it's short. Like a punch.

He follows me into the cages and I move a tee into position. He lets out an exasperated sigh.

"What?" I glance up, tugging the tee's neck to the right height. "Hate tee work?"

"It's torture," he says with flat eyes.

"Then you're not doing it right."

The laugh that crackles from his body is less genuine this time. I drag a bucket of balls to my side and balance a ball on the tee, gesturing with an open palm to let him go first.

"Nope." He moves back to the corner where he can lean his weight against one of the poles, crossing his feet and pulling out his phone, probably skimming through social media.

"You wanna go second?" I ask.

"I don't wanna go at all. I'll wait for you to throw," he responds without looking.

I shake my head as my gaze moves away from him. He's gonna be in a world of hurt next week when my dad moves on to hitting drills. He doesn't believe in skipping steps, even if your only job is pitching.

The best pitchers are the best they can be at everything else.

He put that mantra out there often at my last school. For the most part, the players bought into it all. My ex, Jordan, bought into it hardcore, which is probably the only reason my dad was all right with us dating. He was mediocre as pitchers go, but he was always at his best. Drive counts for a lot more than talent in my dad's eyes. Too bad that sentiment wasn't shared by Jordan's father.

I push that thought out of my head and instead focus on my target, digging my feet in at a comfortable distance and taking a few slow-motion practice swings without my bat. I glance at Cannon as I reach down for my bat, but his attention is still on his screen, probably flipping through pictures of our classmates doing stupid shit and documenting it all for public consumption. I hate social media. It's the downfall of my generation.

Eyes back on the ball in front of me, I rotate my hips and bring my bat back, twisting with a hard swing, leaving my feet in place. Cannon must have stopped his social binge long enough to catch me because he repeats the same simmering chuckle he gave before.

"That's your batting stance?" He cocks a brow.

I open my mouth to explain how tee drills work, but then decide it doesn't matter. I close it into a straight, unaffected line while meeting his stare with a harder one. The familiar competitive growl in my belly mixes with the constant need to prove myself as I place another ball on the tee and repeat the same drill. This time, Cannon snorts a laugh through his nostrils, and by the time I glance up, he's back to his mindless phone skimming.

It shouldn't surprise me, and I guess really, it doesn't. It disappoints me, though, and that takes me off-guard. I expected more from him, and I'm not sure why. Maybe it's because he was so receptive on the track, or because up until this point, other than a really good kiss, Cannon Jennings has been nothing but an arrogant prick.

I power through about twenty more swings, noting the half-empty bucket. I could move on to regular swings, but because I'm stubborn—or because I can't help but engage with this guy—I try one more time to show him the way.

"You sure you don't want a turn?"

I study him until he finally blinks up from the screen. Our eyes would look so good together, I think. If only his didn't make me absolutely mental.

With a slight eyeroll, he bends and tucks his phone under his mitt to protect it and lines up to swing left-handed. I smirk because it always looks weird to me. Honestly, I'd give anything to be able to do it. I look like a fool when I do anything left-handed.

"Don't move your feet," I say, pausing with the ball in my palm, an inch or so away.

He grimaces because he thinks my method is stupid, but he'll understand next week when my dad makes him do this about a hundred times.

I place the ball and adjust the height of the tee up just a tick for his height. He lines his bat up with a few slow swings, stopping right before impact, then clears his throat as he wriggles his heels into the turf and loads for his first swing. Topping the ball with his bat, it dribbles from the tee and travels about six feet to the center of the cage. It takes every ounce of self-control for me not to revel. Holding in the laugh proves impossible.

"Fuck off," he retorts, not bothering to wait for me to load the next ball and instead doing it himself. He repeats everything as before, and the result is the same, including my reaction.

"This is stupid," he says, tossing his bat to the side and undoing a Velcro strap on his batting glove. I reach forward and grab his wrist, my need to coach stronger than my instincts for what is probably a bad idea. His arm petrifies under my touch, forearm flexed with threat. I unwind my fingers one at a time while my eyes are fixed on where they just were. Blood rushes back in to fill the pale spots left behind from my hard grip.

"Sorry. I meant you shouldn't quit after two tries. It's a drill, and you've never—"

"I know how batting practice works, coach. Thank you, but I'm good." He offers a salute along with his sharp tongue and bends down, pulling his batting gloves completely off his hands. He picks up his mitt and cradles it under his arm, holding it like a kid holds a teddy bear but with a tinge of aggression. Phone in hand again, he resumes his position against the pole, leaning impatiently, put out that he has to wait for me to finish my drills before we can get on to doing something he likes. Something he's good at.

Stunned at how quickly he can turn into a child, it takes me a few seconds to regain the ability to move.

"Have you always been this sensitive? Or is that a new thing?" I bend down to get a ball in my hand so my eyes aren't insulted by his sour puss expression, but it's still there when I look up. Rather than back down, I glare right back at him, placing the ball on the tee before taking deliberate steps back. Holding my palms out, I offer him a chance to prove me wrong.

He laughs through his nose and looks to the side, squinting as he stares off into the distance where the mound—his comfort zone—sits empty, dirt swirling in the air around it as the wind kicks up. Cocking his head to the side, he levels me with one more hard gaze before giving in, his gritted teeth and flexed jaw evidence of how much he doesn't want to fall into my trap.

After picking up his bat, he sidles up to the tee, lining up his feet in a position I know in my gut is too far back. I clear my throat rather than say something immediately, which comes off totally passive aggressive. He pushes my buttons and brings out the fighter in me. It's maddening.

"What?" His shoulders sag, the bat resting heavily on the left one as his hands loosen their grip.

I run my hand over my mouth and chin, giving myself a few seconds to plot the perfect words before they leave my lips.

"So, the point of this drill is torque and bat speed. And the reason you're not making the right contact is because . . ." I pause and hold my open hands out while my eyes widen to stop him from thinking I'm being insulting. "I know you know how to make good contact. I know you can hit. I'm only trying to correct this one little thing, that's all."

He gives me a slight nod, tiny enough that if I blinked I would have missed it.

I step up next to him and nudge his front foot with my toe, guiding him forward a few inches. Pacing around his body, I grab the barrel of his bat and pull it around as I walk the trajectory it would take for a normal swing. He lets me guide his hands while his eyes narrow and follow my movement with suspicion. His forearms flex as they rotate and though I don't want to, I swallow at the sight; I know he sees me do it.

"You want to make contact . . . right . . . here." I stop the bat just as it meets the ball, holding it firm and glancing up to make sure he's looking. His focus isn't on the mechanics I'm demonstrating at all. It's on me. More specifically, he's zeroed in on my eyes. He was just waiting for me to finish my silly little show, until I looked up to find his jaded, pursed lips and completely intolerant expression.

"You think this is stupid. I got it," I say, letting go of the bat and backing away. I'm so damn mad at myself for trying. I don't know why I don't give up when I'm faced with these situations. I'm forever that girl who thinks she can change people's minds.

I'm about to give him his out, tell him we can do it his way, go straight to hitting from live pitches, when he rears back and rotates his hips, bat following and making hard contact as it drives the ball like a bullet into the metal posts at the other end.

We both stare at the point of impact for a few seconds, and I breathe out a little laugh to accompany my half smile. I'm not sure whether I'm more surprised by the result or his effort. Rather than attempt more conversation, I decide to simply feed him another ball, silently placing it on the

tee and stepping back as he moves his feet into position—
the *right* position.

Another swing. More great contact.

I nod, whispering a "Yes" under my breath. He's still
brooding, and any celebration on my part is going to come
off as gloating. Not that it isn't warranted, because I *was*
right, but making a big deal out of that won't make things
better. It'll only drive the wedge back in that uncomfortable place between us.

We continue on with this pattern, wordlessly working
out and going through my usual round of drills. Cannon
lets me set the pace and go first so he can copy everything I
do. He doesn't resist when I nudge his feet, but I never
once breathe a word aloud. It's odd, but it's working, so I
don't fight it.

After the fifth time of picking up all the balls, Cannon
kicks the remaining few into the far corner and takes the
bucket in his hand, carrying it to the screen at the end so he
can throw to me.

"You ready?" His voice startles me because we've been
carrying on in silence for so long.

"Yeah," I respond, settling into my comfortable hitting
position and nodding for him to begin.

I have noticed a lot of things about Cannon that I will
never tell him. It's enough that he's already had his lips on
mine, but beyond being the best kiss I've ever had, he also
has the kind of voice you wish could wake you up in the
morning and put you to bed at night. It affects me more
when he says very few words.

Like now, when he said, "You ready?" It came out in
this deep timbre that just hung in the air, the sound of the

y at the end lingering a little longer than it would from any other mouth. And then there's his movement. He pitches as if he's putting on a contemporary ballet, every tick of his muscles purposeful, each pause met with a fluid extension of his arms and legs. The way he draws his leg up and separates his arms before exploding with a slingshot of power that sends the ball exactly where it's meant to go—exactly where I asked for it—is pure perfection.

His talent is undeniable, but there's an undertone of truly primal appeal that I have been fighting every single time we throw together. I find myself growing jealous of the times he works out with his cousin, and not because I think Zack is a threat to my playing time. I'm envious that he gets to watch Cannon work.

Those movements are now on display, and for his first three or four pitches, I'm thrown off *my* game. A smug satisfaction tugs his lip up on one side, and it's enough to shake me out of my awe. I send his next pitch barreling back at him, my ball striking the metal of the L-screen shielding him. He flinches and I shoot him a smirk of my own, flipping the bat in my hand for show. He shakes his head, and looks down at his feet with a quiet laugh that I instantly add to my short list of traits I admire about him.

Lips puckered, he flexes and digs in to throw me another pitch, contributing to this game of batting-practice chess that our competitive sides decided to play. I swing way too early, fooled by the slowed-down ball that seems to float by long after my bat slices through the zone.

"Whoa!" I grin at the path the ball took over the plate, impressed with a pitch my dad should know he can throw.

"You like that?" He tips his chin up, the shadow of his hat leaving his eyes for just a moment.

"That wasn't bad," I say, not wanting to inflate his ego too much.

"Not bad." He chuckles. "Not bad, she says," he continues on, a teasing spirit to his tone. It is hard not to find *this* Cannon Jennings utterly charming.

Swinging his arms around at his sides, he puts on a serious face, leaning forward as if getting a sign from his catcher. I play along and drop my bat to the side, crouching down and giving him the sign for slider, which is what I *think* that was. One of his eyes closes more than the other and his lip ticks up. I heed the warning and shoot to my feet, grabbing my bat and readying myself for the pitch. This one sails through even slower, somehow fooling me so badly that I swing hard enough to tie up my legs and trip myself. It's mortifying, and to add insult to injury, Cannon laughs like a madman at the other end of the cage, rearing his head back and holding his glove against his gut.

"Glad you're amused," I grumble, brushing my palms along the fresh raspberries scraped into my kneecaps, noting the new hole in my favorite pair of joggers.

By the time I'm upright and on my feet, Cannon has made his way to my side. I jerk, surprised by his instant—and *very close*—presence. He tilts his head, maybe curious at my reaction, then lifts his hand, a ball balanced at the tips of his fingers.

"That pitch," he begins, blinking his focus to the ball. Mine follows as he slowly rotates the ball in the air between us, the seams moving at an angle away from me. "It's not quite a full curve. I throw it more like a slider, so the ball tends to . . . go . . . like . . . this." He bends as he gives his description, walking the ball through the air and over the plate along the same trail it took the two times he threw it.

"You make that up?" I ask. He's crouched down, his quad muscles completely filling out his joggers, thighs tight and thick like a man. I swallow at the sight of them. He must notice because he rises, clearing his throat. I've just objectified him. I scrunch my face, embarrassed, while he's not looking.

"My dad used to throw it when he was in college. He showed me how when I was in Little League." He tips his head up and hits me with dazzling eyes that are warmed by this fond memory. It's sweet, and genuine. His mouth quirks up, dimpling his cheek. "I threw that sucker all the way to the championship one year."

He laughs once, eyes narrowing over his growing smile as he looks back to the ball in his hand. He rolls it in his fingers.

"You win?" I ask.

He glances up through dark lashes. My list of things I like about him is ever-growing, though admittedly superficial. His chest quakes with one more short laugh before he shakes his head, tossing the ball in his hand and gripping it with a firm palm, fingers spread along the seams just where they're meant to go.

"Nah. We ended up facing this team from Albuquerque full of massive seventh-graders with no fear. They knocked that pitch over the fence seven times."

I wait a breath before giving in to the laugh his story pulls from me.

"Ouch," I say, tapping my bat on the plate a few times, signaling I'm ready to try and send one over the fence too.

"Yeah, but I've gotten a lot better at it since then," he teases.

"We'll see," I fire back.

We're bonding, and it's nice. I like Cannon, beyond the obvious attraction, which really is a bad idea on all levels. We could be friends, and I meant what I said in our statistics class that first day—I might be able to help him. As much as his dad taught him about the game, mine's taught me a lot, too. About how to make good pitchers *better*.

"Give me what you've got, Smalls," I shout, a little *Sandlot* throw-back that makes him chuckle.

Muscles primed, I shift my weight, ready to hit that strange curveball of his, but instead of getting ready to throw it, Cannon drops the ball into the bucket at his side, his gaze off to the side.

"This your idea of only being an hour?"

I didn't see Zack walk up, and my stomach sours with the instant intensity brought to the air with his company. Everything about Cannon's posture changes with his cousin's presence, and that friendly banter between us grinds to a halt.

"Just taking some swings," Cannon says, acting as if he's packing up and getting ready to go.

"We just started, actually," I interject. Cannon doesn't look at me, instead continuing to kick balls toward the bucket to put them away. Neither of them responds to me, which only makes the beast grow in my belly, the one that tells me to scream and call 'em as I see 'em.

"Cannon." I assert his name, like a teacher would. *Like my dad would.* He spares me a sharp glare over his shoulder. "Aren't you gonna take a turn?"

"Bahahaha!" His cousin accentuates his over-the-top cackle by grabbing his stomach and arching back. I assume he's making a joke at Cannon's expense, because he's a pitcher and pitchers rarely hit. But that's not the case at all.

"What, are you gonna throw to him?" His eyes are squinty, his lips pulled in so tight that there are deep divots where they pucker on either side. It's a truly ugly face.

I open my mouth, the beast ready to engage, then snap it shut, not giving in to the urge. I shift my gaze to Cannon and lift my brow as he hoists the bucket of balls and sets it on a metal chair that looks as though it's been beaten by more than a fair share of line drives and bats.

"I'm done here." His answer is definitive, short and clipped, the kind of response a trainer gives a dog.

A punchy laugh escapes my chest. I'm dumbfounded, and within thirty seconds, I'm also alone. The Jennings boys cross the field without a single glance or goodbye, and I hate that I'm hurt by it. This is always what I expect, yet somehow never fully see coming. I should probably let it go, see them on the field again Monday with renewed armor around my *feelings.*

But that's never quite been me either. I'm always up for a fight, a trait both of my parents have sewn into my fabric. Before they make it to their car, I hustle and pack up my own gear, double-timing it to my mom's van that my dad left behind for me to get home.

I'm pretty sure Zack and Cannon don't notice me in their rearview as they speed out of the lot, fishtailing through the dirt shoulder. Masked by the cloud of dust left in their wake, I feel around the underside of the van's bumper until I find the lockbox where my dad stuck the key. I drop my gear in the back and jump behind the wheel, zipping out of the lot while the trail of dust still lingers in the air, showing me the way. Tail lights in view, I slow enough to not be obvious and follow them. We stop at a house nestled in the woods, the driveway filled with shirtless guys playing basketball and surrounded by the kind of girls who only want to hang out and watch them. Any other girl would either slink low in the driver's seat and pass on by or park and find a friend to ogle with. Maybe that's because they don't have a basketball rolling around their back seat like I do.

The thundering in my chest slows when I recognize Lucas, and I find my footing as I slip one foot out of the driver's side and spot June sitting with a group of girls on Lucas's open tailgate. It would be so simple to hop in the back with her, the ease of it so inviting that my fingers twitch at the feel of the ball. I'm tempted to play this a different way. Be a different kind of girl. Take the easy route.

Don't ever betray the person you are.

My dad's words echo around my head amid my mental battle. He gave up a lot so I never have to diminish who I am. And I'm not the girl who sits on the sidelines. I'm the girl who puts herself in the game, who changes the rules.

I hop out of the van and open the back door. Ball in hand, I slam the sliding door shut and jog across the street, dribbling along the way. It's been awhile, but every step I take bolsters my confidence and comfort with the ball.

June's head pops up when she sees me. Waving her hand, she announces my arrival, inviting me to join her, *over where the girls are.* I smile back and stay the course.

Zack and Cannon were only a few paces ahead of me, and I jog three steps to close the gap, tapping my apparent nemesis on the shoulder until his toes square with mine after he turns. Zack doesn't even flinch in surprise, as if he expected me; his smirk dares to suggest he may have even lured me.

"I've got next game," I announce, fully taking the bait if that's the case. I've learned not to ask permission. They never grant you access if you're timid. That's not how you change minds and break into their exclusive clubs.

Of course, I'm not here on principal. I'm here because my feelings were hurt. Stupid feelings for a stupid boy with stupid, stupid features that I've been thinking about way too often. And while it's his cousin I'm in a standoff with, it's Cannon I want to convince. I'm just not sure of what.

7

CANNON

Hollis Taylor might be more like my cousin than I thought. This is a total Zack move, following people who pissed him off so they have to deal with looking him in the eyes.

I have to look *her* in the eyes, and I don't really want to. Before my cousin showed up, we were . . . I'm not sure what we were, but we weren't holding this invisible grudge that's there now. I have to stop making this my problem, but it's hard when my uncle and Zack will not stop talking about what a huge problem this is, and not only for them.

"Your senior year is going to be overshadowed by some novelty publicity stunt."

That's their talking point. They want to rile me up to make sure I'm invested in their battle, but really, there is some truth to it. Allensville Public is not a small school. It's not one of the mega schools that gets TV coverage, but it's a decent size in a town caught between factories to the south and the big city to the west. A girl behind the plate is the kind of human interest story the media eats up, which makes it hard to shine when you're the one on the mound.

All of that shit shouldn't matter. Deep down, I know it doesn't. Coaches at D-ones aren't looking at news stories, they're looking at numbers. And I've got the stats.

"Alright, how 'bout this—you can have Tory but I get Hayden. I'll take Cannon and you get Lucas." I give my cousin side-eyes because I do not want to be a part of this showdown. Too late, though. He just shoved the ball into my chest.

Hollis tosses her ball to the side, and one of Lucas's friends nudges it into the dead grass with his foot. Friday afternoon basketball at Hayden and Tory's has become a habit for Zack and me. I usually look forward to it, mostly because the twins end up putting on a show and it comes down to the rest of us getting out of the way and passing them the ball to do epic shit. I have a feeling that's not how this game is going to go.

"You know what? I'll be nice. You take it up top first." My cousin jerks the ball from my hands and bounces it to Hollis who accepts it with a firm slap of her palms. She's locked in on this as much as Zack is.

My cousin points to me then Lucas, coaching me on whom to guard. It's a little irritating but he's so far gone in his head, I agree. Hayden and Tory eye each other, and when I get close enough to Lucas to strong-arm him while Hollis dribbles around the perimeter of the three-point line, he mutters, "What the fuck?"

I shake my head.

"My cousin is threatened by a girl. Coach Taylor's her

dad, and she catches, and it's a whole shit show." I glance up in frustration while Lucas snorts out a laugh.

"Right, well . . . this should be good," Lucas responds.

We both shuffle our feet, me guarding him while he jukes for an open position on the makeshift court in the D'Angelo driveway. Hollis dribbles back, crossing the ball behind her body a few times, then once through her legs.

"Oh, look at you. Fancy," my cousin teases, swiping at the ball and easily knocking it away. He coughs out a boastful laugh while she rushes to regain control. She manages, but it's clear by the way the whites of her eyes turn redder that Zack is getting under her skin.

Lucas rushes to the other side of the court, clapping his hands then opening his palms for a pass while Hollis works to shirk off my cousin's handsy defense. She sends a hard chest pass in Lucas's direction, but I've already read the play and intercept it, dribbling up top and passing the ball off to Zack to set up.

"Atta boy, Can. *Yup yup!*" My cousin is obnoxious in his celebration. I've joined these guys for dozens of Friday afternoon games, and while Zack is usually the loudest guy out here, he's trash talking with a little extra venom today. It's obvious, and also embarrassing for him.

Hollis hasn't said a word, but I can tell she's reaching a boiling point by the way she holds her lips closed tight, almost puckering as she zeroes in on nothing but the ball. She's stuck to my cousin like glue, reaching in when he drives to the right. He toys with her for way longer than necessary, then spins, dashing around her on the left and driving the ball to the hoop for a layup. He holds out a fist for me to pound as he jogs by while Tory inbounds the ball back to Hollis.

The ball back in play, Tory gives me a quick glance, a silent commentary on Zack's showboating, and I can tell he wants to put my cousin in his place. I'm not sure he realizes this game has nothing to do with the rest of us.

Sensing that Tory's ready, Hollis passes the ball back to him in a rush, and we all step back as he puts up an instant three-pointer that sinks through the hoop without a sound.

"Oh, damn!" Tory boasts, moving in on Zack with his chest puffed out. My cousin laughs him off and pats his chest with his flat palm. Tory's gone stoic, no longer playing a game for fun. I'm not sure this is the result my cousin wanted. Regardless, it's the one he's getting.

For a few minutes, the game shifts into its normal pattern—the Hayden and Tory show. Zack passes the ball to Hayden, and the faceoff ensues. Each of them drives in against one another in a boisterous round of one-on-one, forgetting that the rest of us are on the court. It's then that I catch the smile on Hollis's face. She came here to prove a point, but now, she's just having fun. *I'm* having fun. Every time I manage to get a pass, I flip it over to Hayden and watch him do his thing. Hollis does the same with Tory, even picking up his signal to set him up for a dunk. The two of them slap hands after he finally lets go of the rim, and the tightness eases in my chest.

This game is back to being what it should be, a way to blow off steam and just *be*. A place away from baseball, away from my goals, away from plans and parents. Right here, for this little slice of afternoon, we get to be a bunch of punk-ass teenagers. The rules are unwritten, but they are always followed.

Until now.

I didn't realize how long it had been since the ball met Zack's hands, but the moment it finally does, the tone of everything changes. Hollis isn't set on her feet yet. She's still hailing Tory's last shot, laughing with her new friends, not even looking as my cousin lowers his shoulder and drills right through her.

I hear the moment the breath leaves her chest, an audible *pop* from inside her ribs, her mouth an instant O shape, her cheeks pale and eyes frightened while a muffled moan crawls up her throat and out her mouth. She falls to her elbows, a good chunk of skin peeling away from the right one. She's too busy gripping her chest and trying to refill her lungs to notice the blood trailing down her arm and dripping onto the D'Angelo driveway.

"What the fuck is your deal, Jennings?"

Tory pushes my cousin back a few steps with a hard shove, and Zack's nostrils flare in response. Stepping into Tory's personal space, my cousin moves close enough for their chests to nearly touch.

"Part of the game, isn't it? I mean, we don't change the rules because—"

"Because I'm a girl?" Hollis interjects, suddenly on her feet and urging Tory to back out of a fight meant for her. She joins the standoff and Tory gives her space, but only a little, his pulse amped up enough to make his jaw twitch.

"You're the one who wanted to play." Zack holds the ball against his hip as they stare each other down, both panting from a mix of anger and racing heart rates. The blood on Hollis's arm is drying, but the thick beading left behind is a pretty good indication of the cut at the heart of the trail.

"Just learning your rules, Zack."

I don't know if my cousin expects her to cry or what, but she's clearly not intimidated by a little pushing and shoving. Hell, I've bruised her up with enough wild pitches over the last week that I could have told him she had thick skin, both literally *and* figuratively. Zack rolls the ball back and forth between his hands, eyes searing into Hollis, tongue held between his teeth, smile faint and ominous.

"Dude, just stop this," I mutter at his side. He doesn't bother to look at me, dismissing me with a flick of his hand.

"What? Hollis is good with it. Aren't you? We don't have a problem here." He nods at her, prompting her to fold or call his bluff. Only, he isn't bluffing. I've seen Zack get like this before. When we were little and playing against club kids from the rich teams, he stood his ground over fights he clearly picked. It always felt as if we were on the righteous side back then, but now he comes off like a dick.

"Yeah. We're good," Hollis says, nodding slowly. Her eyes lazily sweep from Zack to Tory, then to me. She's summing up everyone present, and I'm not sure what label she's assigning me.

"We'll call that a foul, then. Your ball," Zack says, letting it fall from his fingers into a lazy bounce in her direction.

"How very *honest* of you," Hollis bites back.

She doesn't pause for long, catching us all off guard by

faking a shot then driving in around Zack for a left-handed layup. Her move draws praise, some of the guys waiting for the next game whistle, and both D'Angelo brothers bump fists with her. It was impressive, and it was actions instead of words. I expect it to only light more gas in Zack's belly, but he seems equally impressed, nodding with big movements as he says, "Okay, I see you."

For the next ten minutes of play, everything and everyone seems to find a rhythm. Zack holds a stiff forearm against Hollis while he dribbles in, but he never crosses the line into flagrant fouling. It's a contact sport, and it stays contact—hands smacking against arms when shots are fired, inadvertent scratches, tripped-up feet, trash talking spilling equally from all our mouths. I block one of Hollis's shots on a double-team and she nails me right back, punching the ball between my legs and right into Tory's hands. We've battled so hard, nobody's noticed the dark clouds creeping in and the sudden drop in temperature. The only thing that could shake our moods would be the clouds opening up and dumping icy rain on our game—or what my cousin does . . . right . . . now.

Hollis has the ball, working it around the imaginary three-point line, Zack stuck to her like second skin, hands reaching in but never quite fast enough to throw her off or find the steal. Our shoes are loud against the pavement, screeching when we stop hard, and sliding against loose gravel. Tory is nearly impossible to guard, but I'm doing my best, always somehow in contact with his body, be it an elbow matching the one he's got in my ribs or our legs fighting for position. The game's tied, and maybe that's what pushes Zack over the edge. Maybe he was waiting for his moment.

Or maybe . . . maybe he's desperate and angrier and more insecure than I realized.

After long seconds of faking grabs at the ball and getting nowhere, Zack swings his hand around Hollis's side, his hand slapping against her ass with enough force that the sound of skin-on-skin bites through the heavy wind despite the padding of her joggers. He yaps in laughter, practically beating his chest when the ball juts out from the top of her foot, her world visibly thrown.

My arms suddenly go slack, no longer struggling to hold on for defense. Tory's do the same, no longer itching for the ball. Only the people in our game actually see it —*feel* it—but the awfulness of it all actually chokes me.

The ball now in his possession, my cousin rushes the lane, no one engaged enough to stop him, and dunks the ball with enough force that the rim vibrates along with the slow rumble coming from the clouds above.

"I gotta get home. I think it's going to rain," Hollis says, her gaze at no one in particular and her announcement cursory, an excuse to let us all leave and pretend everything is normal. Maybe it is. Maybe that was something playful, like the way Tory slaps Hayden's ass when he does a good job. Maybe I didn't see what I think I saw, or feel what I should have.

The fact Hollis is already in her van and swinging around for a U-turn tells me my instincts are sickly attuned.

I glance to the right, everyone suddenly broken up, gone in different directions—away from my cousin who is still shooting and smiling, proud of his big win. Hollis's ball still sits in the grass. I walk over and kick it up into my hands, rotating it until I see her name carved into the side in thick black pen marks. I trace it with my thumb, a sourness coating my stomach that I immediately try to convince myself is only in my head. I glance out to the road in time to make eye contact with Hollis as she drives by, and I know better.

This problem between her and my cousin? It's only going to get worse. And I'm in the very middle.

8

HOLLIS

I've gotten better at pretending for my parents. For a while, I still had a lot of tells. They could sense that something was under my skin because of the way I picked at my dinner plate or only gave short answers. I've found that sticking with my natural knack of being a smart-ass can carry me through any interaction without questions.

I came home from basketball Friday and pulled into the driveway seconds before my father did. Mask in place, I rushed from the car and ran toward him, greeting him as he stepped out of his truck, and leaping at him like one of those flying monkeys at the Bronx zoo. He had exactly two seconds to prepare for my weight, but he still caught me effortlessly, despite how awkward it looks when we do this now.

I get my height from him, so when I was a kid, I outgrew my mom carrying me pretty quickly. Since my dad's limbs are proportional with mine, he could always manage. Whenever I fell asleep downstairs or was sick or twisted an ankle, Dad was charged with hauling me around. We started doing this again last year when my mom bet he couldn't lift me anymore. Now it's our thing.

Sometimes, I need to be daddy's girl. Other times, I think he needs me to be. Friday night, maybe we both needed it a little.

With most of the weekend over, I've been able to put what happened with Zack into the appropriate mental box, locking it up and tucking it in that part of my brain I don't deal with until I want to. *Until I have to.*

We're not a very formal family. No big Sunday dinners when we all sit around the table and share. Usually, Dad grabs a pizza and we all take slices as we come and go. Sometimes, there's a game on in the living room, and we end up piled on the couch.

This is one of those Sundays when my mom is grading and my dad is nodding off on the couch, having drunk one too many beers while tinkering in the garage. My brother still goes to bed early, so I'm on my own. Having bargained that filling a dresser with clothes, one step closer to fully unpacking, was worth another week of van privileges, I have wheels at my disposal. The problem is I have no idea where to go.

After a good fifteen minutes of roaming aimlessly around neighborhoods, looking at leftover Christmas lights that are yet to be taken down, I pop out from a side street, suddenly on the main drag through town. The glowing orange A&P sign flickers in the mist lingering after the long weekend rains. The roads are slick with frozen mud. So far, winter storms here aren't the picturesque kind. I wait for the few cars to pass before crawling the van out onto the road. I'm used to driving in New York weather, but I've been told over and over again by my dad that the roads and weather here mix differently.

I immediately recognize the lone car parked in front of the gym, and despite the uncertainty of which Jennings drove it here, I pull in and park right next to it. I'm not dressed for a workout, my dad's old college sweatpants rolled up at my waist and my shirt the black Billie Eilish long-sleeved tee I got for my birthday at a concert last year. With one deep breath, I resolve to keep what happened Friday tucked away in my mental box, no matter who is inside, and push open the door, glad I at least have socks on with my bright pink knitted boots.

A bell jingles when I walk in, and the old man I met the first time I came here cranes his neck, peeling his eyes away from the Packers playoff game on the small TV mounted in the corner.

"Aw, hell. You again?" he grumbles. I *think* he's teasing.

I nod toward the TV as he pulls himself up from the chair he was planted in and makes his way to the register.

"What's the score?"

"Packers are up by a touchdown," he says, his groggy words wrapping around the well-chewed toothpick dangling from his bottom lip. The clank of metal plates knocking together hits the nerve at the back of my neck but I manage the strength not to turn and look in the direction of the noise. I don't want to know just yet who is to my left.

"Good." I nod.

He squints in apparent skepticism, a hint of a smile creeping into his dry, cracked lips, evidence from his lunch or dinner caught in his overgrown mustache. A deep cough crackles in his chest twice as he tucks his chin. He coughs with the lungs of a lifelong smoker. I recognize the same distinct sound that came from my grandfather's chest. Leaning on his elbow, he slouches at the counter and observes me with one eye, the other squinted shut.

"You a Packer fan?"

Oh, the temptation to lie, but I just can't.

"Oh, no way. Giants all the way! I'd just rather we play you next week than the Seahawks." I blink at him as he stares at me for a few seconds in dead silence, then huffs out a laugh, standing upright and slapping his palm on the countertop.

"Well, hot damn. I like you, sweetheart. I hate your Giants, but I do believe I like you." He pops open his register and hands me a five-dollar bill, and I look at it strangely, take it tentatively.

"I'm . . . flattered?" I'm really just confused, and maybe a little offended.

I cock my head, missing the opportunity to correct him on the *sweetheart* bit because I'm so thrown by what came after. And then I hear the voice of the Jennings I hoped drove that car here tonight.

"He's giving you a refund because he shouldn't have charged you in the first place. Aren't you, Pete?" Cannon is close by. I feel the heat radiating from his body from his workout, and a certain amount of oxygen leaves the space he enters.

I hold the fiver up between Pete and me and glance from Lincoln to the old man. I flatten it on the counter and slide it his way. "Take it off my tab. I'd like to get a monthly membership."

He gives me a sideways grin and slides the money toward him with a single finger.

"I'll bring the other forty-five when I come next time," I say.

He nods, pulling a clipboard up from behind the counter and tossing it down in front of me. A crumpled paper stuck to the top reads: ENROLLMENT FORM. He taps it with his finger, and I note the small tattoo above his knuckle, two small letters—G and F—faded in green.

"Put your info on here. I've got a fancy program that bills you so I don't have to handle cash. Something about taxes or some shit." He laughs, a little sinister, as if he's maybe gotten away with skipping taxes a few times in the past.

"Sure," I say, glancing up at him while pulling the paperwork and pen close to my body. I fill in my name and tap it with the ball point of the pen until he looks at it.

"Something wrong?" he asks.

"No, just want to make sure you take a good look at my name so you can commit it to memory and quit calling me *sweetheart*." I raise a brow and leave my mouth flat and serious. A short laugh punches out of his chest, but he nods.

"I'll do my best," he says, eyeing the six-foot-plus guy standing next to me whom I have yet to completely acknowledge. I have mixed feelings after Friday. Cannon left our hitting session because Zack told him to, his mood suddenly changing to fit his cousin's stereotypical grudge. Then, when Zack turned our basketball game into a blatant and very public example of sexual harassment, Cannon just stood there. I don't expect knights on white horses; I'm not naïve. I do expect guys of my generation to be a little more enlightened. I remind myself, though, that Cannon hasn't walked in my shoes.

I fill the paper out and spin the clipboard around for Pete to take, but before he carries it off to head back to his chair—and the Packers—I stop him.

"Who's GF?" I gesture the pen I'm still holding toward his right hand. He turns his palm over and looks at his finger, his eyes getting lost for a breath before a tepid smile sinks into his mouth, rounding his cheeks.

"Gini Forenzi. Best damn cook this side of the Mississippi." He leaves his gaze on the fading initials then curls his hand into a fist, almost as if to hold on to them and keep them around a little longer. He knocks on the countertop with the same hand, and I can tell that's the end of that conversation.

My hope that Cannon has moved back to the weights is extinguished the moment I turn around. Hands in the pockets of his black shorts, his white T-shirt soaked with sweat, he jerks his head to the side to flip his curling hair from his eyes.

"Aren't you freezing in here?" It's the only question I feel like asking.

"Give it an hour, you'll be peeling layers off too." His voice carries over the volume on the TV and he looks toward the back of Pete's head. The old man promptly grips a remote and raises the sound a few more notches.

"My place, my thermostat. You don't like it, get your own gym," he grumbles.

My eyes widen and I can't help but laugh as I look back to Cannon. He shrugs at the response.

"Pete lives upstairs, and he keeps things . . . *warm.*"

Warm. Yes, that's the word for what I'm feeling right now. It has nothing to do with Pete and his thermostat, though. My stomach feels the same way it does when I take sips of my father's whiskey on holidays. I'm on shaky ground, and I'm not sure why. I think it's because I want to let Cannon off the hook, but after spending the last forty-eight hours renewing my bad impression of him, it's hard to flip back again.

"You wanna spot me?" He backs away toward the bench he has set up, and at a quick assessment, it looks as though he's lifting about two-twenty-five.

"Sure." I shrug, that line I drew over the weekend blurring with my first step toward him.

He straddles the bench, pulling up the legs of his shorts as he sits, and it's impossible not to gawk at his thick, defined quads. He might be right about the heat in here. I already regret the long-sleeved tee. I push the sleeves up and move into position at the bar while he leans back, resting his head in front of my knees. His hair flops back and if I were in shorts, it would tickle me.

I left without a hair band, so I stuff my hair into the neck of my shirt to keep it out of my face. When I look down and meet Cannon's waiting gaze, I notice the amusement threatening to break his lips into a chuckle.

"What?" My New York accent is thick tonight.

"You are always tying your hair in literal knots. Why do you even have it long?"

I blow at a stray lock that's already fallen over my face,

and it's enough to pull out the laugh he's been holding on to.

"You make a good point, Jennings," I say, pushing the rogue hairs back into my collar, then tugging the neck of my shirt forward to keep them locked behind me for a few extra seconds. I hope.

I wrap my hands around the center of the bar while he places his on the outsides, making eye contact with me when he's comfortable. He nods and blows out, and suddenly I notice his lips. Full, a maroon red brought out by the blend of the cold air outside and the oven Pete's made inside. His cheeks are rosy, and there's a faint trace of stubble along his jawline. I don't think he could quite grow a beard, but for some reason, I imagine a version of him ten years from now that has one.

With a hard upward thrust, Cannon brings me back to the present, pushing the bar from his chest with a grunt. My fingers remain loose but poised, ready to help. Nobody at Xavier ever lifted this much weight. My dad lifts this much. *Sometimes.*

His pace is unflinching, the bar lowering with ease, rising with an equal push every time. He doesn't struggle until the end of his fifth rep, and even then, he only needs a little verbal encouragement from me.

"You got this. This is nothing for you, come on!" I boost. His eyes flit to mine while he holds his breath, his pupils a deep black from the effort, the ring of blue around them practically glowing, as if he's more machine than man. Perhaps he is, because when he reaches the top, he leaves his eyes on mine as he grunts out, "Again!"

I hold his intense stare, gauging his command, rooting

out whether he's simply showing off for me or working to improve . . . *for him*.

I nod when I realize he's going to do this no matter what my response is, and I tighten my hold on the bar, not wanting him to injure himself on my watch. The bar falls more easily this time, his resistance weakened, and as it bounces off his chest, his drained power becomes evident.

"Come on!" he shouts at himself. I help with the lift just enough to give him an edge, his left arm stronger than his right; most of my work is to keep the bar level.

"Almost there," I say, even though he's only a quarter in to the return.

"Come on, push!" His eyes lock on mine again with my shout, and the doubt clears away behind them. He growls as his grip tightens, my hands sliding toward his, holding his fingers in place, not so much lifting as guiding him up. The muscles and tendons on his forearms and biceps roll in waves, working in unison to pass this hurdle. The moment the bar rolls back onto the rack, a hard breath rushes from his mouth, puffing his cheeks before his arms fall limp at his sides.

The smile that stretches his maroon lips is instant, and so very wide. Dimples mark both cheeks and the rush of blood comes back into his face as laughter billows in his throat and through his mouth in apparent relief.

"God*damn*, that was hard," he admits.

My hands are still on the bar as I stare down at him, my hair no longer obeying where I put it, instead sticking to my neck and face. I barely did any work and I'm sweating. Cannon was right, but it's the feel of his hands underneath mine, trusting mine, working *with* mine, that makes me rush with heat.

I suddenly need distance between us. I fall back a few steps to another bench, sitting down to pull my long-sleeved shirt over my head, and wiping away the sweat from my neck and forehead. I'm in my sports bra, which is never weird for me, and usually isn't a big deal for other guys in gyms. But my bare arms and midriff are Cannon's primary focus as he stares at me upside down, his head tilted up and his hair falling from the end of the bench while he stares at me from his lying position.

Leaning back, I place my palms on the bench behind me and stretch a little, fully aware of what this position does to my breasts and stomach. I'm basically a peacock right now, tits for feathers. I'm not a Victoria Secret model, my size modest, but B-cups pronounced from my muscle can draw attention. I've never really wanted someone to look. It's antithetical to what I preach. Fuck hypocrisy, though, because this is the first time since our kiss that Cannon Jennings has looked at me and licked his lips.

"You wanna go next?" He asks the question while still meeting my gaze from upside down. It's somehow easier to look him in the eyes this way.

I nod and get up just as he does. We cross paths, our arms brushing as we pass and he moves to stand at the bar while I position myself on my back, feet flat on the ground and my eyes fighting not to look past the bar and into his. I focus on my hands while shifting my butt on the bench until my lower back finds comfort. I test my grip while Cannon removes most of the weight. He's about to take another twenty-five plate off when I stop him.

"I can do that," I say. It's my max. It took me all summer to get up to one-twenty-five, and I was stubborn about it. I can tell Cannon has reservations by the way his gaze sticks to mine, his head slightly angled. His doubt fuels me.

"I said I can do that, so let's go, pitcher boy." He flinches at my tease but shakes his head while smiling.

"Pretty sure in the short time I've known you I've learned when I can and can't tell you to do things," he mutters.

"And that would be never. You can never tell me what to do," I respond, my mouth a tight, serious line for exactly two seconds before I let my laugh break through.

"I'm pretty sure you're not joking about that." He winces in one eye and smiles crooked. I nod toward the bar and try my damnedest to focus on this heavy-ass weight I'm about to lift up from my chest.

"Alright, Staten Island girl, show me what you got!" His encouragement is genuine, and it's enough to get me through the first thrust, lifting the bar off the rack and into position above my chest. Now comes the hard part.

I flit my gaze to his in a brief panic, and his grip tightens on the bar as he senses I need more help than I let on. He doesn't bail me out, though, which I appreciate. He's going to make me follow through with this.

"Come on. First one; we can get to three," he says, his voice low as he bends forward and speaks at me.

"Four," I grunt back. I can feel his assistance, his hold taking enough of the weight off for me not to crush my ribs, and as I let the bar hit my chest, I'm able to rebound it back up. I grit my teeth and tense my jaw so much that I feel the strain in the sides of my neck as my hands wobble their way back toward him, my elbows locking at the top.

"Okay, that was one. Let's get to three and then we can negotiate that fourth one, deal?" He lifts one eyebrow and I try to laugh. My exertion only allows me a quick nod, though.

"Fine," I bark out.

He chuckles and shakes his head, guiding my hands back down as I work on the second rep. Determined not to get weaker, I groan loudly, the same way my dad does when he maxes out, and the air in my lungs buoys me enough to finish the second rep with a little more energy. Not wanting to lose it, I nod at him to go right into the third. My muscles burn, and sweat glistens on my arms. It's the middle of winter in Indiana but I am burning up.

"You got this," Cannon chants.

His voice invades my head and I take my eyes away from my hands for just a blip. His eyes are focused on my hands, on the bar that is too heavy for me at this point but that he believes I can move. He nods, but our gazes don't quite meet. I'm glad because if they did, I might drop everything.

Lost in his blues, I blow out hard as the weight lands against my breasts. This exercise is so much harder for women. I can't imagine men lifting weights precariously over their balls. It wouldn't happen. I push and grind and my elbows are tingling by the time I straighten them again, arms locked and spent. I don't let go of my grip, though. I don't let the flex slip away either, because now is the time to negotiate. A small part of me wants Cannon to insist and give me permission to not walk the walk I so carelessly talked. But that is not his style. Yet one more thing for the list.

"You ready for this fourth one?" His eyes shift just enough to meet mine, and I can read the challenge in them. It's different than the taunting way his cousin stares at me, or the way parents at Xavier looked on when I took the field. Cannon is looking at me as though he legitimately believes I can do this.

I nod again and pant out a "Yes" as together we bring the bar back down to my body. Cannon helps way more this time, taking a good twenty-percent of the weight for me by the time I reach my chest. The way up is a different story.

"Time to battle," he coaches, easing up so I feel the struggle.

His assistance isn't gone, but he isn't helping me at the same level he did the first three reps. This time, my arms have little to give, so I dig in with my feet and crush the arch of my back against the bench for every extra little ounce of leverage I can get. I start to cry out as the bar falls to one side then the other. Each time, Cannon gives me a nudge back to balanced, continually uttering encouragement.

"You're so close. It's almost there. One more . . . just one more push." He takes over when I'm about an inch from getting the bar back on the rack, and the moment my arms are free, I let them dangle to my sides as relief and pride flush my body.

Cannon claps a single clap and brings his closed palms up to his lips, hiding his grin.

"I can do that," I say, echoing my proclamation from

minutes before. My lips a lazy, open-mouthed smile, I say it again, my eyes meeting Cannon's as he backs away a few steps. "I can do that."

"You just *did* that," he corrects.

His cheeks dimple with his closed-mouth smile, and I cash that expression in as mine—I earned those dimples. Still a little breathless, and hot as hell, I maintain our stare until it becomes uncomfortable. Cannon is the first to look away, glancing down at his feet as he shuffles back until his shoulders touch the wall.

I swivel my legs around the bench as I sit up, straddling it and facing the other direction so we're now looking at one another. His stoic armor slips as his focus moves from my face to my neck, then to my bare midriff. When he looks me in the eyes again, he sees he's caught and rubs his palm over his chin as he lets out a bashful laugh.

"I like the belly button ring," he says, gesturing lazily at my stomach. I tuck my chin to my chest and stretch my skin.

"Oh, yeah. I forget I have it sometimes." I shrug when I look back up at him and he gives a slight shake to his head, breathing out across his faint smile.

"What?" I press.

His eyes dip to my stomach again and his lips part, his expression a little more predatory, definitely interested. I allow myself a glance toward his stomach, and then lower. Training shorts don't mask much, and Cannon is definitely into belly button rings.

I flick my finger against the metal to get his attention, but he doesn't waver, his gaze still on my bare skin, soaking me in like a boy told not to eat desert before dinner.

"I didn't plan on working out." I tap the bottom of my pink boots against the concrete floor a few times, drawing Cannon's stare there instead. He tilts his head back with a short laugh.

"That's a first. Pretty sure Pete's never had anyone lifting in princess gear before!" He lets his hands fall into his pockets as he shifts his weight against the wall, crossing his feet at the ankles.

I lift my toes to gaze at the glitter accents on the knitting, and smirk.

"My little brother bought these for me as a joke because me and pink aren't really a thing. Turns out though . . ." I draw my legs up and fold them on the bench, sitting so my hands can hold on to the tops of my feet. "I really love these things."

I gaze up at Cannon with a cheesy grin and he pushes away from the wall, nodding at my shoes. "They're pretty dope."

I wait for him to pass, irrationally pleased that he approves of my girly footwear. He's taking down the weights from my bar, so I stand and help him. We work wordlessly for a few minutes, leaving things nice by the rack before moving on to free weights. I kick the tire I saw him flipping when I first visited the gym.

"I'd like to try this sometime," I say.

He finds a good spot to stand for his bicep curls then glances from the tire to me and back again. "Shouldn't be a problem for you," he says, sizing me up like an equal. As he begins lifting, I stand by and watch for a few minutes, letting myself live this moment. I'm always either the cool teammate or the girl some boy who has no interest in team sports is into. Other than Jordan, guys in my game don't want to cross boundaries, and my relationship with my ex was living proof of what a disaster it is to blur the lines. But maybe . . . maybe I can be both the kinda girl you kiss at a party *and* the kind you throw with on the diamond.

Lost in this blissful fantasy, I set my feet up a few feet from Cannon, facing the wall-length mirrors as I begin my reps. My weights are about half the size of his, and my biceps are definitely not in the same league, but I keep pace, doing the same number of reps and resting in sync with him. We're about to begin our third sets when his eyes finally find mine in our reflection. He studies me while his arms begin their work.

"Hey, about Friday." He starts a conversation, maybe hoping I'll take it over and navigate the rough waters. What he doesn't get, though, is that this is a conversation I don't want to have. He's in the boat alone.

"Don't." My response is swift and clipped, forming instant ice. "It . . . It's fine." *Not fine.*

The awkward silence seeps back in, and my motivation to lift weights—to even be here—wanes. Butterflies are gone, replaced by lead and rocks that sit heavy in my gut.

"It's just that Zack . . ."

I let my arms fall, heavy with the weights, and look up at Pete's cobweb-covered ceiling tiles.

"Please, just don't," I grumble.

I roll my head to the side, eyes meeting his. He's grimacing as if embarrassed of his cousin, but Zack isn't his job. Cannon is responsible for Cannon.

"It's usually a boys' club out there . . ." He trails off, because there's no great way to finish that statement.

"Except for the girls who sit around and stare at you guys with awe like you're gods. Bare-chested gods." That was smug. My chest is getting tight. This happens when I get frustrated and conflicted. I'm not a very pretty angry person.

"Come on, that's not fair. So what that some of the girls like to hang out and watch us? So what if our shirts are off? And so what if, you know what? Some of us like the attention, and some of them like to give it to us. Fuck, Hollis. You need to seriously loosen up. Not everything is a protest for women's equality. And you can take your shirt off too, ya know. No rules against that out there." He rolls his eyes, a sneer to his lips as he turns away. He's proud of himself, and that tightness in my chest is close to suffocating. The only relief will be letting it burst.

Cannon dumps his weights on the rack and I follow a step behind, dumping mine right next to his. He huffs and moves them to the right place, which is actually a nice thing to do but the way he does it ticks me off, so I groan, balling my fists at my sides.

"Why did you have to ruin this?" I lament.

"Ruin what, Hollis? I was just trying to talk to you, about Zack and what he did—"

"You were making an excuse for him," I cut in, leveling him with the truth.

His mouth opens but promptly shuts. His eyes shift their focus from my right one to my left, his mind working behind them. I pat my closed fist against my hip, antsy and unsure whether I should wait for him to speak or get this weight off my chest.

"I swear, Hollis, I'm not making excuses for him. He

was . . . not cool. Friday was not cool," he says, and I instantly regret letting him go first.

I laugh out and look up again, my jaw slack and my spirit dashed. How can I be so attracted to a guy who I also want throttle until he understands what it's like to be a girl in this world?

My head falls forward and I nod, a pathetic laugh drifting through my parted lips, the faint smile I'm wearing only there to mask that I'm nowhere near happy or really amused.

"You're right, Cannon. Way to sum that all up. Zack was not cool. And perhaps *Friday* was not cool either. That's what happened. Not cool," I rattle off, laughing a little more with every word I breathe because this is so ridiculous. I should have stayed home and tried to paint my dad's nails while he slept or put popcorn in his nostrils.

"You don't make this easy," he finally breaks in. His words stop me cold, my mouth closing while I stare, unblinking, at the space to the right of him, unable to bring my eyes to him fully.

"*I* don't make this easy," I rephrase. I just want him to hear it, in my tongue.

Crossing my line of sight with a heavy sigh, he grabs what must be his towel from a weight rack and slaps it against the metal with one hand. I'm no longer warm in this room. My bones are cold, my skin covered in bumps. Things got cold in here real fast.

"You just stood there, Cannon. Seems you decided to take it easy. I don't make it anything," I say.

He rolls his neck before balling the towel up and throwing it on top of his gym bag in the corner. I recognize his stuff from last time, bag unzipped with his clothes and phone inside. My eyes dart to the place where the towel now rests on top of his slides and sweat pants.

"Your cousin doesn't like me, because . . ." I shrug, not having to say it; we both know. I'm a threat. Short and sweet, very simple. "And he chose to deal with his dislike by demeaning me in front of others, by sexualizing me to point out that I am different from the rest of you. That he has a power I could never have, and that makes me weak and him strong."

"Hollis." The way he says my name and lets his head tilt makes my stomach churn, and not because of the belittling tone underneath, but because for a little while there, I had fantasies of him tilting his head and saying my name for wholly different reasons.

My eyes flutter closed as he speaks the rest, the words I saw coming.

"You're overreacting. It was hardly a statement. He just slapped your . . ."

The fact he can't finish tells me he knows he's wrong, that his line is bullshit. I open my eyes and point at him, wishing I could handle getting close enough to push into the center of his chest. My legs are lead, though. Most of me doesn't want to be near him.

"And you stood there and let him get away with it." I hold his gaze for several long, uncomfortable seconds, long enough for my legs to regain their feeling. I stay locked on his face while I move back toward the benches, to my abandoned long-sleeved tee that I want to crawl inside of and disappear into. Too mad to stick around to put it back on, I instead grab it, glaring at Cannon until I have to crane my neck to do so. I let my anger spill out onto Pete as I pass, knocking on his counter while I walk by and check the score as I utter, "Suck it, Green Bay." That wasn't fair, but I don't like being prodded into uncomfortable conversations. I knew I wasn't ready to talk about Friday, and especially not with Cannon.

His cousin may have felt threatened before, but he has no idea what's gunning for him now. I'm not going to make this look close anymore, and I won't offer advice. I'm going to humiliate him out there at workouts, and when tryouts come in two weeks, I'll make it hard for my dad to justify keeping him on the roster at all. And if Cannon can't throw what I need him to, then he's next. It won't be me calling in a favor from Daddy, either. It will be me showing everyone the difference between serious talent and a bunch of boys playing a game.

9

CANNON

S he was right, righter than she even realizes.

It's Monday morning and I have yet to call my cousin out on acting like a douchebag. Not only did I stand there and watch him belittle her, but I'm still standing by and doing nothing. I thought about it all night, and it's still heavy on my mind now that I'm sitting across the table from him, watching him slurp up oatmeal like a kid still learning how to use utensils.

"Tryouts in two weeks. Who's ready?" Uncle Joel lands his heavy palms on Zack's shoulders and my cousin abruptly drops his spoon. The weight is both literal and psychological.

"We should have a pretty good team," I say, not wanting to give away too many details. I'm not sure what Uncle Joel knows beyond Coach Taylor has a daughter playing. My uncle joined the board recently, probably to have leverage. I don't think my cousin has been totally forthcoming about his insecurities, though, and I sure as shit ain't going to expose them over breakfast.

"They got you throwing to Zack?" He squeezes my cousin's shoulders when he asks that question, and his eyes grill mine from across the table.

"Got me throwing to everybody," I say. It's not a lie, and it's enough to pull a chuckle from my uncle's mouth while I leave the table with my bowl and empty glass to find solace at the sink with my back turned to them.

"Rumor is coach's daughter isn't awful. How 'bout that?" He's baiting Zack. I can tell. He knows more than he's admitting.

"She's all right," my cousin says. His chair screeches along the floor behind me, so I move out of his way at the sink, anticipating him. Our eyes meet briefly at the dishwasher, and a silent agreement passes between us.

Mouths. Shut.

"You throw to her at all yet, Cannon?" Now he's baiting me. I don't like it. This isn't how things work between my dad and me. We say what we mean and don't equivocate. It's a blunt and honest relationship that has never led to fights or distrust, and I'm sad that my cousin doesn't get to have the same thing.

"Eh, a little," I say with a shrug. I don't make eye contact with him on purpose, and his enduring silence gives me the sense that he knows why I'm not looking at him.

My backpack is near the stairs, so I move over to it and unzip and rezip the top for no reason other than to bide time while Zack catches up to me.

"Well, maybe I'll stop in and check out the lay of the land today. I've got a free afternoon," my uncle says.

My cousin's eyes close as he exhales next to me.

"Sounds good. We gotta go," Zack responds, keeping the keys in his palm this time and jetting right toward the front door. I lag behind, and my pulse actually races with fear that my uncle will try to pull one more piece of intel out of me before I can get away. I breathe out in relief at the sound of the door falling closed behind me.

"Take it you wanna drive this morning?" I meet his eyes over the roof of the car.

He nods, getting in without pause and firing up the engine before I have a chance to shut my door. We don't talk most of the way to school, but I can tell he's stewing.

"I think I'm throwing to you today," I finally speak.

"Uh huh." Zack's response is clipped.

It's bullshit, and we both know it. I have no idea who I'm throwing to. I only know that I threw with Hollis on Thursday and Coach likes to rotate us.

"Workouts are pretty regimented anyhow. There's not a lot to see, so your dad will probably get bored and leave in the first ten minutes." I don't know why I'm hell-bent on easing his anxiety, especially since I'm embarrassed for him after Friday's basketball incident. And he clearly isn't interested in anything I have to say this morning.

The car hits the dip into the school lot forcefully and I have to palm the dash to steady myself. Zack's driving like an ass.

"Fuck, dude. Easy," I finally grit out.

"*Pfft,*" he breathes.

I sink into my seat and focus out my window on

anything that isn't my cousin. When I see Hollis and her dad pull around to the back of the school in their van, I make a silent wish that Zack missed it. I'm not ready for him to launch into some snide remark about how nice it must be to live with Coach and get rides to school with him. I won't be able to indulge his grudge if he tests me right now.

Luckily, he's not in the mood to talk. We pull into our spot and he leaves the car before I unbuckle. I laugh quietly to myself as he stomps through the main doors and disappears, probably getting to class earlier than he ever has in his entire life. Turning my attention to the front, my gaze meets Tory's and he nods, leaving our group of friends and walking toward my side of the car. I kick open the door just as he steps up.

"Hey, man. I see Zack is still on his one-man douchebag mission," Tory says, pulling a short laugh from me as we slap hands. I shift in the seat while he folds his arms over the window frame on the door and glances around the lot.

"That was pretty fucked up, yo," Tory says, and I know he's talking about Friday.

"Yeah." I sigh. I don't have much to add because his synopsis captured Friday to a tee. *Fucked. Up.*

"This is about him, just so you know," Tory says, and I turn to look him in the eyes. "Don't get caught up in it and think you have to do whatever he does or defend him. I've learned a lot of things this last year, and key is knowing how to take care of your own shit. Don't get yourself neck deep in his to the point you drown in your own."

"Colorful," I say, chuckling.

"Yeah, well." He shrugs, opening my door fully while I grab my bag from the floor and step out of the car.

We hang close, Tory probably sensing that I'm not ready to talk about Zack's shit with a full group. It would be impossible for people not to bring it up. I'm surprised his ass slap isn't trending on social media. For Hollis's sake, I'm glad it's not.

Hollis.

I've been so caught up in my morning that for a brief bit I forgot I have to sit three feet from her in about ten minutes. I spent most of the night tossing and turning, playing out how this morning would go. I tried out jokes and flat-out apologies. Every scenario I imagined ended in her telling me to fuck off. Maybe I should just get that over with and say it before she has a chance to.

"See? That's how it starts," Tory says, pulling me out of my head.

"What?" I ask.

"You, taking on your cousin's shit. You're trying to work it out. I can read it all over your face."

"*Pshh*, nah. That's not it." I push away from our car and wander closer to the main doors. Tory tags along, waving off his brother who's hanging out with the girls.

"Spill," Tory says when we're far enough away from everyone for there to be no ears around to hear.

I wrinkle my face, a little in self-disgust but mostly because talking about things in my head with anyone but my dad isn't something I do. And even with my dad, it's mostly school, college, or baseball talk.

"My first hour is with Hollis. Think you can pretend to

be my uncle and call me in sick?" I lift a brow at him, half serious about my request.

Tory's shoulders lift with his laugh.

"That's what happens when you kiss a total stranger. Things get messy." He pulls the tab on his energy drink and sucks down half of it, peering at me over the can.

My eyes narrow.

"How'd you know about that?" I query.

He pulls the can away and belches while shrugging.

"Saw you through the window." He holds his can out for me, and I take a shot of caffeine. I'm going to need a jolt of something to get through this.

"Yeah, well, that's only half the reason this is all so complicated. I'm not sure I can avoid drowning in Zack's shit because we have the same mess. Our issues bleed together, and then our dads are involved, and his is on the board for the booster club, and then . . ."

"I'm gonna stop you here," Tory says, hand on my shoulder with a heavy pat. "All that you just said?" He circles his finger in the air between us. "None of that means anything to me, or makes sense. But I can almost guarantee that you and Zack are not in the same shoes. You're making his problems yours, and that is only going to fuck with your head, my friend."

He flicks my forehead with a snap, and it hurts.

"Ow! Dick," I say, swiping at his hand but missing it. He laughs, then finishes the rest of his drink, tossing the can in the recycle bin by the office.

Our friends catch up to us, and June makes her way next to me. The bell is seconds from rescuing me, but it's as if she has it under her control and won't let it ring until she invades my head and space.

"How are you?" I'm immediately thrown by her sincere question and my brow puzzles. I was prepared for a lecture, part two of the things Hollis said to me at the gym last night.

"I'm . . . fine," I say, turning my head further and looking at her sideways. She doesn't budge, her eyes slanting more, and her stare unforgiving. She's a high school senior with mom powers; I swear she's looking right through me.

"I don't know," I finally give.

June loops her arm through mine and squeezes my bicep. She and I aren't close, not really, but she's always struck me as soft and kind. I can see why Lucas loves her. She's . . . *intuitive.*

"Nobody blames you," she finally says, the bell sounding behind her words.

My forehead dents as we move through the corridor, but not because I don't understand what she means. I understand perfectly. What hits me is the way she cut right to the heart of my stress. They don't blame me, but there is one person who does. And she's already sitting in her seat by the time I make it to my classroom door.

I'm a little shell shocked by the time I land in my seat, and I dump my bag by my feet and let my forehead fall into my palms. Rubbing my eyes, I ready myself for the hard part—*the hardest, really.*

My hair curly from my morning shower, I roll my head to the side in my hands and wait, staring on while Hollis busies herself with dozens of little tasks that I recognize as diversions, ways to keep herself from looking at me. Finally, the heat of my attention too much perhaps, she flattens her pen against her notebook and presses her palms on her desk, splaying her fingers out while she draws in a deep breath.

Her head turns and our eyes meet. Mine were waiting. Before she can open her mouth to keep this grudge going, I end it.

"I'm sorry."

Her lips are parted, the path her words were on suddenly diverted with something so simple. An apology. One she deserves from more than only me for sure, but one I owe her. And the only one I have the power to give.

My lips tighten in a subtle smile as I lock in anything else that might slip out on accident. There aren't any *buts* that need to be added. No excuses to make for people who aren't me. As Tory said, I'm taking care of my own shit.

She blinks a few times, hesitantly staring back.

"That's it. No excuses. I'm sorry, and you are right," I expand. The class quiets around us, and Mr. V dims the lights, flicking on the screen up front. He's giving instructions but I'm not listening. I'm determined not to look away from her until she gives me permission, even if it isn't full absolution.

Hollis clears her throat as she shifts in her seat, bringing her hands together on top of her notebook and moving her gaze to her own hands. She taps her thumbs together a few times and flits her gaze to me a few times, as if coming to a decision. I feel a bit as if I'm on trial with a super biased jury.

Leaning to her right, she glances first up to the monitor

and our teacher, then to the floor, where her backpack rests beside her leg. Tugging on the top zipper, she reaches in, feeling around for something, her eyes remaining up front —always the perfect student. The scene makes me smile, even if I feel a bit shunned. She straightens again, a pack of gum cupped in her palm. She works it open in her lap and pulls out a stick, unwrapping it without looking and popping it in her mouth. She turns to me mid-chew, one eyebrow raised and holds the pack out for me.

"Gum?" she asks.

I breathe out a quiet laugh and shift my focus from the pack back to her, studying her eyes and her features for a second or two.

"Sure," I respond, reaching over and pulling out the piece on top. Her gaze sticks to mine through it all, as I unwrap the stick while staring back at her, and even while I pop it in my mouth and begin to chew. I smile with closed lips when the gum goes soft, and she does the same, our jaws in sync as they work slowly.

"Thanks," I whisper.

She responds with a slow blink, her lashes dusting the tops of her cheeks while her mouth curves up into them.

That's all it took. My chest is open, and I can breathe. Hollis is as comfortable with saying I'm forgiven as I was apologizing, and a stick of gum is her olive branch. Now, if only this feeling can stick all the way through practice. Somehow, I'm doubtful.

My relief is short-lived. By the time Zack and I make it to the track to get our laps in, Uncle Joel already stands in the middle of the field next to Coach. I'm not sure which I want more—super powers that let me listen in from a distance, or to never know what they're saying. Zack probably feels the same.

We hit the track at the same time, and even though I finish before him, he's not far behind. I turn to congratulate him with a raised hand as we walk back to our gear, but his eyes are fixed on his father so I let it fall to my side.

Zack slings his heavy catchers' bag over his shoulder, not bothering to roll it. I'm not sure whether it's an act of showing off how strong he is, even after a run, or if he's so angry about his dad showing up that his veins are pumping super-human blood.

"Hey, it's gonna be fine," I say at his back. He's not waiting for me, but I get it.

He turns his head to the side, his eyes not fully reaching me as he nods. I slow my steps and let him gain some distance, maybe subconsciously wanting him to seem more dedicated than me, like he has hustle. By the time I reach the dugout, he's already fastened on his leg guards and is jogging out on the field to stretch with Hollis and the other catchers. I let my gaze wander toward Uncle Joel while I switch out my shoes, glancing up and peeking from under the brim of my hat. He's intently watching his son, arms crossed, while he remains stoic at Coach Taylor's side.

Nothing about this is good for anyone. Coaches aren't interested in parental opinions, but because Joel is who he is, and because he has a say in hiring and firing and funding this program, Hollis's dad entertains the conversation. His sunglasses shield his eyes, but I can read enough into the hard line of his mouth to know he hates every minute of this forced conversation.

No longer able to stall, I grab my glove and kick my gear bag into the corner before jogging out to stretch with the other pitchers. I catch the end of Joel and Coach's talk as I run by.

"Lots of talent, like you said, Coach," Joel says just before putting a hand on Coach's shoulder, somewhere between a friendly pat on the back and an intimidating intrusion of his personal space. "But hey, I know you'll make the right choice."

"The *best* choice," Hollis's dad adds as he draws his lips in for a tight smile. There's an *F-U* behind those lips, and Joel knows it. I glance away before I'm caught staring, but listen to the end.

"Of course. But we all know who the best is," Joel closes with, walking backward in my periphery. I shut my eyes, wincing through my last few steps until I join the rest of my teammates.

That weight I cleared out with Hollis this morning has been replaced by something heavier that takes up every inch of space inside. I feel as though my arms can't move independent of my gut, my pulse controls the pace of my legs, and my head is going to either deflate or pop without warning.

Somehow, I get through my stretches without bending over to vomit, and I remind myself to breathe, hearing Tory and June's advice in my head. I'm in charge of me, and

Zack's shit is his. Only, I'm living with all of this, and his dad and my dad, and Zack—*family*—is the whole reason I'm here in the first place. Lines are hard to draw, and while I get what Tory meant, I don't think he understands how tangled everything is when it comes to this season— this team. Maybe I did get Hollis's forgiveness today, but if I can't walk this line just right, I'll end up betraying my family, and that apology will require a lot more than a pact made over some Doublemint.

"Jennings!"

I turn to answer the same time Zack does, both of us responding with, "Yes, Coach" from either end of the field. Coach Taylor lifts his hand and pinches the bridge of his nose just under his glasses.

"Sorry, I keep forgetting. Cannon," he says, gesturing for me to rush over.

I pick up my glove and do as asked, noting that my cousin watches my every move while finishing his stretches.

"I'm gonna have you throw to Hollis today," he says the moment I step up to him.

My mouth goes dry. My uncle is pacing around the dugout just beyond his shoulder.

I squint from the sun as I look at him. It's bright as fuck out today, the sky filled with puffy white clouds. I never wear glasses, though. I don't like the feeling of anything on me when I'm throwing. Extra swag is always a distraction. If I could get away with ditching the cap, I would.

"You sure about that, Coach?" I question. I know immediately that he's sure, and that I should shut my damn mouth, but that sick feeling taking over my insides made me ask.

He doesn't respond with words, only a look, one I have to read through the sheen of his Oakleys.

"Right, okay." I nod and head toward the bullpen. I get about ten steps into my jog when Coach stops me.

"We're on the mound today."

I pause mid-step and spin on my right foot, coming back toward him. He's making a point, and I'm part of the performance. There are seven of us out here who can throw, and at least three who are going somewhere after this year. He could have led with any duo, but he chose me and Hollis on purpose. I'm the best, but Roland or Jay would have been great choices for this exhibition. *Jay has a better curveball!*

My inner-dialogue continues on a constant stream while Coach calls Hollis out and points to the plate. She rushes into the dugout to grab her mask and chest protector while I kick at the rubber and push the dirt exactly the way I like it. She has no idea that Zack's dad is the weird guy wearing the crisp white dress shirt and deep blue tie hovering around the bench while she gets dressed. She doesn't even glance his direction despite the fact he is practically memorizing everything about her with that judgmental stare.

It's then that I realize exactly why Uncle Joel is out here. *Someone said something.*

I know it wasn't Zack. He was hoping to just win the starting job and have this never be an issue. Too late for that, though. It's the only issue in Joel's sights. My uncle rubs his chin, looking on while Hollis rushes into place, shaking dirt from her mask before pulling it over her head and face. She pats her glove a few times to tell me she's ready, and I circle the mound, stepping up a few feet behind the rubber to do some warm-up tosses while she stands.

I shoot a glance at my uncle before throwing. His arms are crossed firmly over his chest and he's chewing at the inside of his mouth. It's an old habit from his playing days when a wad of tobacco was always tucked inside his lip.

There's no way out other than marching off this field in protest or quitting to go play tennis, a sport I absolutely suck at, so I shuffle step toward Hollis and throw the ball. It hits her glove and creates a poof of dust before she pulls it free and sends it back to me on a zipline. I sneak another look in my uncle's direction while I set my feet again and note how sunk in his cheek is. He's chewing on it harder. He was hoping the rumors weren't true, but it's hard not to see that Hollis is the real deal.

She's not only good, she's *better*.

She and I continue our warmups until the rest of the team moves into the dugout, displacing Uncle Joel. He moves behind the backstop, just over Hollis's right shoulder, and takes a seat in the bleachers, his tie blowing across his body with the breeze. He has to be cold. Even with the sun and clouds reflecting the heat, it's maybe fifty out here. I'm wearing thermal compression pants and a long sleeves, and I feel the slight wind cut through the threads.

"Jennings," Coach shouts. This time I'm the only one who answers, Zack sitting on the bench with his water jug balanced on his knee. My cousin's eyes reach mine when I respond to our coach and the look of betrayal absolutely slays me.

"Yes?" I swallow, thankful I'm out here on the mound alone so no one can read the subtleties in my expression.

"Think you can handle three live batters? I'm looking to give you all three apiece today." He glances to his right where Jay and Roland stand waiting to go next.

I nod, choking down the bile.

"Sure," I say, dipping my chin and kicking the dirt out a little more to find my perfect fit.

I signal to Hollis that I'm ready to throw a few warm-up pitches for real, and she crouches down, ready to take them. We start with a few straight fastballs, and I easily hit her location. I shut out the sounds of players taking position behind me, ignoring my infielders throwing the ball a few feet away. I throw a change up and a curve next, one a little off target, forcing Hollis to drop to a knee to block it. The ball kicks away from her when she does, and she stands, jogging over to get it. I catch the pleased smirk on my uncle's face behind her, his shoulders shaking with laughter at the "silly girl trying to play a man's game."

Suddenly, I'm at another crossroads, not sure whether I want Hollis to shine or fail miserably. Maybe she'll be mediocre, and Zack will be a little *less* mediocre. There's no win in this situation.

"Johnson," Coach calls out. One of the guys I don't know well grabs a helmet and rushes out to the batter's box, the first unlucky supporting cast member in this play called *Get This Nosey-Ass Board Member Parent Off My Field*.

My guess is Johnson is a freshman, maybe a sophomore. His knees are quaking, and it's not only his pants blowing in the wind. Those suckers are skin tight. Hollis glances up at him then back to me, pounding her mitt before reaching down and giving me the sign for a two-seam right down the center.

I nod before winding up and rocketing the ball to her without as much as a blink from Johnson in the box. Hollis throws the ball right back to me while Johnson steps out and adjusts the Velcro on his gloves, as if that's what made him freeze and forget to swing.

I let myself be amused for a moment, also glad that this first batter is nothing special. Hollis handling my straight fastballs is meaningless. Hell, I could affix a glove to a folding chair for this, no catcher necessary. Nothing about this impresses my uncle, which means so far, my cousin is off the hook for having to prove anything in front of his dad.

It takes three pitches to strike Johnson out, and Coach forces the poor guy to stay up there and try to bunt for three more throws. He can't get a single one fair, though, so before my pitch count gets needlessly high, Coach lets him off the hook.

"Madden, you're up," he shouts, patting Johnson on the back as he runs by. If anyone is quitting to join the tennis team today, it might be him. Dude looks shell shocked.

Marcus Madden is another story. I know it, and so does Hollis. Marcus and I played fall ball out here together, along with Zack, which means Uncle Joel knows a thing or two about Marcus's swing. There are two guys who can put the ball over the fence if you're not careful, and Marcus is one of them.

As Marcus takes a few practice swings, my uncle sits up tall, rolling his shoulders and clasping his hands in front of him, elbows on his knees. He rubs his palms together greedily, and I can't help but imagine he's making a wish for one of those dingers right now. Either that or a harsh foul ball right into Hollis's head.

I grumble to myself, my voice a hum only I can hear, then step up on the rubber with my glove shadowing my chin while I look in for Hollis's signs. She asks for another straight fast ball, and I shake her off on instinct because I know better. Maybe I should let it go and get this over with, let Marcus round the bases and gloat. Hollis gives me the sign again and I suck in a hard breath, this time giving in.

"Fine," I mutter.

She moves her glove a few inches inside, crowding Marcus, which is smart, but maybe not pushing him tight enough. I wind up and let loose, both hoping it's enough and *just* enough at the same time. His swing is awkward, and the ball clips off the bat near his hands.

Coach whistles at me, and I turn as he tosses me a new ball. Hollis stands and kicks the other ball behind her before getting set for me to throw again. Her sign is exactly the same, and she sets up in the same spot. I'm tempted to shake her off, but after staring at her for a solid five seconds I decide, "What the hell."

I wind up again and throw the exact same pitch, getting the exact same result. This time Hollis scoops the foul tip and tosses the ball back to me in one smooth move.

If this were a real game, I'd be gloating right about now. Ahead in the count, the clutch hitter one strike away. But it's not a game, and my uncle is now standing. So is my cousin.

My eyes shift to Coach but he keeps his gaze firmly affixed to the clipboard he's balancing on the dugout fence. This is his daughter's call, and he trusts her to make the right one.

"Give him hell, Madden," my uncle taunts from behind the plate. A few of the guys in the dugout lean forward to see who the obnoxious parent is. Coach glares in Joel's direction, the sun glinting off of his sunglasses as the tendons in his neck flex. I'd laugh my uncle off if he were actually doing this in jest, but he's not. The same ugly side his son has when he's challenged is coming out right now.

Hollis flashes me the sign for my slider while everyone else is occupied with Zack's dad. It's a smart call, and if I were on my own, it's what I'd want to throw. Marcus digs in with his palm out to me to give him time. While he's a good hitter, his ego is a bit much. During games, he can drag his at bat out with annoying rituals and time-outs. He's been warned by umps for being excessive, but knows there's nothing anyone can do about it. You hit the ball like he does, you can call time-out to paint your nails with glitter if you want and coaches won't care.

Once he's ready, I waste a few extra seconds staring from behind my glove just to eat at his nerves. He's lined up as if he's anticipating me going back inside. It's a gamble, but one he had to take. If I do, he'll be ready to punish me for it. But I'm not. My only task now will be not to miss.

I wind up and throw, my world switching into slow motion as my back leg swings around with my follow-through, my eyes up while my hand cuts through the air and skims along my shin. I get my glove up and ready, because I know better than to stand there defenseless. But there's no need; the ball cuts exactly where I want it to go, trailing away from Marcus as he swings through hard enough to lose his balance and land on one knee.

Hollis stands and pushes the mask up on her head, flashing me a proud grin that I can't help but mimic. My uncle catches it, too, so I let it drop as soon as she throws me the ball and shouts toward the dugout.

"Next!"

She stands there with her gloved hand on her hip, mask pulled up while wild strands of hair blow in the strengthening wind. They've come loose from what is probably an actual knot she tied with her hair under her helmet. Dirt lines her cheeks, darkened by sweat. And through it all, her blue eyes glitter like sapphires, the one beautiful thing she cannot cover up and hide no matter how hard she tries.

There's something exceptional about her, and I admit that to myself right now. She's not just beautiful, though goddamn is she. It's something more than that—this vibe she has that seems so invincible. While Marcus wears his confidence like an arrogant bastard, Hollis wears it like a queen, every jewel in her crown owned. All of the compliments in the world would be meaningless to her, though. All she cares about is her own expectations for herself. I wonder if she ever falls short like I do.

"Jennings."

The sound of my name shakes me from my trance and I shout, "Huh?" to my coach, only to realize that for once he means the other Jennings.

"Grab a helmet," Coach orders.

Zack stands dumbfounded for a beat, his body rigid like a deer's at the sound of a predator.

I blink.

"Well, go on," Coach barks, his East Coast accent suddenly thick over so few words.

I gulp as Zack rushes to grab his helmet, stuffing it on his head and slipping his bat from his bag. He rushes out toward the plate, forgetting that he still wears his leg guards, and Coach has to remind him by clearing his throat, then pointing at them.

"Oh, for Christ's sake," my uncle mutters, his volume loud enough that I hear him easily. I'm sure most of us did. I recognize the way Zack's jaw tightens and his lips come together in a tight seal. Uncle Joel was merciless when Zack struck out growing up, and as we get older, my cousin bottles his anger in and buries it under that same expression.

I feel trapped, so many outcomes possible in the next few minutes. Nobody knows what I can throw better than the guy at the plate. Zack and I have been apart for two years, but when we came back together, it was seamless. That is, until Hollis ripped things open. I stare into her eyes sixty feet away. She's squinting with thought, probably working out how we navigate this situation her dad purposefully put us in. She bangs her glove against her hip a few times to clear the dirt away then squats, glaring up at my cousin as he takes a few warm-up swings.

Zack is a solid hitter. If I throw anything near the plate without something wicked on it, he'll get a piece of it. And maybe that's what should happen. Maybe I throw for a duel, several pitches wasted, so no matter who comes out of this as the winner, really, we both do. But something tells me Coach Taylor has a nose for bullshit play. He'll see right through it, and do I really want to be *soft?* This is too important for me, but if I humiliate Zack, his world will be crushed, and I can't live with that either.

He creeps into the batter's box, digging his heavy feet into the loose dirt and twisting on his toes. This guy has had the same swing for years, and it's dramatic and filled with all the little mannerisms he's grown up watching the pros do on TV. Uncle Joel eats it up.

"Come on, son!" My uncle claps three times before hooking his fingers into the backstop. He won't be sitting down.

Hollis signals for a fast ball, then sets up low and outside. She's right. My cousin has trouble hitting the outside pitches because of his wannabe-pro-style swing. He's too far from the plate, which makes him vulnerable. I nod, knowing it's the right thing to do for me, but it's going to make Zack look foolish.

I wind up and send the ball flying at Hollis with my usual amount of pepper, but I miss her spot, giving Zack just enough to foul off and please his dad.

"Atta boy. Come on, show him what you've been working on for two years!" My uncle cups his hands to clap this time, amplifying the slapping sound. It's his way of boasting.

Hollis stands and tosses the ball back to me after sliding her mask up on her head. She holds a palm out along with her open mitt. There's a stink on her face, a sourness that has her lips sneering while her nose scrunches up. We've thrown enough together for her to know when I miss my spot on purpose. Damn her father for putting me in this situation. I know he's trying to prove a point to my uncle, but I'm the one feeling the stress.

I turn and kick at the rubber to ignore her stare, though I swear I feel the heat of it in my back. The smart move is to throw my slider, because that pitch starts out looking like the perfect strike then veers right into my cousin's dead zone. Hollis must be in my head because that's exactly what she calls. I breathe in through my nose and pause for a few seconds before shaking her off. Instead of calling a different pitch, though, she gives me the sign again. I shake my head one more time. Any pitch but this one. It will make Zack look stupid. I've gotten so much better at it over the last two years, and he hasn't seen it enough to know it's coming.

Hollis drops her chin, eyes on the plate and her glove hanging limp on her hand. She snaps her head up again to meet my stare while I remain hidden behind my glove. I wish it were bigger, big enough to hide my entire body. I've muted my uncle's clapping, but every now and then it breaks through. I wonder if Zack's immune to it by now. He doesn't seem to be fazed, digging his feet into the dirt while he anticipates my next pitch. He's like a bull waiting to be let loose in the ring.

Hollis gives me the same sign one more time, and when I shake her off yet again, she pulls her mask off and rushes toward me. I can see her gritting teeth by the time she's halfway to me.

"What the fuck are you doing, Jennings?"

Wow, no mincing words.

"I'm not feeling that pitch," I lie.

"Bullshit. You're being a chicken. It's the right pitch to throw. If this were a game, you'd throw it," she seethes.

She pulls her mask down over her face and runs back to the plate, crouching down and giving me the same sign as the last four, insistent and not waiting for me to nod in agreement. She sets up and snaps her glove for the ball a few times, no longer giving me the luxury of throwing anything but what she wants. If I don't throw this, it's going to look like a huge miss on my part. Stuck, I pivot and lift my knee, giving her the perfect slider that leaves my cousin whiffing the bat through the strike zone, not even close.

"Oh, come on! Dude, you hit that! You know how to hit that, don't you?" My uncle comes off like a drunk Little League dad, and if he were any other parent, Coach Taylor would toss him off the field. But my uncle approves his paycheck. Enough *nay* votes at the board meeting would make the principal nervous, and nervous principals fire people to make problems go away. Coach Taylor is stuck, just as I am. The only way he can make his point is by setting Zack up to fail. But I don't want to be the one who stabs my cousin in the back. I don't think I can live with that.

Hollis throws the ball back and gives me a quick sign

for the same pitch, again. It's the right call, *again*. I nod, letting her know she's right, but there's no way in hell I'm throwing that pitch. My cousin needs this win a lot more than the rest of us. He's the one who has to sit at the dinner table with my uncle tonight. Uncle Joel will brag when my dad calls tomorrow too, probably embellishing the tale of his son's at bat against me, but I'll text my dad to let him know I missed on purpose. My dad will get it. He knows how his brother is; Uncle Joel is . . . *intense*. Besides, family comes first.

Right now, winding up and bringing my arms in then separating them with my stride, family comes first. The claps echo in some faraway place, the sound growing faster as the ball exits my nimble fingers. The threads spin line over line. It's an easy-to-spot four-seam fastball that my cousin can't miss. Hollis is already shifting her knees to adjust, her glove moving back to the center of the plate in a prayer that Zack swings through and misses.

He won't, though.

He doesn't.

My cousin tosses his bat over his shoulder with his typical ego-driven flair as he holds up a fist and begins his slow trot around the bases. I maybe shouldn't have made it quite so easy. The ball barely cleared the fence, but barely is always enough when it comes to home runs. My muffled ears clear and my Uncle's whistles break through the barrier first.

I feign disappointment, pulling my hat down on my face for a moment during his victory lap. I smile behind it, just for a second, and that's how I know I made the right choice. By the time I slide it back in place, Hollis has walked off the field and into the dugout, throwing her glove with enough juice to take out five or six bats balanced against the fence.

"Hey!" her dad shouts, snapping his fingers twice. She jerks her head toward him, her face stained with dirt, her eyes slits that glow with her anger. After a short standoff with her dad, her shoulders slump, and eventually, she looks down, pulling her mask and helmet off completely and undoing the knot in her hair. She stares at the water-stained concrete of the dugout for the next several minutes, and I'm glad, because the minute she looks at me, I'm going to quit thinking I made the right choice with that pitch.

10

HOLLIS

I've never understood why people pace. What does walking back and forth in patterns do to solve problems? Nothing, that's what. It does absolutely nothing. Yet here I am, not even sure who I'm the most angry with, and I am pacing.

I bet my dad is in his room doing the same exact thing, maybe even having the same exact silent conversation with himself. This is all so pointless.

Cannon doesn't trust me. That's the one thing I keep coming back to. If I'm ever going to catch for him in a game, when it truly matters, he needs to trust me. That's not the pitch I told him to throw today, yet he threw it anyway. My conclusions are either a lack of trust or he knew Zack would hit it. He did his cousin a favor, and maybe—*maybe*—I should understand the family bond thing better. But wouldn't it mean more if Zack actually earned it?

There aren't enough miles to be walked in this house to

get my brain to stop. I need a better distraction, and homework is not going to cut it. I'll be lucky to slow my mind enough by midnight to finish writing the lit paper that's due in fourteen hours.

"Gah!" I grunt out, throwing my copy of *Macbeth* on the center of my bed. I stare at the cover and laugh maniacally, though quietly. How appropriate that I'm reading a story about the struggle for political power and how it tears people up from the inside out. *Scotland's got nothin' on the politics of high school baseball.*

Restless, I ditch the quiet solitude of my room, closing my door behind me so my mom doesn't mention the boxes still to be unpacked. My dad has finally parked himself on the couch, his feet up on the coffee table and some microbrew bottle in his hand. My mom's sitting at the kitchen table with the reflection of her laptop glowing in her reading glasses. I grab the van keys from the counter and try to be smooth, soundless, but they jingle just enough to turn my parents' heads my way.

My mom pulls her glasses down to the tip of her nose and raises a brow.

"Stir crazy," I answer her questioning look. "I won't be out late, and I will drive carefully, and yes, I am working on finishing my room."

That last bit's a lie.

She grimaces and says "Uh huh, sure."

"Thanks," I say through an exaggerated smile, palming the keys and heading on my way.

"If you see Jennings, let him know I wanna talk to him before workouts tomorrow," my dad says as I leave. I glance at him, but he's already turned his attention back to the television.

"Which one?" I ask.

"Either," he says before taking a long sip of his beer.

His ominous threat gives me a little boost as I leave the house. It's tacky to be happy about other people getting in trouble, but I'm all right with being a little tacky right now. It's better than some of the things I've wished on Zack and Cannon over the last hour. Nothing *too* bad—jock itch or premature baldness. Or getting cut from the team. I know that last wish won't come true. They're too good, and my dad would get called out for retribution. Zack's dad would make sure of it. I've had enough of other player parents getting involved to suit me for a lifetime.

I've yet to check out the bowling alley that June works out. She's been encouraging me to come visit during her work hours for the last week, and now seems like the perfect time. I could use another female to vent to. I shoot her a text to make sure she's there then head toward the main part of town. The lot is pretty full when I pull in. Cheesy eighties music blares through the doors every time someone comes or goes. It reminds me of a joint back home where I used to get slices of pizza with my dad after games.

I check my phone before going in to see if June responded, but nothing yet. She's probably busy. Buzzed on the nostalgia of hearing Madonna's "Like a Virgin," which my dad always points out was my mom's favorite song growing up, I'm smiling by the time I push open the door. The overhead lights are dimmed, and neon-colored lights line the lanes and walls of this place. It's a bit of a dump, but in that perfect kind of way. The carpet is obnoxious swirls of color, some of them glowing more than others from the black light shining along the main walkways. My white socks and shoes are vivid, as is the NYU emblem on my sweatshirt.

I make my way to the counter where a few people are in line for shoes, and I'm relieved when I see June rushing around to check people in. Stepping to the side, I lean against the counter and wait for her to have a free moment to talk. She catches sight of me on one of her trips to grab shoes and a smile lights up her face. Mine does the same, proof that I really needed this—*a person.*

"Hey! Look who finally showed up!" June holds up a finger and rushes back to her register to cash someone out. She clears the line in about two minutes and comes back to me with two large cups filled with Coke.

"Perk of knowing the junior assistant manager." She smirks. I take the straw and pull the wrapper off, blowing the bit left on the end up in the air for her to catch.

"Fancy," I say, sucking in a big drink.

"Mondays are league nights, so it gets pretty busy. You have to come back on a Sunday morning. We can literally bowl while I'm on the clock if you want," she offers.

"Oh, tempting. I'll have to take you up on that. You know, I was Staten Island sixth grade champ with a pretty wicked one-forty-one," I brag. I haven't bowled since junior high, so I'm pretty sure I'd have to work to match that score again.

"Well, I'd only take you by a hundred or so," June teases. I laugh out hard but stop when I realize she's not kidding.

"Another perk of the job, I guess, huh?" I say.

She cracks her knuckles dramatically to show off, then winks.

"Hey, I'll set you up with pool if you wanna stick around and hang out when I'm done here. We can grab a late dinner." She pulls a box of pool balls out from under the counter as more people walk up to her register. I ate dinner already, but I could really use the girl time, so I nod and smile, taking the balls and my drink into the pool hall area, away from most of the crowds.

The neon lights don't glow in here. It's peacefully dim, the room just dark enough to conceal Cannon until I've unboxed the balls at the pool table that's apparently directly behind him. He jumps at the sound, and his movement makes me yelp and grab my chest.

"Oh, shit!" I say through a nervous laugh. My heart is pounding at a marathon runner's pace. "I didn't see you."

He was wearing his hoodie up over his hair but he pulled it back when I startled him. My gut says he's here hiding. For about four seconds, I'm distracted by the adorable way his hair flops around, before I remember that I want to punch him.

"My dad wants you to see him before practice," I say without transition. Cannon's eyes scrunch up. "Just, he said if I saw you before tomorrow's practice. I didn't think I would this soon, and ya know . . . I don't want to forget."

"Uh huh," he deadpans with a slow roll of his eyes. He turns his attention back to the other table, rolling one of the balls across the table and back again.

"Don't throw shade at me just because my dad isn't happy with you. I have nothing to do with his coaching decisions." I mumble the words, irritated at the obvious insinuation Cannon makes. Most people—*all people*— assume that I'm basically my dad's assistant. I must get favors. He must be willing to punish people just for me, right? I mean, I couldn't possibly earn things on my own, and no way does my dad has ethical standards.

"*Pshh*, whatever," I mutter at my own thoughts.

"You just don't get it," Cannon says, suddenly facing me, tossing the cue ball in his palm.

I abandon the balls on my table and lean into the side with my arms crossed.

"Don't get what? That you don't trust me to call your pitches or that you would rather make your cousin look good than let him earn it on his own?" I can tell I've hit a nerve by the way his eyes flinch. He doesn't back away, though, abandoning his ball to the other table and stepping into my personal space until he's close enough for me to smell the mint on his breath.

"Did you take a minute to consider what the rest of the night would have been like for Zack if I struck him out? You saw my uncle out there. Imagine that at home, where there is no place to run off to." His eyes pierce mine, a penetrating stare that challenges me, and my stomach churns at his point.

"That why you're here? Hiding from your uncle?" I change the subject and shove a cue at his chest.

"Something like that," he says, his voice low, words trailing off as if he just realized we're close enough to share each other's breaths. He wraps his hand around the stick I gave him and his eyes flit to my mouth then back up to my gaze.

"You any good?" His head tilts with his question, but I

think maybe he's challenging me as an excuse to put distance between us. The break is welcome. When he's close, I don't think clearly.

"I'm all right." I shrug and face the table to properly rack the balls. I'm being coy. My family has a pool table. Or rather, we did. When I was old enough to hold the stick right, my dad put me up on a bar stool and let me play. I'm not a shark or anything, but I know my way around a game of nine-ball.

Cannon meanders to the opposite end of the table, working the chalk cube at the end of his stick.

"What's the wager?" he says, glancing up at me before tossing the chalk in my direction. I catch it in my palm and squeeze it tight while I hold his stare for a beat. I could play this two ways. It could be a game, for fun, for something silly or maybe even slightly flirtatious. Lord knows there's a thousand butterflies beating in my chest rooting for me to take that route. But the tiger in my soul is even more demanding and pushes me to make a point while I still can.

My tongue gently tastes my upper lip before I suck in and grab hold of it with my teeth, locking in the nervous laugh that's dying to escape my throat. I'm going to make a business deal. The most gorgeous guy I've ever met is daring me to change the course of our relationship over a game of pool I have a really good chance at winning, and I'm going to instead opt to teach him a lesson.

My God, what is wrong with me?

He's literally my kryptonite right now, black long-sleeved shirt with three open buttons at the top, dark fitted jeans that rest low on his hips and show off that tempting bit of skin just above the band of his boxer briefs. His feet are stuffed into unlaced white Vans, and damn it all to hell, even his ankles are cute. Unlike me, he's taken a shower since that shit-show of a practice. His hair is damp, curling into loose waves that he keeps brushing away from his eyes. All of that is enough to make me get all stupid with my choices, but it's whatever that smell is that accompanies him most of the time that's thick and fresh and alluring as fuck right now.

Good thing I'm as close to repulsive looking right now as I can get. I'm still wearing dad's sweatpants rolled down to fit my waist and my Yankees World Series sweatshirt. That knot that Cannon likes to affectionately tease me about is a doozy right now, to the point it's going to take a bottle of conditioner to work it out. I did wash my face, though, so there's that.

Tongue in my cheek, a little amused by my own gall, I let a short, airy laugh slip through my nostrils and dig in.

"What do *you* want if you win?" I need him invested for this to work. He props his stick up against the side of the table, folding his arm and leaning into the edge right next to his cue.

"*Hmm*, I mean . . . there are so many options." His voice is definitely indicative of a guy taking the bait, despite my super grungy look.

I'm really about to ruin this. Damn me and my morals.

"What if . . ." I let my words linger in the air and haze my eyes just enough to tempt him, draw him in. When his lip ticks up, I go for the kill.

"If you can beat me, I'll let you name your terms at any time you wish." It dawns on me as I say this to him that I must feel a decent level of trust when it comes to Cannon Jennings. An open-ended bet like this, especially given my past, is normally way outside my comfort zone. Yet, there's a little fire in my belly at the thought of losing and Cannon coming to collect. And the way he's looking at me, chewing at the inside of his cheek while he considers my offer, that fire is getting . . . hotter.

"Any terms," he reiterates.

I nod but hold up a palm in pause, hedging my offer just a little.

"Within reason," I add, one eyebrow raised.

Cannon's chest lifts with an amused laugh. I lock in on his blue eyes and will myself not to blink, even while he does, once . . . *twice*. His lashes are so long for a guy, like tools used to put whomever is looking at them under a spell. It's close to working on me. I'm a little jealous because mine are so blonde that sometimes they're hard to see except in the sun. Not his—his are *all* I see right now.

"I accept," he says, stepping back and spinning his cue over his wrist a few times.

I point my finger in a circle to mock his circus trick.

"I'm a little worried if that's how you think this game is done," I say.

He shoots me a tight-lipped glare before dropping the base of his stick to the floor with a heavy *thunk*.

"And what is your ask?" He leans over the table and swivels his stick into position, gliding it across his knuckles. I'll admit, he looks comfortable at the head of the table. This might not go the way I want. It's that emphasis on *might*, though, that prompts me to speak up.

"If I win, you have to let Zack know you went easy on him."

And there it is. I did it; said it. Put the challenge on the table. I thought I'd feel better about backing him into this corner, but now that I see the blood leave his cheeks and the corners of his mouth turn down as he slowly stands upright, this doesn't feel like *winning* at all.

I manage to hold my position despite his look of betrayal. What do I owe his cousin? Nothing! That fucker disparaged me in front of my peers. No, he sexually harassed me. He crossed a line, physically, to purposely demean me because he felt small. I owe Zack absolutely nothing, and he deserves to know that his big achievement at practice today wasn't very big at all. All it was is one big, fat gift he doesn't deserve.

My mouth curves the opposite way, a forced smirk inching up into my cheeks and working against the sourness I'm feeling from my neck down to the bottom of my guts. Crossing my arms over my chest, I hug my stick and jut one hip out in a challenge.

"Well?" I lift a brow.

His stare is decisive. No more blinking lashes to lull me into submission. I'm being dissected solely by the dominant glow of his swimming-pool blue eyes. His nose is pink from being out in today's sun and reflective clouds. His wet hair is drying right before my eyes into touchable waves that I imagine in my fingers. I'm thankful my arms are crossed to hide them because I can feel them twitch.

"Fine."

I flinch at his sudden acquiescence, most of me prepared for him to bail on this little wager. By the way he rounds the table and motions for me to step back, I tremble at the knees. Cue ball palmed in his left hand, stick grasped in his right, he steps into the space between me and the table and comes close enough that I can feel the warmth of the breath he exhales from his nose.

"Pardon," he says, and I step back several feet to lean against a pub table.

Cannon positions the ball a little off-center then dabs one more dusting of chalk on the end of his cue, blowing the excess away while he looks at me, his eyes focused away from the tip of the stick and onto my gaze. His mouth quirks on one side, and it's in that small look that I know I'm done. I'm so fucking screwed.

He leans over the table in a smooth pivot, drawing the stick back and getting the feel of the slide before letting it rip, knocking the balls in all directions and immediately sinking one of each—a solid and a stripe. His eyes centered on the table, he rounds it, his tongue sticking out the way Michael Jordan's always did when he was deciding whether to put the game away with a dunk or a little fade-away from the top of the key.

"You got a preference?" he asks.

"I . . . well . . ." I stumble on my words, his sudden confidence nailing me to the floor.

He chuckles then bends down, lining up a shot at a solid.

"It's all right," he says, leaning his head to one side to glance up at me and wink. "It won't matter."

And it doesn't. He proceeds to sink his initial target, and then every other solid ball on the table, sometimes two at a time. I half expect him to drain the eight-ball without even looking. He has to work at it a little, though, what with so many of my balls still on the table and in his way. He calls the side pocket and when the ball falls in easily, I breathe out heavily enough to flap my lips, then I drop my stick.

"Two out of three?" I scrunch my lips up with my pathetic attempt to regain my edge.

"You think it will matter?" He lays his stick on the table and saunters toward me.

My nervous knee twitches, and I find myself rocking where I stand to keep my legs busy and my blood flowing. Cannon stops about a foot away from me, and looks down at the floor as he slips his hands into the pockets of his jeans. I draw in his scent, letting it numb my nerves like the venom of a scorpion. I got sloppy, arrogant even. And that trust I felt so sure of wanes a little now that he's calling in his bet. I gave him a free pass to surprise me, to ask something of me or dare me or— That's the thing. It's the unknown; I did that. *I did that!*

My hands balled into fists at my sides, I roll my shoulders back and lift my chin, determined not to let my worry shine through.

"Bet's a bet," I say, shaking my head with tight lips. I had no idea I was going up against a pool shark.

"That it is," he says, glancing up while keeping his head low. The way he peers at me through the strands of his hair that now shadow his eyes is both ominous and so freaking enticing.

"Five a.m., Saint Peter's Gulch. Tomorrow." He leans in and for a moment I think he's going to kiss me, but instead he pauses while forward on his toes. "I'll let you know what you owe there and then."

I swallow and he sees it, his eyes darting to that place on my throat that betrays my bravado.

"Fine," I gurgle out.

He laughs lightly and falls back to give me space.

"Relax, Hollis. I'm sure you'll be able to handle it." With one last wink, he brings his hands from his pockets and claps them a few times to remove any leftover chalk. I force myself not to look over my shoulder as he leaves, and I keep that promise to myself, spending the next twenty minutes playing out the rest of the balls on our table and realizing I never had a chance.

11

CANNON

I used to have a huge grudge against my parents for forcing me to spend my summer days at the elementary school's recreation program. There were exactly three things I enjoyed about those summers up until seventh grade—all-you-can-drink chocolate milk from the cafeteria lady, time with Sydney Chistensen in the "kissing tunnel" where we kissed like sock puppets, and the pool table.

To say I got good at playing pool is an understatement. I won goddamn ribbons for it. For Christmas one year, I asked Santa for a Predator pool cue instead of the latest Louisville model. My dad was stunned, but good ole Santa came through. I still have that thing, gold case and all, assuming it survives the move here in the storage pod.

Uncle Joel said my dad will be able to head here a couple of days earlier than planned, possibly by Friday. The minute my dad gets here and we unload my truck, I take him to the airport so he can head back to New Mexico and make that drive all over again with my mom and more of our stuff. I'm so close to having a little bit of normal around me. Granted, we'll have to cram our "normal" into a shared set of bedrooms adjoined by a bathroom, but I'll be able to survive my living quarters if it means I have my own truck again. Sharing Zack's very unsexy sedan is seriously grating on my nerves. I'm used to being able to get in and just drive for however long or far I want, but with Zack, I have to constantly worry about how much gas is left in the tank, or if he needs to get somewhere or wants to be with me. *I'm never alone!*

I don't want him knowing about my morning plans, especially since I still can't believe I made them. I've spent the last five minutes silently working the car keys out of the pocket of his jeans that are on the floor. First, I had to find the right pair of jeans. I should have planned ahead last night, but Zack and I didn't hang. I got a lift to Eight Lanes from Tory and after my pool game against Hollis and my dramatic exit, I couldn't have her find me waiting around out front for someone to come back and pick me up, so I walked home. Three miles is a lot farther than you think when it's thirty-one degrees outside.

Of course, I walked in and Zack asked where the heck I'd been. I just held up my cell phone and told him I was talking to my dad. Thank God for video games because he half-heard me and nodded before going right back to shooting some alien thing.

Finally, with the keys loose and clutched in my palm, I creep out my cousin's door, thankful he's still snoring. I'll be bunking with him when my parents get here, and it's going to suck boatloads. I'm a light sleeper, and Zack basically holds a party in his nose every night.

I manage to slip out the front door without making a single sound and roll Zack's car back in neutral with the lights off so I don't disturb anyone. I told Hollis I'd be there at five, and it's a thirty-minute drive. I'm not sure she knows where she's going or what this place is, but if she shows up it means she really wants to be there. I don't know why that matters to me but it does. It's the entire reason I put this out there.

After a quick stop at the service station to drop the last twenty bucks from my dad's deposit into the tank, I race down the highway to make up time, almost missing the turnoff. The sign for the gulch state park is broken in half. When Zack dragged me up here for sledding before Christmas, he mentioned they don't fund this place anymore. I'm tempted to park under the sign and look out for Hollis to make sure she doesn't miss it, but I'm also worried she found her way and is already there, waiting for me.

Zack's car doesn't take the side road as well as my truck will, so I'm slow along the winding road that weaves through the stick-like trees, old snow frozen into solid ice blocks on the ground. It's still pretty out here, the frozen water like jewels that shine under the full moon along the landscape. Everything in town and on the highway has turned to icy mud. The sun won't be up for two hours, but we had to make this trip early to get home before school. *Before Zack knows I'm gone.*

The moon is bright enough to light my way and I travel mostly by memory, though I pull over a few times to check my location on my phone to make sure I haven't gone too far. The piled-rock walls come into view after about ten minutes of driving through the thickest section of trees. Steam puffs out from the exhaust of a familiar minivan parked close to the small ramada.

She came.

I pull into the graveled spot next to her, suddenly feeling my nerves. I blow out one hard breath and kill my engine, stepping out at the same time she does. We meet at the back of my car, our air mixing in a swirl of steam. She's shoved her gloved hands under her arms, and her body is wrapped in this obnoxiously yellow puffy coat. No knot in the hair this morning; instead, she wears a black sock hat pulled down just above her brow and over her ears, the length of her hair wrapped around her neck like a warmer.

"You know it's not snowing, right?" I tease her, but really, she's adorable like this, bouncing on her toes for warmth, tight jeans down her legs, feet stuffed in rubber-toed boots. She looks like winter—my kind of winter.

"It's somehow colder out here, ya know? Like, I mean, I've been cold in the city, and wind off the Atlantic is *ooof!*" She widens her eyes in expression. "But whatever this Midwestern stuff is, it's a whole different kinda cold. My breath is a solid. Skipped right over the gaseous state."

She puckers her lips and puffs out a few times, a tiny train engine coughing out steam. I see the fog clearly, but mostly I'm looking at her lips.

"I see you're tougher than I am?" She pulls one gloved hand loose from under her arm and gestures at my body, not quite as fully wrapped as hers.

I could play it tough, but that's not what this morning is supposed to be about at all. Unzipping my jacket, I twist the front inside-out and step closer for her to feel inside.

She looks at me like I'm a total creep, which, considering how Zack has been toward her, I get.

"Feel my shoulder. I promise, just trust me," I say.

With twisted lips, she studies me for a beat, and her hesitant expression makes my chest ache just a little. I don't want to be the kind of guy that *anyone* makes that kind of face at, especially not her.

After a heavy sigh, she narrows her eyes and tightens her lips, still not sure whether she can trust me. If we can't get past this test, we're in trouble for the rest of the morning. She pulls her hand free from the glove then slips it under my jacket, nervous fingers tracing up over my shoulder as I cautiously fold the jacket back over her hand and my chest.

"It's made for snowboarders. Lots of warmth without the bulk. I think it's the same material they make bullet proof vests out of," I say.

Her lip ticks up and her eyes blink a few times before her gaze hits mine.

"Does that mean I can shoot you?"

"Ha!" I punch out a laugh, but the silence that follows during our brief stare leaves me a little unsteady. She's kidding, but there's maybe a one percent slice of honesty in that barb.

An entirely new feeling takes over when she pulls her hand away. Her movement is slower, and I feel the tiny vibration in her thumb along my chest. She's nervous, too, and not because she thinks I'm going to shoot her.

"We should get to it. I don't want to make you late," I say, nodding toward the head of the trail.

"You mean you don't want Zack to know you're gone," she corrects. She's intuitive—*and right*.

"That too," I admit, glancing over my shoulder, my mouth a straight line to mark my guilt. I slow my steps to look at her a little longer and feel the burn left behind from her calling me on my bullshit. Maybe I crave the punishment to absolve me of my sins when it comes to her.

Eyes forward again, I pull a small flashlight from my pocket and click it on, lighting the way to the edge of the canyon. The walk isn't long, but it feels like a mile with the silence that swallows us. The only noises are the crunch under our feet and the occasional snap of branches.

The makeshift ladder seems scarier now in the faint light of the moon, the pole slick with the deep frost that comes before dawn. I grip the metal pegs that jut out from the pole in my bare hands, the cold stinging my skin. I let go for a minute and rub my hands together, as if that'll help.

"Wait a minute. *We're climbing up that?*" Hollis points up.

"It's worth it," I say, starting my climb without giving in to the cautionary tale beating in my chest. The metal stings and I'm glad Hollis has gloves because at least she'll be able to tolerate the cold. The height thing, however, might be a different story.

She beings to climb behind me when I'm a full body-length ahead, and we both keep a steady pace. The wind is colder the higher we go, and by the time I reach the wooden platform at the top, it's chilling. Maybe this was a bad idea.

"I hope you know my dad will kill both of us if either of

us gets hurt," she says, hoisting herself up to join me in the small standing-room space.

"Good thing we'll go down together, then—literally," I respond, tugging at the sturdy straps dangling loose around the tall pole at the edge of the platform. I keep my gaze on Hollis while I untangle the contraption, and it's hard not to laugh when her eyes widen so big that I see mostly the whites.

"Oh, hell no," she says through nervous laughter, shaking her head.

I tug on the zipline harness built for two with all my weight to prove that this thing is sturdy. I made Zack prove it to me. And if this can hold both of us, I'm pretty sure Hollis and I will be fine.

"I did this last month with Zack. It's a serious thrill, and besides"—I stretch the straps out and step through one section before holding out the remaining two loops for her —"A bet's a bet."

I hit her with a daring grin. The wind is strong enough that it whips the hair sticking out of my knit hat. Hollis's hair twists like tentacles, blonde ribbons curving around her neck then stretching out into the air like fingers. Her nose is pink and her cheeks are red. Her eyes, however, are not quite as wide as before. With a slight tilt of her head, she studies me for a moment more, then places her palms on my shoulders for balance, stepping through the straps.

The second she enters my space, my chemistry changes, and I think maybe hers does, too. There's nowhere for either of us to go, our bodies quite literally tied together on a perch about a hundred feet in the air. Her mouth rests at the base of my neck, and the tiny gasp she lets out tickles against my skin. It's the one part of me that's not sheltered from the cold, and she's managed to scorch it with one breath.

"Hold on," I say, my mouth suddenly dry. I tug the straps around her back and they cinch together with mine.

I peel back my upper body enough to look her in the eyes.

"May I?" I glance down to the space between us, where the last buckles are loose and need to be fastened.

She blinks nervously, but I can tell she isn't scared. She's something else, and I hope maybe what she feels is the same kind of reaction I'm having inside my chest.

"Make it tight," she laughs out.

I breathe out through my nose and smile before looking down between us. Her hands grip my shoulders tightly and she rests her forehead against mine so she can watch as I lock us in together. When I'm done, I freeze in place for a moment, not ready to look up and meet her stare again. She's close, and we're touching, and I've felt her nose brush against mine twice since we've positioned ourselves like this.

Three times.

Four.

Her lips part with another breath, fear exhaled and a leap of faith drawn in.

"Ready?" I ask, still not moving my head away from hers. She nods against me.

My hands tentatively move to her waist, never moving from the invisible guideline drawn by the top of her jeans. She leans into me and circles her arms around my body, and when the weight of her chin rests on my shoulder, I let my muscles relax and flatten my palms on her back.

This is different than kissing as strangers. This is a literal leap, a sign of trust that goes way beyond. When I made this trip with Zack it was more about the thrill and being boys together who like to do daring, dumb shit. I may not have admitted it fully to myself until right now, but I dared Hollis to come out here because I want her to trust me.

"I've got you," I promise just as I push us off from the ledge. Her fingers dig into me at first, but after a few seconds of gliding across the frozen stream below, she relaxes. And then the joyous laughter begins.

"Oh, my God!" she cries out, her head swiveling from where it rests on my shoulder. We're halfway across the line, moving at a good speed, when she drops her hands down to my chest and leans back enough to see everything.

"This is amazing!" Her smile is all teeth and glee, like a kid seeing a true winter wonderland.

I had fun here with Zack, but this trip with Hollis is special. I haven't looked at the scenery once; the only thing my eyes want to watch is her. We rotate as we travel, and her eyes blink from the wind and cold, but the dimples pushed up into her cheeks only grow deeper. The moonlight traces her lashes, lighting them up like flecks of gold. Her eyes glimmer like diamonds, her lips like candy, I lock in on them for a little too long, and she catches me. When her tongue passes over her bottom lip, I give in and meet her waiting stare. Damn that this zipline isn't longer.

"Brace yourself," I warn, glancing up in time to catch the safety rope as we glide over the second pedestal.

I wrap the rope around my forearm with one hand, and stop us as gracefully as I can. Hollis lets out a small grunt then breaks into laughter, her arms limp at her sides.

"Worth it?" I ask.

Her smile hasn't dipped once, and she adds in an emphatic "Yes" with a nod before tilting her head to the sky, ready to climb to the next platform and make our trip back.

My chest is enlarged with pride, but other parts of me are swollen from something else, and unfastening our straps while trying to hide my painful erection is borderline comical. Thankfully, Hollis steps out quickly when I loosen the belt to create slack.

She's already at the top of the next platform by the time I free myself, and the solo trip up the peg ladder gives me a chance to calm down and let the cold air work its magic before I gladly torture myself again.

This time Hollis helps, more familiar with the process and less afraid of what comes next. I expect her to hold on to me less so she can enjoy the ride and take in more of the skyline, a soft glow of the sun hinting at its impending rise. It's like a line of glowing bright blue ink tracing along the slight hills. Rather than looking around completely, though, she holds on exactly as before. Her hands rest more comfortable around my neck this time, and as we slip away from the solid wood base and into the air, her fingers twist some of my hair. Everything I thought I had in check explodes, including my self-discipline.

Slipping back enough to force her eyes to meet mine, I do my best to read what they say. She doesn't blink, her focus moving from my left eye to my right, as mine do hers.

Her fingers curl my hair again, letting the short pieces slip through her knuckles while her nails scratch at the base of my neck. My palms at her waist, I give myself permission to stroke along her sides with my thumbs as we glide across the landscape at twenty-something miles per hour.

I sense the end of the ride coming, and reach out instinctively to slow our stop. I catch her against my body when my feet find solid ground, then let the safety rope go, remaining steady where I am for fear she'll let go completely. Our feet tangle on the wooden planks, hers tucked inside my wide base. Either my eyes have adjusted or the sky is getting brighter because I can see every freckle that dots her cheeks and nose. I'm mesmerized by them, but equally as rapt that she seems as taken with mine.

I had no idea how much I actually won in our silly pool game. I don't think I knew how much I *wanted* until this very moment. As her lips part, her tongue dashing out bravely into the cold to taste her skin, I'm overwhelmed with desire to take everything I can. I won't break this trust, though. Of everything that this morning brings, her letting me help her fly is the most important.

Her fingers curl into fists at the back of my neck, and I'm so damn afraid she'll let go and tear us apart. She doesn't, though. Before I make a move to unfasten our straps, she lifts up on her toes ever so slightly, just enough to bring our heights in line. Her eyes skim down fleetingly to my mouth as she closes the distance between us, and her gaze hits mine again just as her soft lids flutter to close. She leans in, the ultimate of trust, and presses her mouth to mine in a chaste, soft kiss that I let her control completely. My only moment of greed is a soft suck of her plump bottom lip, and it's pure torture forcing myself to let go, but I do.

Our lips part but her forehead remains on mine. I unbuckle our straps and eventually, the harness falls to our feet. Before Hollis steps back, she kisses me one more time, this one on my cheek.

"Thank you, Cannon," she whispers.

"You're welcome," I reply, knowing our words should be reversed.

Despite spending the last hour in the freezing cold, I keep the shower temperature tepid while I erase the feel of her lips on mine and the visual of her body from my mind. It's a good thing we drove back separately, because I don't think my body could handle these thoughts with Hollis just a foot away from me in the warm car. My imagination is bad enough. The minute I pictured laying her down in the back seat, the ride home got really uncomfortable—*and fast.*

Finally somewhat coherent and no longer hard for a girl I'm keeping at arm's length, I kill the shower and wrap a towel around my waist. When I come face-to-face with Zack's sinister smile on the other side of the door, I expect him to make some joke about me draining the hot water or spending so much time alone in the bathroom. But that's not what's on his mind at all.

"The board is meeting about Coach Taylor." He grins, arrogant pride seeping from the pores of his skin.

"Why?" I ask, when really my inner-voice is saying, *What did you do?*

"There are some questions about his techniques, and maybe how he makes his rosters." My cousin passes me in the doorway and we trade sides as I step into the hall.

"But he hasn't made any rosters yet," I explain, my mouth watering with sickness.

Zack's smile grows more ominous just before he winks.

"Exactly," he says, closing the door on this conversation, *and my face.*

I spent the morning trying to earn Hollis's trust and prove my integrity, and with one conversation with his father behind my back, Zack is threatening to burn that trust to the ground. All because a girl might be better at something than he is.

No *might*. She *is* better. And I need to start standing up for her, despite my family.

12

HOLLIS

I wasn't sure my body would warm up after I climbed that pole this morning, but somehow, now I can't seem to cool it down. I've been simmering from the inside out ever since I left the gulch this morning, and sitting next to Cannon in class earlier today rekindled everything.

Things have been pleasantly awkward since. I quite like pleasantly awkward. This time, the aftermath of our kiss is more promising. We went into that with eyes wide open. The only thing that can ruin this euphoria is currently finishing up his second lap, alongside Cannon.

"Looks like I beat you out here today, Double-D," Zack says as he slows to a walk, pacing around me in wide circles while I stretch before my run. I glower up at him from my squatting stretch, waiting for him to finish his lame bra-size joke.

"Oh, no. Not like that. Double-D—Daddy's Daughter." He laughs at his lame joke and I dim my eyes. I mean, that's basically a statement of fact. Most humans are their father's child, biologically at least. I get what he's insinuating, though. Nothing new. Before I can defend myself, Cannon walks up behind him and knocks his hat from his head.

"Don't be a dick."

I look down at my toes to hide my smile. I don't need anyone fighting my battles, but after my morning, it's reassuring to see Cannon do it.

Zack picks his hat up from the track and puts it on backward, which is one of my father's pet peeves. I could warn him, but he deserves what he gets. He shoots me a sour look before he leaves the track and makes his way to the field. Cannon sticks around, but I sense his uneasiness in the way he keeps checking to see if his cousin is watching us.

"You don't have to wait for me," I say, my stomach twisting with gooey butterfly feelings and insecurities galore. *Of course he isn't waiting for me.*

"Hey, I just . . ." He swings his arm into mine as I stand and our fingers catch briefly.

Lightning bolts.

A breathy laugh slips out from his guilty smile. It's sweet, as is the way he's stammering and having trouble looking me in the eyes. Perhaps we got a redo on our first kiss. This one is going much better.

"I want to apologize for him, my cousin?" He points over his shoulder with his thumb. He glances behind him but I reassure him before he fully looks.

"He's in the dugout. He can't see you," I say.

"Right," he says, sucking in his bottom lip.

"You don't have say his *sorrys*, by the way. I know

he's not you. And you aren't responsible for him. He can say them himself, or not. That's a direct reflection on him."

Cannon nods, shuffling backward a few steps to not get caught dawdling. My dad's favorite word is *hustle*.

"How'd you get to be so smart?" He punctuates his flattering question with a crooked smile that turns into a wink.

"Lots and lots of lessons learned," I say, alluding to more that he realizes. He takes it at face value, though, and nods toward the track.

"You better hustle," he teases. I'll have my laps done in time. The one true perk to being coach's daughter is knowing not to fail to meet his expectations. I know what I'm supposed to do and when, which is why letting Zack get a hit he didn't earn yesterday irks me so much.

Apparently, it's still quite a sticking point for my dad, too. Apparently, it's a sticking point for my dad, too. He's pulled Zack aside in the bullpen, and based on his familiar and animated hand gestures, I'd venture to guess he's putting some pressure on him.

Great. Pressure on Zack is going to translate into more hostility toward me.

I finish a little slower than my normal time. I don't check on my smartwatch, but I don't have to. I slowed down on purpose, putting off the inevitable head-to-head competition I know is coming. I was pumped for it until I caught my dad giving Zack the anti-pep talk.

I dump my gear in the corner of the dugout as they return from their chat session, and the glare Zack shoots my way is ice cold.

"Go throw," my dad says, tossing a ball with a little

extra zip straight into Zack's chest. "With her," my father adds, pointing in my general direction.

"*Pssh.*" The annoyed rush of air that slips from Zack isn't meant for my dad, and he manages to keep it just quiet enough for me and me alone.

"Well? Hurry up," Zack says, not bothering to wait for me or look my direction.

I follow Zack to the outfield, where we pair up next to everyone except the pitchers. My dad paces around the duos, assessing form and how serious each player is taking something so simple. It doesn't take more than three or four throws for him to get to us and make an example of Zack.

"Is that how you throw down to second?" My dad asks the question loud enough for nearby players to hear. Zack's cheeks burn bright red, and it's not from the cold air.

"I'm still warming up, Coach," Zack replies, throwing the ball back to me with more energy under my father's watchful eyes.

"Uh huh. Well, we should always practice with the same verve we have when we play." My father's sunglasses hide his eyes enough that it's hard to tell when he's looking at you. He has a habit of never quite staring at someone head-on. It's a trick he uses to see what expressions people make when they think he's not fully paying attention.

He is *always* paying attention.

My dad spreads his legs to get comfortable in his stance, arms crossed over his chest while his head swivels to follow the ball Zack and I continue to throw. My partner's footwork is sloppy, and I notice my father's focus on the ground for several seconds, my clue that he sees it. He's memorizing it. It won't be something that comes up now, but it will come up today.

We manage to survive warm-ups without more commentary from my dad, and as much as I want Zack to get his due, I also don't want to be this close to him when he gets it. I feel a little bit like the tool being used to punish him.

I'm grateful for the distance that comes with my dad dividing up the teams. He puts Zack with Cannon, which could be for a lot of reasons, but it's definitely not because he's letting him off the hook. There are enough of us out here to have three squads, and one of the new assistant coaches takes mine. His name's Ernie Ruiz, and my dad lured him away from a school two towns over. He made the call the moment he landed this job. Ernie Ruiz has one key line on his resume that singled him out and made him my father's number-one candidate—*he was a Yankee*. Only for sixteen games in the majors, but wearing pinstripes for any amount of time is as good as blood to my dad.

For most of the guys out here, today is going to be a good time. That's what will separate the keepers from the cuts. It's a game of three outs, and the three teams keep rotating, scoring as many runs as they can until my father decides time is up. It seems like a silly game to take everyone's minds off of the pressure of warmups and tryouts just around the corner, but every coach out here is watching for the ones who truly work. All games count for something.

It doesn't take long for the first two squads to make their outs, so I do a little strategizing with my squad as we take the field. I didn't get Cannon, but I did luck out with Roland on my team, and the one thing he has in his arsenal is a really good curveball. Zack might have gotten the pitch he wanted yesterday, but today he won't be so lucky.

"Look out, DD, here comes your nemesis," Zack shouts from the dugout. I glare through my mask in time to catch him stretching out his hands as he puts on his batting gloves. His joke carries to a few of the other guys, who laugh at my expense, pitifully trying to cover their snickers with fists over their mouths.

Fools.

Any sympathy I had for Zack drains. I get the rough spot Cannon is in, but it's like I told him—*he* is not his cousin. I won't treat them the same. Zack hasn't yet earned my respect.

"Batter up, Big Z!" I say, pounding my glove as I crouch into my squat. I can tell by his swagger as he steps up to the plate that he thinks I'm complimenting him, feeding his ego.

"You like that homer yesterday? I got plenty more in here. It's gonna be a long season, babe." I'm not sure whether his voice is as snarky as I hear it, or if it's the filter I seem to wear whenever he speaks. I'm not sure I could hear him any other way.

"I bet it is, Big Z," I say, echoing the nickname.

He sniffles out a laugh and digs his toes in. Everything about his approach is so affected, so cartoon-like. His feet are so set in their position, there's no chance for him to move them at a moment's notice.

"Come on Zack, you got this," Cannon calls from the bench. His encouragement hits my gut in a curious way. I'm a little soured by it, which I know isn't fair. He is being positive, which is what he should always do. And that's his cousin, so there is that extra pressure. It's just . . . I truly want Zack to fail this time.

I signal for a fastball low and outside, just like before, knowing it will work. And like yesterday, he swings himself off balance, landing on his knee as he twists.

"Strike one," my dad says, marking it on his scoresheet from behind the backstop. My dad likes to watch scrimmages from off the field, to see how people react to him being present but not in their face.

"I got this. Come on," Zack says, sniffing again, but this time as a show of how tough he is. He digs his feet into the exact same spot and I stare at them for a beat while a wave of tightness twists my insides. He isn't learning.

"You sure you don't want to make an adjustment?" I cough out my suggestion, keeping my voice low enough for my dad not to notice. I'm not sure why I'm helping, and I know before his reaction that he won't take my advice.

"Thanks, Double D. I got this, though," he says, spitting on the plate.

My eyes fall shut for a moment as I tuck my chin, acting as though I'm thinking about what to call next. Really, I'm just dreading the ass-chewing Zack has coming his way. Spitting on the plate is disrespectful, and there's no way my dad didn't see that. No matter where Roland throws this next ball, it'll be called a strike simply because Zack just hit my dad's nerve.

My head up, I send the same sign to Roland and line him up in the same location, maybe an inch or two more outside just to be safe. At this point, Zack would swing at the ball if he rolled it in. He's too jacked and ready to show off his muscles.

Roland isn't as good at hitting his target, and he ends up throwing the ball enough inside that Zack gets his bat on a piece of it, foul-tipping it right into my chest. It hurts as much as it always does, but the sting is gone by the time Zack is done chuckling. That guilty weight in my chest is gone now too.

"Strike two," my dad says. I glance over my shoulder to catch the reflection off of his glasses. I squint at the brightness, but I give my dad a nod. I shouldn't, because it's these little communications that can get both of us into trouble, but I can't help myself. Zack is under my skin, and he's under my dad's, too.

"Alright, Big Z. Time to show up or shut up," I say. I rarely devolve into trash talk, but the guy brings out the worst of my personality.

He scoffs at me and digs in, his leg twitching with what I assume is a sense of urgency pulsing through it. He's going to look ridiculous in about six seconds.

I signal for the curve, and Roland has a hard time hiding his smirk. If Zack were paying attention, he'd see it and be prepared. But he's too far gone inside his head.

I set up dead-center of the plate, knowing that Zack will see me in his periphery and probably think that he's going to get a fat meatball to rocket over the fence again. His swing comes almost a full half-second before the ball, the bat flinging end over end toward the dugout from his failed grip.

"That's one!" I shout, counting the outs as I throw the ball around with my team.

I'm still standing on the plate when Zack leans forward and spits again, purposely targeting my cleat. The act is purposeful, spiteful, and cruel. And he is about to wish he weren't in his own shoes.

"Bad move, Big Z. I mean, Big Zero." I give in and let any hope for mercy slip away.

"Jennings!"

There's no confusion about who he's calling. My dad's glasses are off, tucked into the front of his shirt by the time I spin around. He throws the clipboard down on the metal bleacher seat behind him, the clatter echoing around the field. My dad takes long strides around the backstop, through the gate, and into the dirt behind home plate where he steps in close enough to Zack that he could literally bite his nose if he wanted to. What surprises me, though, is the level of bravado puffing up Zack's chest and drawing him just as close to my dad. This is how wild dogs get into fights.

Knowing I should, I walk out to the mound to give them some privacy. The distance doesn't matter much, because my dad can be heard clear as day.

"Do you even want to be out here?"

His hand claps against his thigh, a gesture he makes when he's truly frustrated.

"This is a team, not Zack Jennings play time!"

He turns to walk away but pivots almost immediately, pointing.

"Uncoachable. Disrespectful. Not the kind of athlete I want on my team!"

The quiet before the storm is thick, palpable, and we all taste it. Zack shuffles back a few steps, angry laughter bubbling from his chest as he glances to his side and stares in Cannon's direction. There will be regret, probably on his part, and he will think he can repair the damage he's about to do, but he can't. My father is basically the Mr. Darcy of coaches, his opinion of someone gets set in stone pretty quickly.

Zack unvelcros his batting glove, making a show of it, his tongue pushed so hard into the crook of his cheek that I can see the lump it forms from several feet away. He leans over and spits on the ground between where he and my father stand, and before it hits the dirt, my father shouts, "Get off my field!"

My dad points to the parking lot, and his stare at Zack is hard. He rarely looks people directly in the eyes, but there's no mistaking the point he makes right now. It'll take a miracle for Zack to set foot on this field tomorrow, and I have never seen such a miracle happen in all my years of watching my dad coach.

It takes Zack a good fifteen minutes to pack up and lug his gear out to the lot, making a show of everything in front of the rest of us while we all do our best to play as if my father didn't just lose his shit. To add insult, Zack peels out from the lot, fishtailing the back end of his car enough to send burnt-rubber-smoke into the air. The squeal was his ultimate F-U to my dad.

That miracle he'll need just keeps getting farther and farther away.

Despite the sudden and very present tension felt on every square inch of the field and dugouts, we all manage to get through another hour of games until my dad calls the rest of practice and makes the next day's workouts optional.

I linger, not packing up until everyone has cleared the

field. I have to wait for my dad to finish talking with the other coaches anyhow, but I also want to talk with Cannon. He's been abandoned here.

"Do you all live far?" I have a vague idea where their house is, but I've never been.

"Far enough," he says, punching out a laugh. He lifts his bag up over his shoulder and breathes out heavily through his nose, his tired gaze landing on mine.

"You can't walk home," I say.

"I'll be fine—"

I don't let him bother with the lie and march over to my dad, calling him out of the circle of coaches and doing my best not to eavesdrop. I hear enough to clue me in on things perhaps getting a little messy after today. Drama tends to do that, especially in high school sports.

"Cannon's stuck here now," I explain.

My father's eyes flit from me to where Cannon stands beyond my shoulder. His shoulders slump and he glances back to the coaches waiting on him to finish their talk.

"I can't give players rides. You know that," my dad says. I understand. Especially now that he made such a public stand against Zack's attitude. I also know enough to get why Zack's father makes this messy.

"I'll take him home. I'll be back before you're done." I lean my head to the side and droop my eyes just enough to prey on his weak spot. I am just a player out here, but in all other aspects, I truly am daddy's little girl.

He sighs and drops his hands in his pockets, looking off to the side before bringing the keys out and holding them out for me to take. Before I can grab them, he clutches them in his palm.

"Come right back. And this has nothing to do with practice. This is a friend driving a friend home." He's very literal, and given everything we've gone through in the past, I understand why.

"Got it." I nod.

I take the keys and march back to Cannon. "Come on," I say as I pass him, urging him to join me.

"Thanks," he finally says when we're halfway across the field. "Think he'll be long? Should we just drop our stuff in the van then come back?"

"My dad can't drive you, so I've gotta take you then come right back to get him," I explain.

He scrunches his face as I hit the button that automatically pops open the back.

"That's kinda weird. Nobody really cares," he says.

I drop my bag inside and turn to face him as he shifts his to rest next to mine. Our eyes meet and I do my best to portray exactly how serious this is.

"Everybody cares. They always do, but only bring it up when they need to," I say.

His brow knits as I close the back hatch, and I leave him there puzzled until I get inside and he joins me.

"My dad follows rules and regulations to a T. He documents everything, and he gets witness statements. Everyone in that circle out there talking today is going to be asked to write down their account of what happened. My dad doesn't mess around." *And it's all because of me.*

Cannon gives me general directions as I pull out of the lot, and the first few minutes of the drive are spent with him alerting me where to turn and when. We're turning onto his street when he brings the subject back to the one weighing on both our minds.

"My cousin is just really wound up, and the stress comes out poorly," he says.

I put the van in park a few houses away from his and lean back with a sigh, letting my hands fall to the bottom of the wheel.

"Quit making excuses for him," I say, rolling my head along the seat back until our eyes meet.

He blinks rapidly, as if computing my words, but instead of the argument I expect, he says, "You're right."

I offer a crooked, sympathetic smile.

"I know this isn't fair for you. I'm so sorry." Zack's car isn't in the driveway up ahead, which means he's gone somewhere to blow off steam.

"He's probably with Tory or Lucas," Cannon says, pushing the lever to lean his seat back a little. He props a leg up and holds his knee, his eyes darting around the landscape beyond the van, as though searching for a way to make all of this right.

"Why does your dad play by the rules, like you said?"

I do my best to mask the sick expression I want to make. The way I feel inside can't be helped. This subject was bound to come up, and I need to learn it's simply part of the journey of a female athlete in a man's world. It doesn't make me hate it any less.

"Back in New York . . ." I pause to draw in a deep breath, to swallow down some courage. "Well, I'm sure you'll be shocked to hear this, but not *everyone* wanted me to be on the team."

He chuckles, but when he realizes it's actually a sad statement on human behavior, he lets go of the humor, his laugh lines fading with the fall of his mouth back into a straight line.

"The weird thing is, most of the guys on the team? They were fine with it. My ex—"

"Ex?" he pipes up. Of course that's the part he pays attention to.

"Yes, *ex*. Meaning, not my current boyfriend." *Are you my current boyfriend?* This sudden question tangles in my head while I sort out the details of my sophomore and junior years at Xavier to share with him.

"His name is Jordan, so let's just call him Jordan," I say.

"I don't like him."

I laugh out and grab Cannon's arm, and can't help but smile at this sudden possessiveness. Also, it's strange to reach out and touch him like this. It's both natural and terrifying, a sensation only amplified by the way he reaches over with his other hand and weaves our fingers together.

"Oh," I stammer out, staring at the way our hands look together. The story I was telling slips away, but Cannon brings it back to the forefront.

"I'm listening," he says. And he truly is. This would probably be easier if he weren't, at least not so intently.

I swallow.

"Jordan's dad, his name's Bill. He's this big donor— Xavier's a private school."

Cannon nods, understanding.

"Anyhow, he basically ran the school's sports department. He wasn't the athletic director, or an employee. He was nothing more than a guy with one vote on a board of trustees. But he was—*is*—big on tradition. And girls should be on the sidelines, and in the stands, or . . ."

I pause to snort out a laugh because the thought is so ridiculous.

"In the kitchen, learning how to be a good and proper wife. A girl playing ball was, well, in his words, 'a travesty.'" I add the air quotes to drive it home.

I can think of a lot of things that are travesties. Homelessness, hunger, a truly great person being murdered in cold blood. Me playing ball? Not even close. My presence is an inconvenience to sexist assholes who were probably never half as good as me.

"So, what did they do, like, make a rule or something against you?"

I shake my head and look out my side window, the memories still crystal clear in my head.

"Our field was about a block away from the campus, which is kinda normal for Staten Island. Our locker room was in a basement under the gym, and the coaches' offices were buried in the back, behind the showers. No matter what time of day it was, when the power went out, it got pitch black in there. We had a big game against our rival, and one of the other players' dads caught me during my walk to the field and told me my dad left his scorebook on his desk."

The self-blame weighs down my insides the way it always does. No matter how many times I rationalize what happened, the small inner voice I try to keep quiet pipes up and tells me I let it all happen.

"The locker room was clear. I made sure because I was only supposed to be on the women's side. I was just going to run in, grab the book, and go. I didn't even suspect something when the lights went out because, like I said, that stuff happened all the time."

I can tell Cannon expects something worse by the way his eyes are locked open yet slanted with disappointment. Thank God it wasn't worse. That thought repeats in my head a lot. Really, though, what I'm doing is giving them all an excuse for what they did do to me.

"I couldn't find the book."

"There was no book," he concludes.

I breathe out through my nose and look down at the place where our hands still touch, at the way his thumb is now stroking my skin in careful, slow circles. I shake my head.

"There was no book," I echo him.

His fingers twitch as his muscle tense.

"Nobody was in there," I add quickly, taking the *worse* scenarios out of his imagination. "They locked the door. It was made of thick, heavy metal and it was old. Nothing about my old campus was to code, and that was the only way out. The most important game of the year was about to happen and I was buried below ground a block away."

"Damn, Hollis." His head falls to the side in sympathy, but I also see the relief in his eyes. I understand it because I feel the same relief whenever I remember what happened. I'm coming to terms with the fact it was a truly awful thing, even though it wasn't *worse*.

"I missed the first two innings. Jordan finally came looking for me with my father's keys. There was a scout for the local community college there who never got to see me play. Maybe for a lot of players that isn't the end of the world, but for a girl who wants to play this game in college, any school open to the idea of putting me on their roster is a big deal. They took that away from me.".

"Did the guys get kicked off the team? Expelled? Suspended at least?" His questions are so full of hope. I'm about to dash his outlook on humanity.

"It was parents who locked me in there. Three in particular, including Jordan's dad, Bill."

The way Cannon's mouth hangs open isn't rehearsed or pretend. His eyes drill into me, unblinking, waiting for me to say, *"Psych!"* or, *"Just kidding."* Oh, how I wish I could.

Cannon twists in his seat, letting go of my hand for a moment while his gaze drifts off into the place where the pavement meets the horizon.

"You deserve to play, Hollis. No, you deserve to *start.*" He's so resolute in his words, his mouth closed tight to punctuate the finality of them while he shakes his head. His eyes haze and it's almost as if he's playing out an argument with someone else in his head, preparing to defend me.

Before I can talk myself out of it, I lean over the console and press my lips to his cheek, holding his jaw with my hand. His head moves in slow motion, turning to face me, his mouth opening with a faint breath. Our eyes meet briefly, his falling lashes my only clue that his close just before mine. He palms my cheek as his mouth captures my bottom lip, and in a single heartbeat, we're kissing.

Nothing about the moment is rushed, and every pass of his lips against mine is tender and sweet. Light tastes of my tongue with his are tempered by measured suckles of my top and bottom lips. He takes his time, shifting enough in his seat to steady my head in both of his hands. The way he holds me makes me feel cherished, and this is now one more thing that's going on my list of things to really, truly adore about Cannon Jennings.

13

CANNON

W alking in on a conversation and having it go stone-cold silent is never a good sign. That's what just happened, and I know my uncle and Zack were talking about pushing out Coach Taylor. I heard enough before I came down the stairs to get the general idea of their discussion.

The fact they aren't bringing it up now, in front of me? That means they don't trust me to know the details. That's both good and bad. Good morally because I don't want to be a part of something I don't believe is right, and bad because I can't prepare anyone for what might be coming.

Would I warn Hollis, though? Should I now, even though what I know is really just a bunch of bitching and whining over runny eggs at the breakfast table.

I don't know what time Zack got in last night, but I know he was drunk. I heard him vomit, twice. After Hollis dropped me off, I called Tory and spent most of the night playing video games with him and his brother and Lucas. I suspect Zack was out with a few of the baseball guys, getting support for his bruised ego.

If anyone tries to take this out on Hollis, I am going to lose my shit.

"How'd practice go yesterday?" My uncle tests me with that question.

"Ask Zack," I say without meeting his gaze. I stuff a mouthful of eggs and potatoes in my mouth.

"I wouldn't know. I got *sent home*," Zack grits out, shoveling food into his own mouth to avoid talking.

Clearly, they've already talked about what happened. Everything about Zack's tone is rehearsed. The awkward silence, broken by the occasional scrape of a fork along a plate or the clunk of a full coffee mug on the table, is meant to flush me out. I don't fall for any of it.

"What do you think your dad will think, Cannon?" My uncle changes up his route.

I shrug, eyes focused on my now half-empty plate as I scoop up more food.

"You think he'll be okay with moving your family across country so you can throw to some girl?"

I drop my fork at that comment, my chest tightening into a thick ball right where my ribs meet. I push the plate away, done, and unfurl the napkin my aunt always rolls up for us at the table. I run it over my mouth and chin.

"I guess we can ask him when he gets here," I say, standing and taking my plate to the sink. I meet my aunt's eyes as I do and get the sense that she's had to suffer through this conversation all morning.

"Speaking of, he might get in tomorrow," my uncle says. His chair drags along the floor as he stands.

My buzzing nerves instantly calm at that bit of news. My dad is sensible, even if he's competitive. He and I have had long talks about what might happen if I get recruited by places where Zack doesn't have a shot. My dad's helped me realize that even though Zack and I formed this dream together, I can still forge out on my own if that's what's best for me. Uncle Joel seems to think carrying Zack is my responsibility. I finally see the difference between loyalty and being taken advantage of.

"Is he driving straight through?" I drop my rinsed plate into the washer rack and turn to keep my back to my uncle as he steps in close.

"Yep," he confirms.

Finally looking up, my gaze runs smack into my cousin's. He's leaning back in his chair, rocking it on the back two legs while balancing a steaming cup of coffee on his propped up knee. The way he's eying me pushes my guard up like an invisible wall. When we were kids and I got a better Christmas gift than he did, he made the same smug face he's making right now—as though he has secret plans to sabotage whatever I have that he doesn't. Back then, it was a bike chain breaking or a wood bat splintering after too few uses. The things he could ruin for me now are far more important.

"There's a big meeting today. Isn't there, Dad?" My cousin's eyes remain on me despite his question.

"Hopefully," my uncle responds, his answer cut short from a phone call. He walks between us and holds up a finger as if I'm supposed to stick around and see what this call is all about. My gaze follows his path down the hall and through the front door before I return my focus to

Zack, who is still staring at me, his hint of a smile the kind a villain wears while he watches his victim drink down poison. I do my best to ignore his silent plea for attention, but when a quiet laugh slips from his mouth while I haul my backpack up on my shoulder, I break.

"What's your deal, dude. Just spill it. I don't have time to play the *What's Wrong with Zack* game this morning. I have a test to get ready for." I don't have a test, but there's no way I'm hanging out in the parking lot with him all morning just so he can glare at me and say cryptic shit.

"Board's not really happy with Coach Taylor's preseason, and it seems *someone* at the district found out." Zack leans forward and sets his mug on the table, then folds his hands together near it, pleased with himself, as if he did anything other than act like an asshat at practice.

"What's wrong with preseason?" I shake my head and pinch my lips tight.

"Uhm, maybe that he's not pulling the team together and building a sense of unity? Or that he's broken up the core group of players who have been incredibly successful the last three years in a row?" I can tell by how foreign these words sound coming out of his mouth that he's probably parroting talking points that my uncle already said. I'm also guessing Uncle Joel is the someone who told these same talking points to the district.

Instead of gratifying Zack with a response, I just stare at him and quirk up one side of my mouth and corresponding brow, a gesture that says "Seriously?" without having to utter the word.

"*Pfff.*" Zack rolls his eyes and stands, sliding the mug to the other end of the table. His mom takes it, and I'm upset for her that she's expected to clean up after him.

"You need a ride today or is your little girlfriend coming to get you?" His shoulder bumps into my chest with an extra thrust as he passes and asks that question. I tilt my head to the side and wait for him to turn back and look at me, but he doesn't.

That knot in my chest pulls tighter, but I stay on my path and don't give in to his passive aggressive quips. I'm not sure whether he says that because of something he suspects about me and Hollis or because of something he *saw,* but he's being a douche.

Without a word, I follow him out the door and get into the passenger side, dropping my backpack between my legs and buckling up. He pauses to stare at me for a few hard seconds, finally letting out a dismissive chuckle and buckling up himself.

"Whatever, man," he says. And thank God, we drive the rest of the way to school in total silence.

My plan to head straight to class and fake a bullshit test gets cut short the moment we pull into the lot. My gaze tracks Hollis's movement as she picks up her steps and speeds over to the last row of parking spots. Zack sees her a few seconds after me and lets out a muffled grunt when he realizes she's trying to catch up with us.

"What the fuck does she want?" he grumbles.

My stomach sinks. I've been riding a rollercoaster ever since I snuck out yesterday morning to meet Hollis at the gulch. Maybe I got on this ride at that New Year's party. It's hard to tell anymore, the line's so blurred. I've gone from being pissed off that she dares to exist in my carefully made plans to wanting to fight like hell to make sure she stays in them. Hollis, she makes me a better person.

The car stops hard and I lurch forward, slapping my palms on the dash.

"Dick!" I bark.

My cousin's arms are locked at the steering wheel, and he has yet to kill the engine. When I survey what's happening just outside his window, I spot the reason why. Hollis is making a gesture, and my cousin is going to shit all over it.

"This your idea?" Zack rolls his head to the side and hits me with lazy, annoyed eyes. I lean forward enough to read the logo on the box Hollis is holding: CUPPIES.

Shit. She brought him cupcakes.

I shake my head and cross my finger over my chest in an X.

"Swear to God, man. This is all her." *Give her credit for being nice,* I continue in my head, knowing he won't.

Cuppies is in the mall on the outskirts of town, one of those places where you can get oversized cupcakes and personalized cookies for special occasions. They're over-priced for cake, in my opinion, which makes this peace offering she's holding in her palms that much more thoughtful.

As my cousin pushes open his door, I sit with my back firmly pressed into my seat. I can't bear to watch, and maybe, if I'm lucky, he'll close the door before I have to listen.

"Awe, shucks, Double D. It's not my birthday," he says, leaving the door wide open behind him. I breathe out through my nose and close my eyes. He has to stop calling her that. It's harassment, and it doesn't help his cause. More importantly, she doesn't deserve it.

"I know, I just— I don't know why things between us are so . . . you know," she stammers. Fuck, I should get out and help her through this. I should be her wingman, make my cousin accept this gracefully. But I am still sitting here. All I've been able to muster is the strength to reopen my eyes so I can watch this disaster go down in flames.

"Well, how do you want things to be between us?" He leans into the side of the door, blocking my view. I lean forward to catch Hollis's gaze. Her eyes flit nervously to me then back to him.

"I don't know. Cordial, I guess?"

My lip ticks up with a stunted laugh. Ten bucks says Zack has no idea what the word *cordial* means.

"So you bought me cupcakes?" He steps forward, taking the box from her hands.

"Everyone says this place is good, and I wasn't sure whether you liked vanilla or chocolate, so I got both."

Goddamn, she's being so thoughtful. I'm not sure why she's trying so hard with him, but I can't help but feel this has something to do with that board meeting and the whispers at the district level about her dad and his coaching position. Not to say that Hollis isn't capable of doing something nice for Zack for no reason, but from what I know of her and from what I've seen of my cousin's behavior, I would say he sure as shit doesn't deserve it.

"Let's see," Zack says, tucking the open box in the crook of his arm, pinching it between his side and elbow while he pulls the paper from the bottom of a gooey, chocolate cake. I can tell by the movement of his head and jaw that he's taking a bite.

"Nope, don't like chocolate," he says, letting the cake fall from his hand to the ground. The thick frosting spatters. Hollis's lips part in disbelief as she blinks slowly at the wasted cake.

"Zack, knock it off," I finally say. I hate that I let it play out as far as it did. The liar inside me wants to say it's because I was giving Zack the benefit of the doubt, but really, I'm just a coward.

I get out of the car and pull my bag up on my arm as I step around to meet my cousin and the girl I'm maybe starting to like too much. Her jaw is flexed in a way that has the offended, open-mouthed smile locked in place.

"She's just trying to be nice, dude. Say thank you and take the damn cupcakes." I sigh, shaking my head and wondering how this is the conversation I'm having this morning. Hollis is still staring at the discarded cake on the ground.

"Was she, though? Being nice, I mean." My cousin tilts his head to the side and glances at me then back to Hollis again, practically daring her to stare back at him.

Lifting her chin, she closes her mouth and lets it fall into a stubborn, hardened frown.

Not wanting to see this escalate further, especially given the many places my mind is taking it, I intervene completely, taking the box into my own hands, closing the lid, and shoving it into my cousin's chest. I step into the space between him and Hollis, cutting them off from one another.

"Yes, she was. Now, say thank you and go to first hour."

I hold his stare for longer than I want. His eyes swirl with something truly hateful mixed with unwarranted betrayal. He didn't give me a choice with this. I will stand by him when he's right, but I've never been about signing up to be part of the school dick squad. I've got enough of a label floating around out there from being an introvert who doesn't like parties and small talk. Just ask that girl, Abby.

Zack finally gives in and breaks our stare, but only so he can look down at the mess he made on the asphalt.

"Thanks for the shitty present, Double D," he says, and I shove his chest, crinkling the box when I do it.

"Her name is Hollis," I seethe.

His smirk is faint and cynical, and it's the only thing I'm going to get in return. My body teems with aggression, and if he were to let loose and take a swing at me, I might knock him out. Maybe he senses that, or maybe he likes the attention he's drawn from people standing nearby. Roland and a few other guys from the team have gathered on the walkway that leads to the school, and they're entertained, trying to choke off their own laughter. All I keep thinking is how disgusted Coach Taylor would be if he saw them, even if it wasn't his daughter they're targeting. The fact it is Hollis only makes it worse.

Zack steps into me, his hot breath in my face. A few more inches closer and he'll be crushing the box into my chest.

"Whatever," he grunts out, crashing his shoulder into mine again, harder than he did earlier. My shoulders swivel but my feet remain firm where I stand. I reach forward and slam his car door shut, then trail his steps with my eyes as he joins the laughing group of trolls who have picked the wrong side in this war. Without looking back once, he tosses the crumpled box of sweets into the trash as soon as he reaches the flag pole, and all I can do is laugh out loud and apologize for him.

"Hollis, I'm sor—"

She shakes her head, and I get the point before she even has to ask. I'm always apologizing for him. That needs to stop, and it stops here.

14

HOLLIS

I'm not the kind of girl who has, well, girl kinda problems.

I've had seven major crushes in my life, and six boyfriends to complete them. Granted, the first four were all before fifth grade, but still, they count. I mean, it's hard to resist the girl who always gets picked first in dodgeball; at least, it used to be. That's all it took for me to make Ridge Howard, Miguel Velasquez, Shawn Sutter and Logan Sutter—*that's right, both Sutter brothers*—declare their love for me in the good ole days of elementary school.

My freshman year was all about Angus Lowenstein. He was smart, and completely unlike my usual type. He was into theater, and even convinced me to try out for the high school musical with him. He got the lead. I got cut. (Newsflash: I can't sing worth a damn.) It didn't matter, though, because Angus was perfection in the boyfriend department and on the stage. He was also gay. When I told him I didn't mind, he explained that the problem was dating me kinda got in the way of him being his true self. He's studying in France now, and he's got a French boyfriend who isn't vague or grumpy or mixed up in messy family drama that involves my dad's coaching and my passion for the game. Nope, Angus is in a normal, healthy relationship where everyone knows exactly where they stand and who they are. In essence, he's still perfect.

And this brings me to my two most recent crushes. Jordan was mutual love in every single way, except for the part where his father tried to intimidate me into quitting by locking me in the basement of my school and Jordan refused to stand up to him about it. I recently stopped blaming Jordan, and I have the Cannon situation to thank for that. Going against your family isn't easy, and in many ways, it feels impossible. That's basically what I asked Jordan to do when the Dean of Students called everyone in for interviews after the basement incident. I asked Jordan to turn on his dad, and despite the broken relationship he had with his father, the thought of severing it completely was too much. His lack of testimony was enough to give the powers that be at Xavier an excuse to not do a damn thing except, of course, fire my dad.

And now I'm looking to Cannon to do something very similar, to step away from blindly supporting his cousin to stand with me instead. He seems so willing, and yet I know the damage this will do to his relationship with his cousin and probably his uncle too. Maybe even his dad. I'm not sure making out with me in a mom van is truly worth the sacrifice.

"So, let me make sure I got this straight. You brought Zack cupcakes even though he's a dickhead and he threw them away—because he's a dickhead." June takes a bite of her carrot while her eyes stare at my lunch tray as though she's reading notes to help her process the facts about my screwed up life.

"Yes, that pretty much sums it up," I agree.

"And Cannon called him out on it, but you guys aren't a thing, or maybe you are, you don't know, but you've made out twice." She snaps another bite, her eyes still focused on my tray.

"Three times, actually, if you count New Year's."

"Oh, you always count New Year's," June says through a devious laugh. She takes a deep breath and tosses what's left of her carrot into the open cup of ranch, then pushes her tray to the middle of the table, folds her arms, and sets her gaze on me.

"That's pretty much it," I say, reaching to her tray and commandeering the leftover ranch. I flick the carrot out of the cup and dip the crust of my pizza in to see if that will make this poor excuse for a slice of pie any better. She wrinkles her nose and tells me I'm gross.

It's actually better this way, but no matter what I dip this crap in, it's still not New York pizza.

"I'm not seeing the problem. Lola?" June looks to her friend, who still owes me some beachy waves.

Lola sucks up the last few drops of her smoothie while she shakes her head, her lips puckered around the straw.

"There's no problem. And you totes know I think Cannon is an asshole. But it sounds like he's actually being kind of chivalrous."

I knit my brow at Lola's odd word choice.

"She's reading *Canterbury Tales* in English. Excuse her obsession with knights in shining armor," June explains.

"*Mmm*, armor," Lola adds, swiveling side-to-side in her seat, her lips curled coyly beneath her dreamy eyes. I half expect a white horse with a knight riding on top to bust through the cafeteria doors and whisk her away.

"I know he's being a good guy, and doing the right things, but I still feel like—"

"Like the house of cards is going to collapse at any moment," June finishes for me.

I look down and consider her visual, quickly deciding she's right. And that I'm probably not being fair, but I've watched cards fall before.

"I do. His uncle is the kind of loud guy who refuses to back off quietly. And his son is an apple that did not fall far from the tree. Zack is not going to like me—ever. He's never going to think I deserve anything I earn, and Cannon is trapped right between us, fruitlessly trying to convince him otherwise. And maybe—"

June cuts me off, drawing a line over her lips like a zipper.

"Don't you dare say you aren't worth it." Her expression is serious, and it's the first time I've seen her make a stern face to put someone in their place. Weird that she's making it at me.

"It's just a lot to ask," I relent, discarding what's left of my pizza crust on the tray and flopping back into my seat. I glance down at my pegged jeans, ripped holes in both knees, and torn-up skate shoes with stick figures drawn on every square inch. It's hard not to feel inadequate sitting this close to a girl like Lola, who Cannon already snubbed, uninterested. My sweatshirt is two-sizes too big because I like it that way. Lola's clothes are painted on, her curves made for race cars and the boys who drive them.

"He likes *you*." June interrupts my negative thoughts, leaning forward with her hands one on top of the other, resting on the tabletop right in front of me. "You are Cannon Jennings's type, based on everything you have told us. Mystery solved. That grumpy SOB has a weakness, and it's a girl who can keep up with him and put him in his place. Don't sell yourself short, Hollis. You're a hottie, and nothing like anyone else."

Well, shit. I might be in love with June just a little. I smile at her bashfully because that was a pretty big string of compliments to sit and take in all at once.

"Thanks," I eek out. I'm more accustomed to someone telling me, "Nice line drive."

Emboldened by June's killer pep talk, I walk into study hall and take the seat to Cannon's right, ignoring my usual self-imposed rules about sitting next to him. There's no reason it should be any different in here than it is in our first hour, where we talk and laugh and sometimes—*sometimes*—brush fingertips over arms or thighs when the teacher isn't looking.

"Hey," I say, reaching over and squeezing his shoulder as I sit. He stiffens and immediately shifts his posture to lose my touch and put a few more inches of distance between us. It's obvious, and his acting is bad.

"You scared me," he lies. I'm starting to recognize the differences in his laughs, and the thin ones with more breath to them are definitely forced. Like this one.

"Yeah, I'm stealthy like that." I look at him sideways, a little judgement in my squinted eyes.

"Right," he says, shutting his mouth into a tight smile. He holds up his notebook and points to it, as if it's some exhibit to prove he's hard at work on his studies. The page is blank, and I can't wait to see what he fills it with.

"Uh huh," I say, pivoting in my seat so I face him more than not. Wearing my wry smile, I rest my elbow on my desktop and hold my chin while I glare at his mundane tasks.

He writes his name at the top, then the date. He taps the point of his pen on the next line a few times, finally writing down the word Canterbury.

"You're not in Lola's class," I point out quickly. I know he's not because he and I have the same teacher, just opposite hours. And we aren't studying Canterbury right now; we're still on Shakespeare.

Cannon blinks a few times while staring at the page, finally drawing a scribble of lines through his fake essay title before laying the pen flat on the page.

"Oh, hey, Hollis. What's up?" Tory reaches over my shoulder as he walks in, holding out a fist. I pound it, already accepted into his circle. He takes the seat in front of Cannon but remains sitting to the side while the rest of the class filters in. His gaze bobs between the two of us— me staring at Cannon and Cannon pretending he sees nothing at all.

"Things weird here?" Tory wiggles his finger in the air between us, and I laugh out once, hard.

"Seems so." I shake my head and right myself in my

chair, leaning the opposite way to pull out my own note-book—for *actual* homework.

"Oh, I get it. You two hooked up," Tory teases. My cheeks burn and I know without looking they're florescent pink. I cough, unable to get the words out to put up an argument, and Cannon takes care of it for me, slapping his friend on the shoulder with his notepad.

"Dude, don't be like Zack," he grumbles.

"Ah, I see. Didn't we already have this talk?" Tory waits for Cannon to lift his chin, and when he does, they spend a few seconds in a staring competition as though neither wants to give in.

"You aren't responsible for your cousin, and your life is separate from his," Tory finally says.

I draw my attention down to my notes and doodle, and wish I'd sat at least one more seat away. The smile inching into my cheeks is hard to hide. I like Tory, and I like what he said even more.

Cannon flattens his notebook again and brings both his hands to his face, rubbing his eyes then moving his fingers into his hair, kneading his scalp.

"I know that, man. I know. He's just in this super fucked up place, and I don't know what's going on. I'm sorry." He rolls his head to the side in his palm and reaches toward me with his free hand, fingers stretched out wide for me to weave mine into the empty spaces. I do and he squeezes a little, shaking our hands together in a gentle movement that's also reassuring—and very, very public.

So does this mean we are a—we?

"Well, for the record. I like you two. I like her more, but I like the two of you as a thing," Tory says, pointing to me when he makes the joke at Cannon's expense. We both breathe out a small laugh, and before our hands separate, Cannon's thumb runs along my knuckles a few times for added reassurance.

The door clicks shut behind us and we all straighten in our seats out of habit. So far, Mr. Orson has been a cool study hall monitor. In the nearly two weeks I've spent with him, I've learned that as long as you remain fairly quiet, you can do whatever you want in here. You can also walk out for restroom and water bottle-filling breaks anytime you want. A girl I know does lines in the bathroom and goes missing for the middle twenty minutes of class every single day.

Maybe it was my power lunch with June, or perhaps the little tease of Cannon's hand on mine—whatever the root of it, I decide to test the liberal in-and-out policy for people who aren't ditchers and drug-addicts. Well, not *full-time* ditchers anyhow. I would say I'm more of an extended-leaver who wants to make out with my maybe boyfriend.

The idea doesn't feel stupid when I bite my lip and glance over my shoulder while nudging Cannon, and I still feel pretty bold and confident all the way out the door. The humiliation doesn't creep in until I've been leaning against the wall just outside the culinary arts room for five full minutes and my stomach rumbles because the bread smells so freaking good.

I'm close to giving up my nefarious plan and head back into class when the door swings open at the opposite end of the hallway and Cannon steps out. I push off of the wall and tuck my hands into my back pockets. He stops in his tracks and drops his hands into his front ones, tilting his head to the side before nodding toward the building exit on his end. I nod back and we maintain eye contact while we leave the farthest building from the main office.

Our doors open in sync, but I hold on to mine for an extra second or two while I take in the view of him as he makes his way closer to me. A sly grin pushes a dimple into his right cheek. He cocks his head to the left a few feet from the exit and soon disappears behind a brick wall.

Nervously scanning the area around me, I rush to duck around the same space, freaked out that I'll get caught doing something I shouldn't. My smile is almost manic over this tiny moment of social and academic recklessness. My cheeks are pushed high and my lips stretched as wide as they'll go to accommodate my aching grin when I round the corner and run into Cannon's chest head-on.

"Oh, door locked?" I laugh out nervously. His hands grip my shoulders to spin me around, and he cages me like a defender keeping me from getting to the goal line. It only takes a second for my mind to switch gears and realize he is ushering me away from something.

"What is it?" I force my body to face him, working against his efforts to turn me around.

"It's nothing. Door locked, so let's go somewhere else."

He's a bad liar. His tone betrays him easily, the even volume and guarded choice of words indicating that something set him off. His caginess ratchets up my frustration so I push past him, flinging his hands from my waist and arms until I break free and step into the walled-off space he was hiding from me.

Someone called me a cunt.

Wow.

"That must have been a pretty fat Sharpie," I say, my arms going limp to my sides while I take in the scribbled words on the maintenance door.

HOLLIS IS A CUNT

"I mean, it isn't very original," I say, quick to pretend I'm unfazed. "He's just playing off of tropes and sensationalism. And there's a pretty big movement among women to take that word back and redefine it, make it our own."

The tears come regardless of my brave face. I shudder, and choke on the emotion that rises up my throat faster than I can push it back down. The insult burns and I hate that I let it.

"Hollis." Cannon's arms are around me before I can protest. I rock as he holds me from behind, non-stop sniffles and guarded breaths working to wipe away any proof that this affected me whatsoever.

"It's fine," I say, pulling an arm free to wipe my palm across my cheeks and eyes. "I'm fine. Whatever. It's stupid."

Trembles have set in. I'm both hurt and livid, and both fight to rule my emotions. The one thing I'm not, though, is surprised. And in a moment when all I want to do is erase this experience from existence and rush back to the safety of my desk and the walls of study hall, I can't because the distant sound of male laughter and a golf cart motor gets louder by the heartbeat.

Cannon and I both duck behind the wall, his body flush against mine as if shielding me from oncoming enemy fire. His fingers move to my chin then slide up my lips, holding my mouth closed lightly as he breathes out, "*Shh.*"

I mean, it's not like I'm going to shout, "Hey, here I am —ditching class to check out the mural smearing my character."

His touch on my face softens, but his hand stays where it is. I'm quickly more comforted by it than I am offended, especially as the voices of the two men in the cart become clearer. This part of campus is the most private. That's why it's where students go to vape, and it's why a minute ago I thought maybe I was going to make out back here with a guy I'm quickly letting every guard I've ever had down for.

For our school's athletic director, Tom Wallis, and Cannon's uncle Joel, though, this spot is the perfect spot to organize a coup.

"You think you have enough players willing to go on the record that Taylor's breaking code of conduct? This can't be some *me too* shit show."

My breathing becomes harsh, my chest quaking with fury as my hands grip the front of Cannon's sweatshirt, forming fists around the fabric.

"Yeah, it'll go way beyond him playing favorites with his girl. The man just isn't the right fit for our program, and it's a plain and simple fact. His methods aren't going to work out here, and we have to make the fix before tryouts." Joel Jennings's tone is even. Calm, in fact. He's had this plan brewing for days. For the life of me, though, I can't fathom anyone other than Zack who'd back the crazy idea that my dad isn't the kind of coach who builds great programs. He's either bluffing that he has the numbers behind him or he's paying players to take up his cause.

"He'll lawyer up, you know," our athletic director says.

A muffled voice breaks through on the radio in their cart, something about being needed at the front office.

"Let him. In the meantime, Coach Gage is ready to take over."

They drive off, finishing their conversation too far away to be heard. Those few words Cannon and I heard are enough, though. Coach Gage is a nice guy, but he's seventy-two. He's been volunteering out here for decades. My dad was talking about him at dinner the other night, joking to my mom and Ben and I about how impressive it is that he can still hit pop flies so well. The guy has no interest in leading a team, but he's also a pushover, which is probably how Zack's dad pressured him into taking over my dad's job.

"I have to tell him," I realize aloud, pushing from Cannon's cover and slipping out into the open.

The golf cart is nowhere to be seen. I bite the back of my hand, teeth gripping my knuckles while I sort out the rush of thoughts. Cannon is never more than inches away from me. I'm shaking mad.

"Hollis." He spins me and palms both of my shoulders to catch my gaze and stop the world from spinning. I'm having a panic attack.

"Breathe," he says.

So I do.

15

CANNON

I knew Hollis wouldn't be able to wait for the end of the day to see her dad. I'm only glad she didn't rush over to his office in the state she was in. When she skipped out on weightlifting, I figured she was probably talking to him. Now that his door is locked shut and she's out on the field throwing with Zack and a few of the other guys, I'm not sure what to think.

Today was optional. It's my cousin's fault that Coach called off the remaining organized practices for the week. Next week is the last one before tryouts. I'm not worried about myself, but I am worried about Zack. It's not that he needs the practice, as much as he needs a serious personality adjustment to make sure he doesn't get himself benched—or worse, cut.

Or course, if Coach Taylor goes away, maybe that's not an issue. I can't buy into the idea that Coach Gage will like my cousin any better, though. I guess that fact is moot, since Coach Gage will be manipulated into building the team as my uncle sees fit.

I miss my dad.

My gear bag slung over my shoulder, I pull my phone from my pocket and send my father a text while I walk out to join the others. I wonder if they bothered to run? I'm sure Hollis did.

I message my dad to see where he's at, and when he replies with *100 miles to go,* my lungs open up, taking what feels like the first full breath I've drawn in ages.

A hundred miles puts him in town tonight. It means I'll have a rational set of ears to talk to, and wise advice to help me navigate this clusterfuck of a senior season.

With a clearing breath, I tuck my phone in the side pocket of my bag and head down to the field to join the others.

"We ran already," Zack says before I drop my bag and change my shoes. He's robotic with his throwing, and equally so with his words.

I glance to Hollis for verification and she quirks a brow and nods. That fucker really did run.

I stare at her for a few extra seconds while she throws, long enough to get a read on her expression to see how things are after talking with her dad, if she even had a chance to. I'm not able to read much from her expression, but I can tell she isn't exactly happy. She doesn't look as worried as before, though, so I leave them to finish throwing while I get in my run.

My times are getting faster every time I do this. I think about the difference I've seen in myself since I met Coach Taylor—and Hollis. I'm more than faster; I do things with purpose, and that thinking is beyond the field.

I wonder how I would react to the way my cousin acts if I didn't have a personal connection to Hollis. What if I never went to that New Year's party? What if she was simply coach's daughter, no connection to me at all? Would I have bothered to form one?

I never would have liked what Zack has done, but shamefully, I'm pretty sure I would have tolerated it—more so than I already have. I would have drawn a line and made it not my problem. My dad is like that. He doesn't approve of a lot of things, including the way the CEO of his engineering firm back home treated his female coworkers. My dad never said anything to anyone who could do anything about it, though. I suppose I haven't, either. I have made my point to Zack, though. I realize that's not enough, especially after what we saw—and heard—outside the study hall rooms.

I'm pacing after my run, checking the time on my smart watch, when Hollis jogs over from the infield. My instinct is to rush back with her, to avoid giving my cousin more reason to talk about us being alone, but then it hits me.

Fuck it.

Let him hate on me too.

"Hey," I say, leaning into her and kissing her jaw. She's sweaty, but I don't give a damn.

Her eyes are wide when I pull back, and her mouth is a hard line.

"What are you doing?" she growls in a whisper.

I scrunch my shoulders and tilt my head, a little

thrown that she's not game for throwing the PDA in my cousin's face. If he's part of my uncle's plans, then he can deal. In fact, he can deal no matter what.

"Zack's being weird," she adds.

I glance over her shoulder where my cousin is dragging mats out for hitting on the field. He seems super motivated, especially compared to the half-assed effort he's put into workouts so far.

"I'll give you that, yeah," I agree, picking up my gear and walking with her back to the field. She holds my mitt to justify walking with me.

"Did you talk to your dad?" I ask.

"That's the thing."

My head swivels to meet her gaze, and I can tell by the slant to her eyes that something changed.

"Yeah?" I question.

She walks close to me as we enter the dugout, constantly scanning to make sure we're alone enough for her to share details. She nods to Roland and I study him while he pulls his water jug to his mouth and chugs. He laughed at her this morning, which speaks volumes about his character. *Would I have been different? I like to think so but honestly, probably not.*

Hollis waits for him to jog out to the base path to help Zack unroll the mats. Not wasting a second of our time out of earshot, she leans over the back of the bench and looks me in the eyes.

"Coach Gage told my dad he's going to have to retire. Said he and the wife bought an RV and plan to visit the grandkids in California. He's done after tryouts."

We blink at one another while I digest the new information and form an opinion. I'm not sure what to make of it, and I can tell neither is she. One thing is certain: the school won't be able to count on Coach Gage to fill a last minute coaching vacancy this close to tryouts. It means we have time, though I'm not sure how much. My uncle works quickly, and secretly. He's good at making connections; part of his slick marketing savvy.

We make a pact to play along, to play dumb and let Zack lead out here. Giving him a little bit of authority might be a good way to reach him, but my gut says we have to play this careful.

Hollis warms up my arm and we spend the next hour and a half taking live at-bats. About a dozen players show up, and between Roland and me, we throw a good eighty pitches. The rest of the at-bats are taken off the tee or the machine, which must be about as old as the clubhouse. The metal plates are warped, which makes every fifth pitch come out a little wild. One buzzes my cousin's head, and as he collapses to his ass and tosses his bat to the center of the field, I brace myself for him to think Hollis did it on purpose, simply because she dropped a ball into the feeder.

"Damn, girl. You trying to mimic Cannon's pitches with that thing?" My cousin gets to his feet and claps the dirt from his hands, his laughter pulling up his cheeks into a huge smile. It's as if he's a pod person. Or knows his initial plan with my uncle fell through.

Maybe it's both.

"That my nephew all grown up taking hacks out there?" My dad's voice is like salve for a wound I didn't realize I was nursing. Damn, I've missed him.

"Uncle Mike!" My cousin tosses his bat to the ground

and jogs around one side of the backstop while I saunter around the other.

Zack's strong enough now to pick my father up, and he does. For a moment, watching them embrace, I soak in the genuine laughter and slaps on the back with big hugs. I forget that I have a lot of shit to catch my dad up on when it comes to my uncle and cousin. I keep that pushed to the side a little longer as my dad lets go of Zack's neck and opens his arms wide to me. It's been a few long months since we've seen each other in real life. Video chats just aren't the same.

"Hey, Dad," I say through an earnest grin.

"Come here, kiddo." He tugs on the shoulder of my shirt and we fall into a warm embrace, his large hand slapping against my shoulder blade while mine does the same. He's been calling me kiddo since I could understand language. It's nice to know that some things you don't grow out of.

"I got in a few hours early and figured I'd come find you in your element." He steps back and to the side, giving me a good view of my truck. It's filthy from its trip across the country, but damn, I'm almost as glad to see my wheels as I am my pops.

"I'm guessing you're gonna need my help unloading that?" I gesture toward the full load tied down with ropes in the back of the truck.

"Well, since most of that is yours—"

"Like hell it is. That's Mom's shoes and clothes and you know it," I joke.

We both cough out a good laugh before a brief moment of awkward quiet settles in among all of us. It's in this beat, right now, that I remember how messed up everything has become, and how much worse I fear it might get.

"Mr. Jennings, it's nice to meet you," Hollis says, stepping in next to me. She reaches out her hand for my dad to take. He knows very little about Hollis other than the big picture—we have a girl on our team, she's good, and Zack doesn't like her.

"Ah, so you're this big hitter I've been hearing about." My dad speaks through a practiced smile, maybe sensing the bitterness wafting off of my cousin like fumes.

"She hits all right," Zack pipes in, leaving our small circle and moving back toward the plate to his discarded bat. Hollis glances at his back as he walks away and lets out a short laugh.

"I hit better than he does," she whispers, cupping her hand as if she's sharing a secret with my father.

My dad chuckles.

"I bet you do," he whispers back with a wink.

I want my dad to like Hollis. Whatever this thing is between me and her has been cast under a dark cloud because of all the shit with Zack and my uncle. It'll be nice to admit out loud to someone that I really like this girl.

"We about done here?" I ask over my shoulder. My cousin scans the area. Most of the other players are gassed and already packing up. I can tell he wants to go more, probably to show off in front of my dad. But all I want is to get in my truck and talk with my father alone for the first time in way too long. I've missed him.

"Yeah, guess so," Zack says, tossing his bat on top of his equipment bag before jerking one of the Velcro straps of his batting glove loose.

"I can stay, if you want to take a few more swings?"

Hollis's offer is only within earshot of me, Zack and my dad, and I wish someone else heard so they would give in and stick around, too. As it is, I bristle at her suggestion and Zack seems poised to ignore it.

"I don't mind sticking around, watching for a while," my dad offers. He's bound to be exhausted, and since he got in early, he shouldn't have to leave for the airport for an entire day. I'm sure he wants to sleep.

"No, seriously . . . I'd like to work on a few things, too," Hollis adds. Her gaze strikes a deal with mine, and I don't like the dangerous gamble she's making. Plus, I'm not certain how she's getting home. The thought of her on this field alone with Zack, in a car—alone, with Zack—makes my stomach fold up into itself.

"I mean, I'm about done," Zack says, building up an excuse of his own when Hollis cuts him short, grabbing his wrist with her hand. His eyes zero in on the enemy threat, and mine flash protectively, a sour feeling coating my insides and pulling down the sides of my mouth.

"Just another round, two tops," she says.

The two of them stare at one another, only inches apart, and my pulse jackhammers in my chest, tempting my fist into action. But Zack doesn't do anything. Why Hollis is making this offer—*wanting* to spend time with a guy I've been ashamed to call family lately—is lost on me. Unless . . . she really is just good. Stubborn, perhaps, is more fitting.

"You want me to come back in a bit, give you a lift home?" My motives are obvious to everyone, and Zack shoots me a snarky glare that's his way of calling me pathetic.

"I can get her home." My cousin holds my gaze for a solid beat, and our eyes briefly war. While his seem to tell me to trust him, mine warn him not to push me too far.

"Great. Okay, well, I'll catch up with you later," Hollis says, ending the discussion. She squeezes my forearm, this touch more tender than the way she grabbed Zack's, and again, my cousin and I zero in on it. My body rushes with heat at getting caught, a sensation that sinks my stomach with the G-force of a roller coaster when my dad elbows my side and lifts a brow.

"See you at home, cuz," Zack says, his smile falling into an ominous, relaxed line that reads like a devious plan. He lifts the bucket of balls and heads toward the tee to join Hollis. *She's strong, and she's safe.* I keep those two thoughts on repeat until my dad and I pull out of the parking lot and head toward our temporary home.

"So, you didn't mention that Hollis is—"

"Hot," I sigh out. I punch out a laugh before my head falls back to the head rest and rolls to the side to meet my dad's waiting gaze.

"Pretty much that, yeah," he says, giving me a crooked grin that tilts his thick mustache up on the right. His familiar laughter is a welcome sound, as is the endearing, soft punch he presses into my shoulder.

"Zack hates her," I say, shaking my head.

My dad's brow knits and he chews at his lips.

"Didn't seem so bad back there." My dad got the performance of a lifetime, from both of them. There's way too much to get into for this short time we have together, so I don't dispute him outright, but I don't completely agree.

"Yeah, well, you were watching. You know how he looks up to you." I wait for my dad to glance my direction again, and his faint smile lets me know that he gets how rough life is for my cousin.

"Yeah," he agrees, moving his eyes back to the road.

My dad and I have never talked about it openly, but I think there's a silent understanding between us that Zack had it harder growing up under my uncle's rule. It's always been the little things, like the public displays of discipline when we were little, or the immediate excuses my uncle made any time my cousin failed at anything.

"Zack would have gotten more hits today, but I had him up late last night practicing," my uncle would say. Or, *"I told him to only go seventy-five percent for this game since it didn't matter as much as the championship will."*

Then, if Zack wasn't perfect for the championship, he got his ass chewed out all the way home.

It was the same for everything we did—if he got a B in school and I got an A, if we went bowling and I scored higher, if my birthday cake was bigger than his. The competition was this constant undertone, but I was never an active participant. I'm pretty sure my dad never was, either. Zack had no choice, though, and I guess that's why he is how he is, because my uncle bred him that way.

"When you and Uncle Joel played together in high school, what was that like?" I'm feeling things out with this question, and I think my dad senses it. He shifts in his seat and wrings his hands around the steering wheel a few times while his eyes haze into the distance of the road ahead. I point to the intersection coming up to let my father know where to turn.

"It was good," my dad says.

"Ha, that's a non-answer." I dip my chin and challenge him with a glare. He gives in to the heat of it and finally looks in my direction, rolling his neck and rubbing it with his palm.

"Yeah, it is. But mostly because that was so long ago. I mean, we had a good time, and our team went to state twice. We both got to college on the game, so that was pretty cool."

"Was he better?" I challenge.

"Joel?" My dad's head swivels in my direction and he blinks before gurgling out a laugh. "Uh, no. He was good, but I was—" My dad shrugs.

"Better," I finish for him.

He smiles at me with tight lips and I point to the next turn ahead.

Deep down, I've always known this was the case. None of us ever talk about it, mostly because my dad is not the kind of guy who has to keep score against others. For him, the memories of playing with my uncle are more about living life and having an experience. The greatness of the two of them together is always played up more by my uncle. Nobody, though, ever compares the two. My grandmother, before she passed last year, always gave everyone equal everything. That spirit sorta bled out into the rest of the family, because nobody ever feels the need to compete with one another or brag.

Until Zack.

Moving to Indiana did something to my cousin and his

dad. It's as though this time we've been apart unleashed a kind of envy. If Hollis weren't here, I sort of wonder if all of this rage would instead point toward me. My aunt steers clear of the topic, praising Zack for doing his best. Deep down, however, my uncle never quite got over no longer being my cousin's number-one coach. He still wants to be the only voice he hears on the field. And if Zack isn't playing because someone better steals his spot, what will Uncle Joel have to do with his spring afternoons?

We pull into the driveway and my aunt and uncle are waiting in the driveway.

"Mikey!" Hearing my uncle call my dad by the little kid version of his name always makes me laugh.

My dad gets out of my truck and moves toward my uncle, both of their arms out like wings. I wonder if one day Zack and I will be like this, or if I'll resent him forever the way I do right now. I hate this feeling taking over my body, like tar seeping through my insides making it hard to breathe. Maybe Zack isn't the one who changed. Maybe I have.

I'm caught up in the reunion in front of me and lost in my thoughts when they're interrupted by the low idle of a car pulling into the space behind my truck. My immediate reaction when I see Zack and Hollis in the car together is to protect her, but after a blink I realize they are both smiling.

My face puzzles as Hollis gets out and Zack rushes from the driver's side toward my father and uncle.

"I thought you were getting in extra work?" I'm still on guard, and my face must show it because Zack calls me out.

"We catch you in the middle of something? You look surprised." he says.

"Yeah," I huff out through a suspicious laugh.

"I could tell he changed his mind and was sticking around for me, so coming here was my suggestion," Hollis answers.

I shift my focus to her, giving her my perplexed expression. She laughs silently and steps in close.

"I'm fine," she reassures. "Just trying to build a bridge, maybe stop the fire before he starts it."

Nodding slowly, I make room for her to stand next to me and be a part of the conversation unfolding in my driveway. Upon seeing her, my uncle's eyes light up in a way that makes my skin crawl. I hope Hollis doesn't notice.

"So, you're the female phenom, huh?" Uncle Joel reaches out a hand as if he doesn't already have a file on Hollis stashed somewhere, filled with nefarious plots to bump her out of his kid's way.

"I'm trying out for the team, if that's what you mean. Yeah." She shrugs off his compliment with a polite laugh, and I realize she's playing the game too; I'm proud of her for it.

"Oh, I hear you're pretty much a sure bet," my uncle says when their hands touch for the shake. He winks in that car salesman way of his.

I glance to my cousin to get his take, but his eyes are focused on the ground, his face void of giving anything away. He must know about Coach Gage retiring.

"Oh, this is my brother, by the way. Cannon's dad, Mikey," Uncle Joel continues, shaking my dad by the shoulder as he shows him off. My dad is only a year younger, but my uncle always gives the impression there's more age and wisdom between them. He only quit calling him baby brother after an awkward family fight at Thanksgiving four years ago. It's one of the few times I've seen my dad snap at my uncle, and it makes me wonder how long it bothered him before he finally broke.

"We met," my dad explains, smiling and nodding toward Hollis.

My uncle's face dims at the news, but he quickly masks it.

"Oh, right. Out on the field. Did you get to see any of the action?" my uncle asks.

"I mean, they were pretty great at putting balls in the bucket," my dad says through a chuckle.

"Ah." Uncle Joel nods, clearly hoping for a better scouting report.

"Well, Hollis. Now that you're here . . ."

I tense at my uncle's lead-in.

". . . You should stay for dinner. Meg has a roast going. We're a big meat and potatoes family. You can tell us about New York and your dad. Being coach's daughter, I mean. That must be—"

"A lot of pressure," Hollis throws in.

"Yes, right," Uncle Joel agrees.

There's clearly a game of chess in play and everyone seems acutely aware. We're all doing our best to stay off the board and just let Hollis and Uncle Joel battle it out. I refuse to leave her in this alone, though. Without giving her warning, I reach to her side and find her fisted hand pressed against her thigh. It twitches at my touch, and she turns her attention to me with a flinch.

I give her a slight nod. I'm willing to make a grander gesture than this if she refuses. Thankfully, she doesn't. Her hand unfurls and her fingers stretch out for mine. Our palms meld together as I bring her hand to my mouth and kiss the back of it in a blatant show of solidarity—and an enormous F-U—to my cousin and uncle. They mask their reactions poorly, their eyes seething in a way that shows the connection between the apple and the tree.

"You'll love my aunt's cooking. Her roast is seriously the best, like magazine cover-worthy," I brag. It's not a lie, and Aunt Meg has no part in this grudge-match. And judging by the approving smile I just got from my father, neither does he.

16

HOLLIS

C annon wasn't wrong about the roast. It was the literal definition of Midwestern home-cooked amazingness. I didn't think I liked carrots, but it turns out the ingredient I've been missing to completely appreciate them is marinating them for hours in a bath of greasy beef broth.

For a little while tonight, I forgot about the weirdness. We all sat around the table laughing while Cannon's dad and uncle swapped stories about the dumb things they did in high school. Like the time they dragged their team's field in the middle of the night using their dad's old Jeep with a bunch of random yard tools tied to the back. Took them an entire weekend to repair the tire grooves and divots they left behind, but they both swear the party dare that led them to do it was worth it.

Cannon's dad is nice. And not in the way you call someone nice because you don't think you'll ever get to know them well so it doesn't matter. No, he's truly kind. And when Joel is in the environment we were all in tonight—together, with family—he seems nice, too. It brought out a better side to Zack, as well. It would have been easy to erase the last two and a half weeks and start over, but just as we were leaving, Zack's dad reminded me that none of them are to be trusted.

"Hey, tell your dad I'll be giving him a call about that town hall he needs to hold with the board. Routine thing. We'll just be asking him some questions. It's good for the public to buy in on things. Helps with fundraising." He practically whistled out the last few words like a snake.

All I did was nod and say I would. And I have spent—*no, wasted!*—my short ride home alone with Cannon in his truck thinking about all the things I should have said instead. I should have probed, asked about the last time they held one of those, or subtly hinted how it's too bad Coach Gage is retiring. Just one little hint to make him wonder if I heard his plan, if I know something.

"So, I can't tell if that was fun for you." Cannon sighs and lets his weight fall back into his seat as he shifts into park outside my house.

I texted my dad earlier to let him know I was meeting Cannon's dad for dinner, and my gut tells me my father's been waiting for me to roll up to our house ever since. When the blinds at the front window dip and spill out light from the television, I smile and nod to myself. He's waiting.

"It was *mostly* fun?" I lift one shoulder and smile on one side of my mouth.

Cannon laughs.

"Okay, fair enough."

He reaches over and takes my hand in his, turning my

palm over and drawing soft lines along the ones in my palm while his mouth hangs open with indecision.

"You're thinking about apologizing for your uncle and cousin again, aren't you?" I close my hand around his thumb and jiggle it teasingly.

He laughs again and wiggles his head.

"I am," he confesses.

"They were fine tonight. I made it through the fire. I survived. And their plan we overheard—"

"Is going to move on to Plan B," he finishes.

I shrug, pretending I can't guarantee he's right, but honestly, he is.

"I liked your dad," I say, changing the subject to the positive part of the evening.

Cannon grins in response, and I can tell his relationship with his dad means a lot to him.

"You must miss him," I prompt.

"I do."

The last thing I want to do is go inside my house right now. Not because my dad will grill me with overprotective questions. He won't. He's more the "pretend my daughter doesn't date" kinda dad. I don't want to go inside because I don't want to leave this truck. It's so warm in here, and being near Cannon without pretense for once is so goddamn nice. A quick glance out my window tells me that staying out here for a few extra minutes, though, is all I'm going to get. My dad has actually fully opened the blinds, and I can make out his profile as he sits by the window fake reading a book.

"I'm a bit afraid to kiss you." Cannon laughs out

nervously, leaning against his steering wheel and nodding toward my dad's figure.

I sigh.

"Is it because he's your coach? Or is it because he's my dad?"

Cannon mulls it over for a few seconds, drawing his brow in before meeting my gaze in a snap.

"Definitely both."

He takes my hand again and brings it to his mouth, pressing his lips to the inside of my wrist and lingering there just long enough to signal that in any other situation, this would lead to more. *Way* more.

"I really, *really* like you, Cannon Jennings from Indiana."

A soft smile plays at his lips as he lowers my hand, his thumb grazing along the tender skin where his kiss left coolness behind.

"I really, *really* like you, Hollis Taylor from Indiana . . . by way of *Staten Island.*" His attempt to mock my accent is adorable, despite how bad he is at playing New York.

"You are so accent-less," I tease.

"Hey, I'm from the southwest." He pushes my arm playfully and I push back, my fingers raking down his arm and snagging on the material of his hoodie. I grab on and tug gently before letting go of his shirt and picking his phone up from the center console. I hold it up to his face to force it to unlock.

"Are we already at the snooping-on-each-other's-phone stage of the relationship?" He laughs off his comment, but the sound fades quickly and his eyes go wide and dart away.

Relationship.

I tuck my bottom lip under my teeth to quash my nervous grin threatening to ruin my bluff while I pretend to be unfazed by his words. Inside my chest, though, is an epic house party, complete with strobe lights and twelve-inch woofers.

"I'm giving you my number," I say, sending a text to me from his phone. I hold it up to face him when I'm done, showing that I typed the word RELATIONSHIP. The best thing about Cannon's thick eyelashes is the way they shudder like butterfly wings when he's nervous. He stares at the word without breathing for a few seconds. I hold it in the space between us to give him the opportunity to take it back. I'm not sure why I expect him to. Maybe because I know how many issues come with us having that word.

"You got a text message. You should probably answer that," he says in a low voice that's close to a whisper. His eyes flit up to mine, and I let my lip come loose so I can show him the smile I've been keeping in.

I take comfort in knowing the buzz in my back pocket is a message I sent myself but that he let me send. What's strange is that I still plan on reading it—staring at that one little word—all . . . night . . . long.

"I should get in. You know, before my dad comes out."

We both bow our heads with a nervous laugh.

"God yes, please. Don't let him come out here," Cannon says.

"I'll see you tomorrow? Maybe, you want a ride to school?" He cocks his head to the side, leaning into the steering wheel, and the party in my chest puts on another song to keep things going.

"I'd like that," I say.

No kiss. Not here where we're being watched. Honestly, it's not even that he is one of the players on my team, one of my dad's players. It's that I'm daddy's girl, and having your father catch you getting a good night kiss is mortifying and cringe-worthy for everyone involved.

"You can leave your gear in the back, then. I'll lock it up and bring it when I come get you in the morning."

We nod our good-byes and I slip out the door, pushing it closed while I stumble backward like a drunk in from a bender.

Per the norm, my dad is relaxing with his feet up and one of his favorite coaching books cracked open in his lap. I'm no longer sure if the man has ever actually read it. I'm starting to think the only time it gets pulled out is when I'm in the driveway with a boy and he's playing studious by the window.

"Have a good time?" He doesn't look up from the pages as he asks. This is part of his act, too.

"I did. We ate roast. It was oddly delicious," I say.

"Better than Meno's?" He quirks a brow with that question.

"Let's not get crazy now, Dad," I say, putting on a serious tone. Meno's was *our* pizza joint. It's the place where my dad took the team after big games, win or lose. No amount of grease-soaked carrots in the world could ever compete with that.

"Well, I'm pretty beat. See you in the morning?" He stretches with a yawn as he stands from his chair, dropping his fake-read book on the side table.

"Actually," I begin, waiting for him to pull the string on

the small lamp to kill the light enough for me to tell him this. "Cannon is picking me up."

His lack of response is almost worse than any word he could have said out loud. I'm relieved with he finally utters, "Oh."

"Just tomorrow. I'm sure. Ya know, to be nice." I'm babbling, making excuses, and thankfully he lets me off the hook. It's weird to crush on a guy and want to admit it to your dad and gush with him the way you would a girl-friend. I do, though. Probably because Cannon is totally the kind of guy my dad would pick for me out of a lineup of eligible bachelors. I've seen the way he works with him, coaches him; he's grown to respect him. They respect each other.

Then there's Zack.

Folding his big flannel-covered arms around my shoulders and neck, my dad pulls me close and kisses the top of my head.

"Good night, angel," he says.

"Good night, Daddy."

With the lights out in the house, I wait in the darkness downstairs while he climbs up and shuts his bedroom door, probably to spill the beans about everything he thinks he knows to my mom.

My pocket buzzes before I hit the stairs. I hook my bag on the finial at the end of the staircase and pull my phone out to read the text message I expect to be some razzing tease from my nosy little brother, or maybe June checking in on me after our girl-chat lunch today. Deep down, I hope it's from Cannon, but hope is a lot different than expectation.

How do you feel about one block away? Surely your dad's window seat doesn't look out that far.

My lips tug up at his text. I'm out the door in three seconds, feet pounding pavement in a near sprint toward the glowing tail lights just beyond the stop sign. I climb into the passenger seat I vacated only a minute or two before, yanking the door closed behind me. Before I breathe another word, Cannon's hands are on my cheeks, fingers sliding into my hair as his mouth meets mine in a hungry kiss that we've both been holding back for far too long.

I crawl toward him on my knees, and his hands slide down my arms then over my ribs and around my waist, guiding me over the center console until I sit sideways in his lap with my head resting on his driver's side window.

"Goddamn, have I been dying to kiss you like that since our missed opportunity in study hall," he says, pulling back for air while holding my forehead against his. Our noses touch, and it makes me giggle like a girl with a crush when he playfully wiggles his against mine.

"Imagine if our New Year's kiss was like that," I say.

"What, this?" He again tickles his nose against mine and I laugh harder, chastising him with a flat palm against his chest. I leave it there, feeling the heat pour from his body, the hard beat underneath his shirt.

"No, silly. I meant like this," I say, sitting back enough to focus on his eyes. They're blue like the sea, like dusk back home. I reach to my side and turn the music up a little to fill the nervous gaps in the air, the song some alt-pop tune by one of those new female artists who sings as though she's broken. These songs are my favorites.

Propping myself up to face him, I push the button that slides his seat back enough to make room for the two of us. When his hands slip to my hips then down to my thighs, fire burns in my belly. And lower. I'm swallowed up in layers of clothes, and more than anything, all I want to do is *feel* him. I want to see if that beat in his chest matches up with mine. I want them to be close, to beat together or echo on constant repeat.

Straddling his lap as he lays back in his seat, my hands tremble as I reach down for the bottom of my sweatshirt, my tummy tightening with a rush of nerves as I peel the tattered cotton up and over my head. My hands reach behind my neck to find the thick band holding my hair together in a twisted knot. I tug it loose, but pause to laugh at myself when it gets tangled in my hair.

"You and this goddamn hair," Cannon teases, swatting my hand out of the way to help get the band out of my wild mane.

"I should just cut it." I sigh.

The band finally free from my hair, he rolls it onto his wrist, then holds my chin with his thumb, forcing our eyes to meet again.

"Don't you dare. I love your knotty-ass blonde tangles." He makes a serious face that doesn't break for almost a full five seconds, but when I see the curl tempt his lips, I squeeze his shoulders and press my forehead into his.

"You liar!" I laugh out.

His hands press into my sides, tickling me, and I squeeze my thighs around him while we wrestle in this tiny space, taunting each other like grade schoolers who haven't quite discovered puberty. Only, we aren't kids at all. We're both seventeen, almost eighteen. Our birthdays are two weeks apart in February—I checked.

Cannon's birthday is on Valentine's Day. Perhaps St. Valentine or Cupid or whatever gifted him with arrows because of it. Whatever the case, I've been shot with something, and the drug quickly fills my veins. As I rock my body forward to feel Cannon rock-hard beneath me, I can tell that he is drunk on our physical chemistry as well.

"May I?" His eyes scan down the length of my neck and chest to the bottom of the blue jersey I wore to practice today. His fingers flirt with the hem.

I love that he asked.

"You may," I say, cheeks heated and voice quiet. I'm bashful.

Cannon gathers the bottom of my jersey into his hands, lifting with his thumbs while I slowly raise my arms above my head, helping him to remove my shirt completely. I'm still scuffed with dirt on my elbows and legs from our practice, and though I haven't told him, he's worn a smudge of dirt on his right cheek the entire night. I trace it now with my thumb, wishing it were permanent because I love the tough appearance it gives him.

Dipping down, my hands weave into his hair, grabbing hold of thick waves. I wonder what his hair feels like when it's wet, like in the shower. The tension hugging my chest loosens suddenly and I tuck my chin to confirm that his thumb and index finger have tugged the zipper at the front of my sports bra down about two inches.

"Up? Or down?" His eyes haze, thick with want and clearly rooting for option number two. My body begs for that as well.

Sitting up to put a few extra inches of space between us, I wrap my hand around his to nudge it lower. Together, we lower the zipper until the sides separate, and I gasp from both the cool air and the release. I lean back until my shoulders touch the steering wheel and hook my thumbs into the band of my sweatpants, tugging them down enough to show that I am mad with want, and give him permission to touch me.

His eyes smolder in the faint light as he drags the edges of both palms up the center of my belly and chest, peeling away the unzipped bra from each of my breasts one at a time. His thumbs rub over my hard nipples as they pass and I arch and moan.

"Fucking goddess," he says, his voice deep and not shy. He sucks one of his thumbs, coating it in his saliva, then rubs it over one of my raw, pink tips while he reaches behind my back to pull me into him, covering my other breast in his mouth. His teeth grip the tender skin, and his lips wrap around my nipple and suck so hard it burns. He soothes it by blowing on the tender skin, then taking gentle swipes with his tongue.

His hands roam to my back and follow my curves, fingers dipping inside the band of my sweatpants and teasing the tight wrap of my sliding shorts still on underneath. His mouth forms a devilish smile that I can't help but dust with my curious one.

"What's so funny?" I ask, peppering his lips with teasing kisses before holding on to his upper lip with my teeth. It pulls free as his smile stretches larger.

"Most girls probably have some sexy little panties on underneath their sweats and you've got sliding shorts." He laughs lightly, but I can tell he's not laughing *at* me. Cannon sees me for who I am, and I've never wanted to be something I'm not.

"Mizuno sliding shorts are hella sexy," I boast, rolling my hips.

"*Mmm*," he hums, lifting his chin just enough to lock gazes. "That they are."

His hands run down the taut fabric around my waist until his hands cup my ass and he pulls me snug into him.

"Oh!" My breath hitches at the sudden surge of electricity that jolts my core. Wanting to touch his chest and feel its warmth against mine, I flatten my palms on his stomach and slide them up under his long-sleeved tee and sweatshirt until he helps me remove them the rest of the way.

Cannon holds me close, one hand firm on my butt, the other carving a warm line up my spine until I'm flat against him. His hand continues its path up my neck and into my hair. Hidden behind fogged windows in his pickup parked just out of the glow of a nearby streetlamp, we kiss breathlessly, our mouths finding the perfect fit against one another with each nip and every pass of the tongue.

Friction builds as I rock against him and he pulls me close—tight—my swollen center finding relief, even through the layers, against his hard erection. This could so easily transition into something more, but there's no sign from Cannon that he expects it, that he needs it. This here, feeling each other like this, it's enough. *For now.*

I gasp as he pushes up against me and I hungrily rub against him, both of us chasing a relief that's eluded us for longer than I realized. Cannon does things to me, makes me feel things, that are somehow more than anything ever before.

"Make me come," I beg, my bold words dragging a growl from his chest that spills out into a grunt against my neck. The sharp edge of his teeth pierce the skin below my ear as his hips push up into me and his hands hold me to him, anxious fists clutching my tight shorts as he rolls me back and forth in the sweetest rhythm ever.

I look up, feeling the sensation building to the cliff, and his tongue flicks against the base of my neck. He licks up to my chin, then bites at my swollen lower lip, holding me hostage between his teeth as he playfully growls. His hands have pushed inside my shorts, his warm palms melded against my bare skin, fingers moving closer and closer to my desperate center with each rock of my hips until I finally feel the tips of them brush against my soaking wet center.

I break our kiss long enough to meet his gaze and nod, begging for him to continue. "Yes!" The word comes out without my control when his hands reach around me completely, one of his fingers sinking inside of me and pressing against my swollen insides. The quivers come hard and fast, an uncontrollable rush of waves that makes my body convulse and fall into him completely.

"So fucking hot," he whispers harshly against my ear, his voice strained with his own need to find relief. I sink into him harder, still riding the swell of pleasure from where his finger presses on my insides. I ride the next wave, my own orgasm extended with every touch of Cannon against me. My body is a time bomb of sensations, ready to explode with every touch, and his is near the same. A small whimper from my lips is all it takes to push him over the edge, his eyes fluttering closed, his lips parting in a satisfied groan.

I rock and he flicks his fingers against me until our bodies are drained of feeling, numb from satisfaction, and hot from pleasure. It's freezing outside this truck but in here it's an inferno. The thought of how this must look from the outside pushes a giggle out of me, but I don't move. There are no feelings of shame or embarrassment at wearing what I wear. I don't feel inadequate or unworthy or used. I feel close to Cannon. A bond of trust and faith that has been brewing is sealed in place with our physical deed, an act that tells him as much as it tells me that I trust him.

"I really, *really* like you, Cannon Jennings from Indiana," I say, repeating my words from before. The hoarse tone of my voice carries a different vulnerability to it this time, though, and I think Cannon knows. Pushing away the sweat-strewn locks of hair from my cheek and forehead, he lifts his chin and presses a long, tender kiss against it. He's quiet, leaving his lips against my skin for several long seconds before finally replying to my raw and honest declaration.

"I like you more, Hollis. I like you a whole lot more," he whispers, and in this very moment, dare I say, I believe maybe he does.

17

CANNON

I left home early, before the sun was up in fact, and drove to the same corner where Hollis and I gave in to everything last night. Well, not *everything*. I didn't need it, though, my God, did I want it. I wanted every inch of her, to touch and taste her body in all the places, and mark her as mine in every place I'd been.

I'm attracted to every trait she possesses, from her physical form to the confidence that radiates from her. Her raspy voice, her shortened words coated in her native New York roots, her feistiness.

I managed to avoid talking to Zack when I came home after dropping her off. He was locked in his room with the music up annoyingly loud. I gave my dad what's been serving as my room for the night and slept on the couch. I have to take my father to the airport after school today, and I hate letting him go, though he'll be back in a few days. I'm done being here, in this house. I'm ready for our own walls, my own rules. This constant air of suspicion I have for

Zack and his motives makes my stomach hurt nonstop. There are moments it's downright hard to breathe.

I can't lie. There have been moments when begging my dad to move back home have crossed my mind. We're here for more than just me playing my senior year with my cousin, though.

My dad misses family. My grandparents are dead, and he and my uncle are all each other has. Despite how different they are, there's a bond between them that's unbreakable, forged from memories and time. One day, Zack will be all I have, at least in blood. And now that I have Hollis, well, leaving has lost its appeal.

Ready?

I send her the text then pull my truck up closer to her house, but still not directly in front of it. My hands still buzz with the feel of her, and the thought of making eye contact with her father right now is a torture I don't have the balls for. The man is intimidating, and he still holds my future in his hands.

Yes. Be right out. Also, uhm. Need a favor.

I cock my head and stare at her message for a full breath. It's that *uhm* part that's got me a little nervous. I type back *ok*, but two full minutes pass without a response.

Rolling up to her driveway, I brace myself for a lecture from her dad as the garage door rolls up. When I see her legs, tight black jeans and bright white Nikes on her feet, I grin. Then there's a matching version, only shorter and topped with a New York Islanders sweatshirt that's about two sizes too big.

I roll the window down so I can talk to her and her brother.

"So, uhm," she says, a continuation of her message. "Can we give Ben a lift to school? My dad has a meeting, and my mom is already holding office hours online."

"What's up, Cannon?" her brother says, giving me a nod but not a glance as he rolls an over-stuffed hockey bag toward the back of my truck. I've never officially met the kid, but he's immediately made us bros. I laugh and have to admire him.

"What's up, Ben?"

Shit, I hope I remembered his name right. He doesn't flinch, so I feel more certain than not that I nailed it. I hop out of the truck when the latch releases in the back. He's hoisting the bag by the time I join him, but he's struggling. I slide it the rest of the way in and pull up the tailgate, locking it in place. I'm about to jog around to the driver's side again when Ben reaches up and squeezes my bicep with his much smaller hand.

"Whoa, serious guns there. A'right, a'right. I feel ya, Cannon. I feel ya." He winks and backs away, leaving me there speechless with the dumbest smile on my face. I think I'm actually flattered by his compliment.

Ben climbs in the back seat of the full cab and Hollis slides into the passenger seat. Our eyes meet briefly and her cheeks blush, likely remembering what we did in here just a few hours ago. Awkward thought now that her baby brother is buckling up in the back.

"Sorry," she apologizes for her brother.

"Dude, no problem. Ben and I are buddies now. Aren't we, Ben?" I look into the rearview and wait for him to lift himself enough to make eye contact with me. The kid twists his lips, considering my offer, then reaches forward, patting my shoulder with three heavy slaps.

"Let's take things slow, Cannon. That's my sister, after all. I'm watching you," he says, pointing with one hand at his eyes then flipping his fingers to point at me in the mirror. *This kid is unreal!*

"Got it." I agree to his test. "Slow it is."

My gaze automatically moves to Hollis, a double meaning on that promise. She slides her hand across the console for me to take, and I do, even through her brother's remarks that we're making him vomit up his oatmeal.

I like this kid.

We get Ben to school and I help him wheel his bag up to the entrance where he leaves me with a handshake he suddenly decides to invent for just us. By the time Hollis and I get to school, the bell is ringing so we have to rush from the faraway spot where I had to park, peeling into our first hour together with laughter as we race to our seats.

Everyone's eyes are on us, and I don't care. So much so that I hook my pinky with hers to form a bridge between our two seats. Neither of us sees Dr. V approaching behind us, so when he taps our linked knuckles with the end of his ballpoint pen, we both startle.

"This is not a school dance, thank you, Mr. Jennings. Miss Taylor." His tone is more teasing than angry, so we shrink in our seats and suck in our smiles. "Though, I do find the odds of this fascinating. Have to admit, I didn't see this coming."

His joke draws a few laughs from the class, but he doesn't dwell on us after that.

The rest of the day flies by, but this new normal seems

to have crawled up into my chest cavity and helps keep that pitted feeling I've been living with at bay. Hollis makes me happy. Liking Hollis so much makes me happy.

I have to take off to drive my dad soon. In fact, I'm probably a little late, but it's worth it to see her one more time in the daylight. I'll miss practice today, and even though it's optional, I let her dad know. *Coach*. That part is going to take a while to get used to. The things I did to her, *want* to do to her, need to stay on lockdown when I'm in Coach Taylor's presence. I have this unearthly fear that he can read minds. Last night, I had a nightmare that he kept piling on the laps, making me run faster and faster by shocking me with a cattle prod, all because he thought he saw us kiss. I'm all for keeping us secret from him for a little while longer.

My entire body lightens when Hollis walks around the corner. I don't even mind the way her freshman shadow, Maddy, squeals about how cute we are.

"Hey, I thought you'd be gone," Hollis says as I take her hand and pull her into my chest.

Catching her jaw with my hand, I tilt her head just enough to get kissed.

"Uh uh," I say through a smile that hasn't left for almost twenty-four hours. "Couldn't leave without one more of these."

I catch Maddy's blush over Hollis's shoulder as I go in for a deep kiss, taking her mouth over completely and walking her backward a few paces so she bends into my embrace. When I pull away, she's left breathless, and I'm beat-my-chest proud. Also, a few of the other guys who I *know* have been checking her out now know not to bother.

"Hi, Daddy," she says, looking over my shoulder and waving. I swallow my heart, feeling it lodge somewhere in my throat while I forget how to breathe. I turn to find nothing but a closed door and a long, empty sidewalk.

"That was so mean!" I poke her side where I know she's ticklish. Her laugh is loud and free, and she rushes at me for one more kiss on my cheek while she and Maddy pass to head into the locker room.

"Keeping you on your toes, Cannon Jennings from Indiana." She winks just before the door closes behind her, and I am slayed.

My grin carries me all the way to my truck, and I wear it all the way back to Uncle Joel's where my father is waiting anxiously, slapping the boarding pass he printed out in their den last night against his open palm.

"Cutting it close, aren't we?" He gets in while he gives me the mini lecture. Rather than make up an excuse, I decide to give it to him straight.

"Had to see a girl." I hold his stare while I back out the driveway, his stupid sideways grin sliding up to match mine.

"Yeah, I thought there was something more to this whole Hollis thing." He settles into his seat, smug as if he knows it all. He probably does, clever old bastard that he is.

"Your mom's gonna love her." He chuckles, unfolding his boarding pass to check the gate and time for the millionth time.

"You know you can do that all by phone now," I explain. He quirks a brow because he's old school. The man still has file folders for everything. It's a wonder he's an engineer because I don't think he likes computers all that well. He just likes math.

"What are you going to do if they change your gate?" I glance his way in time to watch his mind work, and he finally gives in and pulls his phone from his back pocket to open the browser.

"Fine, I'll modernize," he grumbles.

I laugh and already miss him before he's gone. That feeling tugs away pieces of everything that's been so good. The moment my father is gone, I'll be left with Uncle Joel and Zack and all of their opinions. Aunt Meg won't be the voice that stands up for me; she avoids conflict. But I know it's coming. I feel it in my bones.

"Spit it out," my dad says, his sudden break in the silence jarring as I maneuver onto the freeway on ramp.

I draw in my brow as though I'm not sure what he's questioning, but after he shakes his head with a grimace, I know it's no use.

"Uncle Joel and Zack aren't big Hollis fans. And before you bring up dinner, I know, they weren't blatantly mean. At least, not there. But Uncle Joel feels threatened, and so does Zack, and I—

"Is she better?"

My dad breaks in with a succinct question. I don't have to think about my response, but I let the pregnant pause build because the minute I answer, my dad will work to convince me that all problems are solved. He sees things black and white, right and wrong. If Hollis is better, which she is, then she gets the job, and Zack has to work hard to take it away from her. But in that gray is all the stuff that makes me sick—my cousin hating me for rooting for her, him maybe improving enough to take that starting position away from her, me resenting him for it down the road. And then, Uncle Joel playing politics. *That* is perhaps the heaviest blanket of them all.

"She's amazing."

Now it's his turn to let my words linger, followed by silence. He never addresses them at all; in fact, just nods when I finally glance in his direction. I meant what I said, and it covers all things Hollis. My nagging worry over my father's relationship with my uncle finally scratches at me enough that my new worries come out as I exit the freeway.

"I'm afraid Uncle Joel will try to do something, I don't know, illegal?" I scrunch my shoulders, tucking my neck in at how foolish that sounds. It only gets worse when my dad laughs.

"He's not going to do anything illegal. Is he going to be loud? Oh, for sure. Will he complain that life isn't fair? My brother has been doing that since the first time he got in trouble for punching me in the arm. But in the end, it's all noise. If Hollis wants to walk this path, I'm sure she's gotten used to hearing a lot of noise. You just need to train your ears on when to tune it out."

My brow dents at my dad's incredibly wise advice.

"You sound like Mom," I compliment. He breathes out a laugh because we both know Mom is the one with the most level head of all.

"I learned a lot from that woman." He glances out his window and I can tell he's thinking of her, his mind on getting back to her and making this trip again with her by his side.

I've learned a lot from Hollis, too. I've known her for a month, not quite even, and when I compare the man I am right now with the one who didn't think he had much to learn, I'm kinda proud of my progress. Turns out a faster mile time isn't the only self-improvement on my resume this year.

Full breaths no longer elude me by the time I drop my dad off at his terminal, and I manage to slip back into highway traffic on the verge of rush hour, which puts me back on campus before the sun is down. There's an off chance Hollis is here still, but when I see my cousin pulling from the school lot with Roland and Jay, I know there's no way she'd let them quit workouts before her.

I pass Zack and roll down my window, figuring he'd stop to talk, but he doesn't even glance in my direction as he drives by with the guys. I spend the next few seconds, as I pull in and find a spot, convincing myself he didn't see me or that he waved and I missed it. That's not the case, though. With nobody here to witness, he decided to be a dick, and those knots I finally untangled in my chest? They're back again, and a fuck-load tighter.

Deciding this parking lot is too damn far, I pull onto the curb and drive along the wide sidewalk between the buildings and the fields, getting as close as I can to the places where Hollis could be. My chests thumps with worry, and the quiet out on the baseball field leaves my stomach unsettled.

Goddamn, Zack. What did you do?

I don't know when her dad will be here, or if she planned on walking or having her mom come. I wasn't supposed to make it back this fast, so she's not expecting me, but if something is wrong, she would have called, right? She would have called.

I'm out of my truck in one second, jogging toward the clubhouse with my phone clutched in my hand, hoping to feel it buzz with a text from her that tells my gut I'm wrong. I can make it to her faster than my call would go through. The more strides I take without feeling a vibration from a text, the more my pace picks up until I'm sprinting toward the freezing metal door that shouldn't be so easy to lock.

Gripping the handle, I pull it open hard, not mentally prepared for what might be on the other side. I don't know if he hurt her, if they all did, or something . . . worse.

Worse.

It takes my eyes a few seconds to focus on her, my next breath filled with relief that her shirt doesn't look torn, that her body doesn't look bruised. Fuck, the evil thoughts were so bad that I'm honestly glad she's clothed. I feel sick, and arrange my features before she turns and faces me, but I let everything go when I see how soaking wet she is.

"Hollis, are you okay?" I rush to her, expecting tears or rage, but when she spins to face me, her expression is nothing but even.

"Oh! Hey, I didn't think you were coming." She grips the front of her T-shirt and undershirt in her hands, twisting to wring out some of the water. It pools on the floor between her feet. Her pants, socks, everything is plastered to her body as if she jumped, fully clothed, into a swimming pool.

"I made good time. Why are you . . ?" I reach forward and tug on a soaked sleeve.

"Oh, yeah. So, just me being silly. I was in the showers, and I thought I'd rinse off some of the dirt in my hair. You know, by leaning forward?" Her laugh is suspicious and my gut tells me she's making up some bullshit right now. I say so with my face, my head cocked to one side while my eyes grill her for the truth.

"What? Oh, just me not thinking clearly. I'm fine, maybe cold, but . . ." I swear there's a slight quiver in her lips, but she stretches them into a smile before I can call her on it.

"And you're in here because?"

Her eyes flare briefly with her quick swallow. She's thinking of an excuse. This doesn't add up.

"Clothes. I thought maybe I left some in one of the cubbies, or maybe there were some shirts in storage." She wraps her arms around her body and bounces on her feet, letting her mouth shiver with the chill. She isn't making up being cold.

I glance around the space, then move to the corner where boxes from past seasons have been stacked for what looks like years. There's a layer of dust on them that is scoopable. I slide one box to the ground and it sends a cloud of shit into the air. I wave it away from my face, coughing.

"There might be some in here," I say, flipping open the cardboard flaps to reveal yellowed long-sleeve shirts. She's probably screwed in the pants department.

I toss her one from the middle of the stash and she peels her clothes away without warning, saying thanks as if this isn't a big deal.

"What? You've seen all this," she says, laughing

through the words. Her hands shake as they work to pull her wet shirts away, and I swear there is more to it than just her being cold.

"Oh, I remember." I smile as I move closer to help her pull the rest of the sodden mess over her head. The wet fabric keeps rolling. I play along with her, flirting. But now that I'm close I study her bare arms, her neck, the small of her back, looking for signs that something else happened here. Her skin is blotchy in places, red spots on her arms that could either be bruises forming or a reaction to the cold and the wet fabric.

I ready the dry shirt for her to slip her arms inside while she pulls her sports bra down her arms. My damn male instincts can't help but look at her breasts, nipples puckered into tight tips that make my mouth water. She reaches her hands into the bottom of the shirt I hold up, the length gathered in my hands, and I help her work it up her arms and over her head.

"Maybe . . . two of these," she says through chattering teeth.

I breathe out a short laugh, her hard nipples practically cutting through the cotton shirt. I nod, knowing in my gut that now is not the time to respond to this physical craving I can't help but feel. She's comfortable with me, but she's not okay. Something else is going on.

I grab another shirt from the box and help her layer it over the first, then flip through the rest of the boxes in the pile, coming up with old scorebooks and helmets but nothing that will warm her.

"Alright, well." I shrug, tugging my sweatpants down so I'm in my boxer briefs and a black hoodie. I toss my sweatpants at Hollis and she catches them in one hand while holding the other against her mouth in a fist, poorly hiding laughter.

"What?" I hold my arms out, knowing how funny I probably look. Also knowing that my reaction to her naked body is very apparent. When her eyes lower to my erection, I shrug, and her cheeks redden.

"I was fine wearing these home," she says, her teeth still chattering from the cold.

"Liar," I say, kneeling in front of her to help her roll the long socks down her calves while she slides her pants down. She leaves her sliding shorts on, for modesty I'm sure, and even though they're soaking wet, I don't press the issue.

I take over pulling the wet pants down over her knees, her pale skin beading up from the instant chill, and that's when the bright red scratches along the inside of her thigh come into view. I freeze my position and stare at her skin, my mind racing through dozens of awful scenarios. The one conclusion that I know is certain—she struggled.

Hollis stops breathing and her body goes incredibly still. I lift my hand and brush my knuckles along the line of abrasions that run from the curve of her knee up to the middle of her inner thigh. I lift my gaze but she's stoic, clutching my sweats to her chest while she looks straight ahead. So much work is going into her expression to hold it at peace. She's doing her best to give nothing away, but it's her breath—or lack of—that speaks volumes. Leaning into her, I kiss the bruise forming along her knee and shut my eyes when her hand pushes my hoodie back and sinks into my hair.

"Tell me what happened." My request is soft, and I get the answer I expect.

"It's nothing. I'm fine."

I kiss the deepest red line again and blow to cool it, the goose bumps far from this part of her. With a hard swallow, I finish helping her pull her legs and feet away from the wet pants, then let her balance herself on my shoulder while she steps into my sweats. When I stand, we're inches apart and her mask is not prepared. It's only a glimpse, but her eyes are glassy. It's a different kind of emotion she's feeling; there's a simmering to it. Those aren't tears from fear or crying. No. That's from anger.

"Hollis."

"I said I'm fine. It's nothing," she snaps.

Foolishly standing in our frigid clubhouse in underwear and a hoodie, I have to take her at her word. It doesn't mean I'm not going to make people pay.

We had plans to meet up with June, Lucas, Hayden, and Tory at Eight Lanes tonight, but I'll let that be her call. I know how hard it is to hide how you *really* feel. It's exhausting, and I've never had to do it for reasons that are meaningful and real, as I suspect she is right now.

"Take you home?" I lean my head toward the door and give her a moment to take in how ridiculous I look. As her lips curve, I know she's let her guard down just a little, so to keep the bad thoughts from breaking in, I decide to dance. In the time my hands make it from the back of my head to my hips, she's laughing hard.

"What is that?" She points at my legs in a circling motion, the sleeves of her double shirt tucked over her fingers.

"It's the Macarena," I pronounce, rolling my hips like an expensive stripper. In my head, I'm totally Magic Mike. I'm guessing by the way she covers her mouth and holds her stomach, though, the actual visual is a lot less sexy.

"No . . . it's not," she busts out mid-laugh.

"Oh, I beg your pardon," I say, feeling challenged to sell it. I make my body perform every awkward stripper move I know, knowing full well this is a mess, but it makes her laugh. It keeps her warm. It makes her smile for real instead of the pretend one that was stamped on her face.

Now, I need to keep it that way until I can even the score for her. I know exactly where to start, too, but for right now, I'll drive her home.

18

HOLLIS

Every girl just needs a good cry sometimes. I spend a lot of time holding mine in. Even when it's earned and I have every right to be weak and ugly, I suck it up and fake that everything is fine. I say I do it for others, to protect them from guilt, from feeling responsible or spending all their empathy on me. Honestly, though, I do it because I'm embarrassed. That thought in and of itself is shameful. It's also true. I'm embarrassed that I let something break me, even a little. I'm embarrassed by the attention. I hate when people ask if I'm okay. So, rather than cry, I shove that feeling and all that sparked it deep into the pit of my soul.

I should have known that one day, something would finally be too much.

Cannon is waiting outside in his truck, the engine running. We're going out with friends. It's like an actual real date, in front of people, and I want to feel the same on the inside that I've been pretending to be on the outside.

I didn't feel the tears coming. I ran upstairs for a quick shower and to change, because Cannon needs his pants back. And I want to look nice, to smell nice, to have goddamn beach waves in my hair!

Instead, I have been full-on wailing into my bath towel for five minutes straight, praying that the spray of the shower masks any sounds I let slip out.

It's a good cry.

An ugly cry.

A necessary cry.

It's all mine, and I'm taking it. I've sold myself short so many times, but no more. I'm tired. So fucking tired.

The hardest part is stopping myself from giving in to the same excuse I always use—*at least it wasn't worse.* Truth be told, I've been through worse. I've had guys throw fastballs at my face on purpose when I'm in the batter's box. I've had things stolen, had my name disparaged, been called insults that no guy on any of my teams would ever be called. They don't spray paint those same insults on school walls about the guys, either. In the grand scheme of things, a little hazing by three guys who have fragile egos and feel threatened should not be the thing that breaks me.

But it is.

It is. It does. And it continues to while I stand with one leg in the shower and one out.

I hate that I saw it coming. I hate that I still gave them the benefit of the doubt when Roland and Jay took opposite sides of me in the dugout while we packed up. I knew they were going to grab me. I even braced myself for it, prepared all the things I would say, practiced the face I'd make to pretend I was having as much of a good time as they were. It happened like clockwork—the two of them taking me by the arms, lifting me high enough that my feet couldn't reach the ground. It had to be them. They're the only two tall enough.

I laughed while they dragged me through the dugout, my thigh catching on the loose chain link while I kicked.

I didn't kick enough.

I kicked *just* enough.

Zack was only pretending to roll up the hose after watering the field. The water was still on. I heard the pump; the hose was taut from the pressure; the spray nozzle was leaking.

The first blast of water stung. I didn't shiver until at least twenty seconds passed. I was still laughing, still playing along and taking this rite of passage that I know no other guy on this team had to go through.

"You wanna be one of us, don't you?" Zack shouted.

Yes. yes, I do!

The words were internal, only for me. Outside, I laughed and played along.

"Don't! It's cold!"

Of course it was. They knew it was. I struggled to break free, but they held me down and Zack moved closer, the spray harder, the water colder. My skin was numb, already ripped apart as much as it could be from the blast of cold water. It hit my face next, and I coughed from the drowning sensation.

I stopped laughing. I started kicking in earnest.

"Come on, Double-D. It's just a little water!"

His cackling laughter was muffled by the water, by the rush of blood over my eardrums, by the pounding in my chest, and the screams of anger clawing their way up from where I'd buried them for far too long.

The cry was coming. They were going to see it.

I wonder if Zack's eye is black? I hit him so very hard.

"Honey, everything all right in there?" I drop the towel on the floor at the sound of my mom's voice.

"Just cleaning out a strawberry from sliding today!" She'll buy the lie. She always does.

"That boy has been sitting in his truck in the driveway for a while now, so, uh, Dad went out to talk with him." That thought actual breaks through the noise in my head. The puckered smile on my lips feels good.

"He'll survive," I shout through the heavy rain that I let hit my face. With every drop of water, my eyes free themselves. The puffiness is disappearing; the redness will go away soon. This cry has come to its end.

I'm able to pull myself together with the aid of five more minutes of hot water, and after a half-assed attempt to scrunch my own hair into beachy waves, I rush downstairs to save Cannon from my father's company.

"Sorry, I had a lot more dirt than I realized," I lie as I slip into the passenger seat. I lean over the console to meet my dad's gaze through Cannon's window.

"Hey, Daddy." I smile at my father, everything from before neatly packed away where it belongs.

"Take it easy on him," my dad jokes. He pats the open window frame twice with his heavy hand, and I stifle my laugh because that's his way of warning Cannon that he could end him if he wanted to.

"Good night, sir."

My dad's expression as Cannon rolls up the window is

priceless, his brow pulled in tight and his mouth twisted in a very distinct version of, "What the hell was that?"

"He intimidates you." I snuggle into my seat, glad to be dry and warm and clean.

"Yes. Very much," Cannon agrees without flinching.

For the short drive to Eight Lanes, I get to live in this little bliss. There's no need to pretend, no threat to my pride lurking around the corner.

Only, *there is.*

Cannon doesn't know Zack's joining us tonight. I can tell by the abrupt stop that sends me forward into the dash. I plant both my palms against it to stop myself. The jarring action is too much to keep my bliss in place.

"I'm gonna kill him," Cannon seethes. It's just a thing people say, but I think perhaps he means it.

"Please, Cannon." The sound of my hard breathing is strange to my ears. I'm struggling with this. It's too big this time. I feel Cannon's eyes on me but I force myself not to look into his until I'm in complete control of myself. I don't know that I could ever be fully prepared for all I see in his eyes when I finally do.

I'm not alone in this.

It isn't about baseball, or about his season or his broth-erhood—hell, his family! It's about a wrong, and doing what's right. And I'm asking him to ignore that feeling in his own chest. I don't want him to. I don't want this to be anything. I want it to go away so I can win on the field. I'll do it that way, the only way it ever should be between me and any other teammate or competitor. Equal—*even.*

"What did he do, Hollis? You can trust me," he says.

"I know," I answer without hesitation. I grab his hand

and squeeze it hard. My eyes focus on my grip, the way my veins bulge with the strength of my clasp on his hand. When I loosen my hold, he tightens his, and that small gesture breaks me just a little.

"It was just hazing," I begin, knowing in my gut that I'm starting out with a lie.

I shake my head.

"Tell me, Hollis. I promise you, I won't betray you."

His words are direct, and they cut deep. My dam breaks, and those tears I worked so hard to bury, the embers I put out in the shower, they come gushing out again.

Cannon pulls into the lot and drives to the opposite end, to an area where the lights don't fully glow. We're protected by the darkness and fully alone. He kills the motor, shifts in his seat and cups my face in both his hands, erasing the tears with his thumbs as fast as they fall.

"He hurt you."

I shake my head no, because he didn't really. None of them did. Not physically, other than some scrapes and bruises. Emotionally, though, yeah, Cannon is right. The only way forward is to share what happened, but the last time I did this, committees met, parents got together and made alliances and cast votes. My dad was out and we were on our way to Indiana.

Without pause, Cannon leans forward into me, pressing his lips on mine softly, as if sucking away my struggles and making them his own.

"Promise me you won't tell my dad," I say. It can't become his battle again. He's fought for me too many times. He's lost.

"I won't do anything you don't want me to." His words come out in soft kisses against me, whispers as he closes the space between us even more, ensuring our privacy.

I breathe deeply and let the silence settle in, looking down as I sit back because I think it's easier without staring into his perfect blue eyes. No more excuses at my disposal, no more fear of judgement. Just one more abusive, sexist, small-minded moment in an unfortunately long teenaged history of such moments.

"Jay and Roland picked me up first."

I swallow before continuing, feeling the weight of his eyes on me even though I'm not looking at them. I deliver the rest of the story—an event that lasted seven minutes at the most—with very few breaths. Once the words begin to flow, they don't stop, and details I made excuses for, like the way Zack pushed his knee into my thigh and lifted the bottom of my shirt to expose my stomach so he could see if the harsh spray tickled.

Are you ticklish, Double-D?

By the time I'm done with the story, I'm no longer crying. My breathing is normal, and my rage is under control. I've given the power to someone I trust, and he's struggling with it, his hands gripping the steering wheel as if wringing someone's neck.

"You promised you wouldn't say anything," I repeat.

"I did, and I won't." His voice is hoarse, that familiar anger I've felt so often brewing in his throat.

"We don't have to go in. We can just stay here, in the truck. Or somewhere else—"

"I don't know how you could stand to see him . . . any of them? Hollis, I don't know how you can do this. I'm not strong enough." He shakes his head in disbelief of it all.

"You don't have to be strong enough. I do." It's a simple fact, something I learned young and live every time I play the game I love.

His eyes close and his nostrils flare for a few deep breaths, a move I also recognize.

"You don't have to be nice to him," I relent, a give that makes him smile slightly on one side. I figured he wouldn't be able to keep his mouth shut with Zack, but it's everyone else who I don't want involved. Mostly, I don't want this to be my dad's obligation. Not again, however wrong that is for me to think.

Cannon glances up to his rearview mirror, scanning the lot for several quiet seconds, then finally cranks the key and shifts his focus to me.

"You sure you still want to be here?"

I contemplate my choices. I can go into that bowling alley and be with my friends and have a great night with a guy I'm falling for more every second he blinks, or I could let Zack win. I could go back home and sulk about all the things I'm missing out on. I could think about what happened today and how I reacted. I could replay it and think of all the ways it's coming at me again.

"I choose to live my life, and I want to be here with you. If Zack wants to go home, he's more than welcome."

I'm committed. Clearly, so is Cannon.

His eyes harden on his rearview mirror as he shifts into reverse. We fly backward in a straight line, and I test the tautness of my seat belt just in case.

"Hold on," Cannon says, and I should probably be

afraid and tell him to slow down. Those words don't leave my lips, though, because I know exactly what comes next. And though I didn't ask for it, I want to let it happen.

I'm *going to* let it happen.

It's probably wrong.

I don't care.

We're maybe going twenty-five, tops, on impact. It's enough to completely crumple Zack's trunk and tear the bumper from his car. Cannon pulls forward just as quickly as he smashed into his cousin's car and whips around the parking lot, eyes scanning for witnesses. He finally comes to a stop in a spot near the front of the alley, close to the door—dozens of spots from the scene of the crime.

Is it a crime when it's family?

"I think I can keep my mouth shut now," he says.

A slow grin creeps into my cheeks. I unbuckle and lunge at him, wrapping my arms around his neck and shoulders and kissing him so hard he laughs a little at the force of it. Within seconds, he's kissing back, cradling me over the center console and running his fingers through what in my mind are the most awesome beachy waves.

"Thank you," I say when we break away. I make the awkward crawl back to my side of the truck, but before I step out, Cannon flips up the center console into the seat-back, making a smooth bridge between us for the ride home.

"Huh. So, you're saying I could have done that, like, a while ago?" I quirk a brow, my energy still buzzing with adrenaline. I feel like a justified delinquent, and it feels amazing.

"I like watching you climb over the center." He shrugs, not one bit ashamed.

I hold on to that beautiful blue gaze while I slide the rest of the way out of the truck and close the door on his stare. We meet at the front of his truck, wearing matching smirks reserved for people who share epic secrets. Cannon slings his arm around me and holds his key fob up over his other shoulder, beeping his truck locked as we make our way inside the alley.

"Don't you want to check the damage to your truck?" I ask.

"I don't give a fuck."

I believe every word.

19

CANNON

I want to punch him. His car is barely drivable, but that's not enough. I want to rip his perfectly combed hair from the roots of his scalp and feed him the clumps. He's a disgrace to our family, to our name, and I'm not going to let him get away with this.

I won't break Hollis's trust. I won't go to her father. But I *am* going to tell someone. And if this goes down the way it should, none of this will touch any of them and justice will get served. It's going to require some faith from me, though. And the things my father told me will need to be true.

Tory's the first to see us walk in, and his arrogant grin brings me out of my angry euphoria enough to interact with humans like something other than a Neanderthal.

"Look at you heeding my advice," he says, grabbing my hand and bringing me in for a bro-hug. Hollis slips into a seat between Lola and June, who quickly checks the size of her shoes, then rushes to the counter to swap them out for larger ones.

Hollis Taylor does not walk on dainty feet.

"Are you actually going to take full credit for me and Hollis?"

I quirk a brow at Tory, testing him. A breathy laugh shakes his chest while he pops a pretzel into his mouth. After chewing for a second, he says, "I sure am," then winks before punching my arm.

"Oh, I see how this is." I chuckle, sliding into the seat across from him and slipping off my shoes. He kicks over the pair he grabbed for me when I texted him from Hollis's driveway, then tosses a pretzel about a foot in the air, leaning his head back and catching it in his mouth.

I know his weak spot, though. Tory and I have hung out a lot, and he's told me enough that I have pieced together his secret.

"So, when are we all going to see Abby again?" He kicks the plastic of the chair between my legs with enough force that it cracks. My only response is laughter because I've hit a nerve. He's dating a soon-to-be mega star, and he's keeping it on the down-low because one, they aren't in the same country right now, and two, he's still terrified that something'll mess it up.

I get it, because I'm a little worried about that too.

The month is ending soon, thirty days that I've known Hollis. We're too new for something to mess us up so soon, but it's hard not to feel the threat when our biggest obstacle is cutting lasers into my chest with his eyes across the alley.

Zack was finishing up a pool game with Lucas when we walked in. I'm not sure whether Hollis saw him, but I did, catching his glare in my periphery. He stopped lining up his shot and straightened to watch us pass like some bully who thinks he owns a biker bar. Zack doesn't own shit. In fact, he hardly owns a car now, thanks to me and my short-wick temper.

The air gets cooler somehow when my cousin joins us. I feel him before I see him, and the ice in his stare is as frosty as I expected.

"Nice shiner," I say, my quip earning me a warning glance from my girl a few seats away.

I promised not to say anything about what he did to deserve it. Doesn't mean I can't comment on the obvious.

"Hardly feel it," he says back. That means it smarts like hell.

"I bet. You don't feel much." I yawn my words out and turn my body to create a physical barrier to end our conversation. Despite my literal cold shoulder, I feel him watching.

"There's too many of us, so who wants lane seven?" June asks, tapping her fingers on the computer.

Hollis stands, volunteering, and takes June by the hand, picking her alliance and moving to the chairs that give her the most distance from my cousin.

"But I wanted to make a little wager, Hollis," Zack teases. He must know she shared everything with me, because even though his taunting is directed at her, his eyes are on me.

"She'll just embarrass you," I say, unable to stop myself from defending her.

My retort must have crossed a line in our unwritten contract, though, because before I can make it worse,

Hollis steps over my lap, letting her hand drag across my chest possessively as she passes.

"Oh, we can wager, Zack. I'm not afraid of you." Arms folded over her chest, she stops right in front of him, and I realize she isn't afraid of him at all; she hates how he made her feel. That he has the power to do that, period.

"Winner buys loser's beer at the party next weekend."

I open my mouth in protest—she's Coach's daughter and that's not a cool ask—but Hollis flashes an open palm behind her back to stop me.

"Fine." She pushes her hip out with an extra flair, her exposed thigh popping through her ripped up jeans. I never got this style before, but seeing it on her gives me a new perspective.

Zack is a decent bowler, so I'm a little conflicted about this wager. With everything that's happened, my mind immediately unravels his motive. Somehow, Hollis having alcohol will turn into a scandal.

She's already locked herself into this battle, one of many in her exhausting war. My only option without being *that* boyfriend is to stand by her side, so I hold my palms up and back away. I'll let this play out fair and square, and watch from over here on good ole lane seven.

"Zack's a prick, bro. How are you two related?" Tory asks, flipping the top shut on the pizza box and carrying it to the open seat near me. June went back to join Hollis, leaving my cousin surrounded by the girls while Lucas, Tory, Hayden and I take turns daring one another to find the most embarrassing way possible to push the ball down the lane. I have it in the bag with my repeat of Magic Mike, but then Lucas actually gets down on all fours and pushes the ball with nothing more than his nose, somehow rolling that sucker dead-center with enough speed that it knocks down every freaking pin.

We slap hands and celebrate his mini-victory, but while nothing is serious on lane seven, it's intense over on lane eight.

I keep tabs on Hollis's game, glad she's up with each consecutive frame but wishing that gap between her and my cousin would widen a little more. By the time it's down to the tenth frame, I'm too invested to care about finishing my own, and let Tory throw my last two balls. He earns me a whopping seven to bring my score to a non-brag-worthy ninety-six. If I were over on the other lane, I'd be battling Lola for last place. June is clearly wiping the floor with everyone, but those two scores in the middle—they are neck and neck.

Zack holds his hand over the blower on the ball return, his eyes flitting up to the scoreboard then back to the pins lined up in front of him. I can envision his brain working the math. If he bowls a strike, he can make things pretty tough.

I might not be able to help Hollis with her tenth frame, but I can do something to tilt this environment in her favor. While my cousin brings his ball into his hands, I reach forward and hook my finger in the belt loop of Hollis's jeans. She yelps with surprise, but lets me tug her toward me until she falls into my lap. I catch Zack's glare, so I push Hollis's hair over her shoulder and kiss the curve of her neck.

Most people would chalk up the look on his face to jealousy, but I know better. He feels betrayed. I picked her over him. He never thought I would sell him out like that, but then, I never imagined he'd assault a girl and demoralize her in front of two other teammates, so I guess touché. We ain't even, though. Not by a long shot.

That little wedge I drove into Zack's head works. His shoulders scrunch while he lines up his ball, and his footwork is sloppy from the start. When he ends up only knocking down four, he lets his emotions boil over, screaming, "Fuck!" so loud that families turn to look from several lanes away.

He's already blown it; he knows he has. He doesn't even wait for his ball to return but grabs the first one available and chucks it down the lane before the pins are reset. Hollis doesn't even need her turn, but she takes it, maybe a little to make my cousin watch and suffer while she finishes with a one-sixty-three, bettering him by twenty.

Zack pretends not to care while he pulls a slice of pizza from the box, tipping his head back and biting off the end. Hollis brushes her hands together, gloating because she earned it, and she stops on the other side of the high top that Zack is sitting at, pretending as if he isn't there.

"I like the hard lemonade shit," she says, peeking in the box but scrunching her nose at the pizza inside. My cousin doesn't react to her. He takes large bites of his slice, chewing methodically, his eyes focused on some commercial playing on the TV mounted on the wall. After a full minute of being ignored, Hollis slaps her hand down on the table. That gets his attention.

"I said I like hard lemonade," she repeats.

My cousin tosses his crust on top of the box, then brushes the grease from his fingers with a crumpled napkin. I expect him to walk away without responding. He doesn't necessarily need the last word in things, he just needs to leave a mark. I've been in enough arguments with the guy to know how he fights, and sometimes it's his refusal to engage, period, that drives me to my maddest. He's doing that to Hollis.

I'm not ready for his next move. Nobody is. That's why he makes it, casually flipping the full pitcher over so the bulk of the liquid splashes on Hollis's pants and onto her feet. I want to blacken his other eye so badly that I lunge at him. The only thing stopping me is the touch of my girl's wet, sticky hand gripping my forearm.

"Ooops," Zack says, no sign of the cousin I used to make future plans with in his dead eyes. He's let this animosity take over his soul. I mourn him.

He leaves his mess for us, backing away until he turns and pushes through the double doors that lead out into the lot. In about thirty seconds, he's going to see the smashed back end of his car. About a minute after that, he'll realize he can't open that trunk. And when he drives away from this place, he's going to see a whole lot of white paint on my massive rear bumper. Thing is, though, as spontaneous as it all was, I knew what I was doing.

Between my father and me, we've backed into some pretty heinous things, including a horse trailer in Santa Fe and a cactus somewhere outside Albuquerque. There are so many colors, dents and dings on the back of my truck that it looks like a painter's palette. The hitch also gives me a solid steel buffer that I'm sure punched a hole right through his sedan.

Deep down, my cousin will know it was me who

rammed his car. He won't be able to prove it, and that will make him mad. That part is almost more satisfying than the impact was itself.

No matter, though, because by the time I'm done telling Uncle Joel about the moral and ethical lines his son has crossed, a hit and run at a bowling alley is going to feel like tee ball.

I'm the first to breakfast this morning. I'm never first on Saturdays, and already that has suspicions raised. I scared my Aunt Meg when I slid the stool across the tile floor, and she ended up turning around and throwing her spatula at me. She's used to about twenty more minutes of alone time in here, something I just realized she cherishes. She always hums when she cooks, and hearing it this morning while sipping on coffee that's mostly cream leaves me at peace with my decision.

I've already finished a plate of pancakes by the time my cousin careens down the stairs. I stare at him over the steaming mug in my hands, but he doesn't give me a single glance. I know I'm not transparent. It's killing him to keep his anger bottled inside and to avoid gaslighting me in front of his mom. He'll wait for Uncle Joel to join us. I'm waiting for Uncle Joel, too.

"Have you heard from your parents yet?" Meg takes my dirty plate from in front of me and smiles. In all of the drama I forgot that my parents are already on the road, my dad's second trip across country to get here.

"Not yet, but if my dad's driving, I'm sure they'll get

here ahead of schedule." We both laugh at the truth. My dad has points on his license from speeding tickets, and I'm pretty sure he's banned from ever taking traffic school again. If he hasn't learned his lessons by now, he's hopeless in the eyes of the law.

"What's on your agenda today?" She loops her arm with Zack's, squeezing his bicep while he eats his breakfast at the counter, his back strategically to me. He stiffens at her touch, and the cold shoulder leads her to sag her arms and let her hand slip away.

"Someone hit the car. Jay's dad owns a garage though, so . . ." He turns his head enough to convey he knows exactly what happened.

"Oh, no! Does your dad know? We have insurance. Did the person leave a note?" My aunt's questions barrel out, and I take a longer than normal sip of my coffee in an effort to hide my smile. I feel a little guilty because in the heat of the moment I didn't consider that my aunt and uncle would be the ones paying for the damage. My uncle does make Zack work in the summer to help pay for things, though. That's my guilt loophole, and I take it.

"No note. Fucking coward," Zack says, shoveling the last of his pancake into his mouth. He rushed through breakfast to get out of here. *Good.*

My aunt smacks him lightly on the back of the neck for his swear, and he halfheartedly apologizes while dumping his plate in the sink. My cousin won't call me out for being his hit and run in front of my aunt. The information I have is a lot more damaging. And now that I let that notion simmer in my mind, I realize I'm going about this all wrong. It isn't my uncle I need to talk to; it's my aunt.

I'm patient, waiting for Zack to guzzle down his juice and rush out the door to drag his cracked-up car to Jay's house. When my uncle comes down and joins us for breakfast, I let him tell me what he knows about tryouts, what he's heard is on the agenda for Monday and Tuesday. I play along while he makes his own predictions, noting the way he always puts Zack in the starting catcher's job, reminding him of Hollis only once.

"Yeah, she'll make the team, I'm sure. I mean she has to, right?" He easily dismisses her talent, assuming daddy's girl is only there for one reason. Fury builds in my chest because of how clearly I now see it all. Hollis lives with this, and now that I see that double standard, I realize it exists everywhere.

My aunt clears the table and does the dishes all on her own. She works as an intake specialist for high end orders at a lumber yard six days a week, yet her weekend time is somehow not as sacred as my uncle's. My mom was always the one to take off for everything when I was little—when I got sick, when I had appointments, when I needed to go somewhere for travel baseball. My dad got to show up for the big things, be there for game time. Often his chair was ready and waiting for his ass to sit in it. When my mom was finally promoted to IT director at the financial company she works for, it was a big deal that she was a woman—the *first* woman. It took her eighteen years to move up to a salary my father got to in five. My uncle, my dad—they don't live the double standard on purpose. I don't think they see it because it's routine for them, but I bet there are times when my mom and my aunt do. I bet they'd like things to be easy just once.

I wait for my uncle to leave the room before I broach the subject with my Aunt Meg.

"What do you think of Hollis?" I'm not sure why this is how I break into this subject, but I know it's the right choice by the way my aunt settles her gaze on me as she finally sits at the table to drink her own damn cup of coffee in peace.

"She seems like a pretty strong girl." She stares at me over the top of her cup while she sips. She knows more than she lets on, she just doesn't dive head first into the drama. I can learn a lot from this woman.

"Yeah," I agree, hugging my now-empty cup between my hands while I lean forward across from her. I tap my fingers against the ceramic while I ride the mental teeter-totter of what to say next. Telling my aunt about her son's behavior puts the burden on her, something else I realize about this situation.

My struggle, though, is with what's right. What Hollis is enduring isn't. That much is certain, but am I taking the power away from her by starting this chain reaction? My aunt will confront my uncle. Together, they'll confront Zack. My cousin will blame me, and the issue will get tied up in this ugly knot that never leaves this house.

But I promised her I wouldn't tell her dad.

"You know, sometimes, Cannon . . ." My aunt busts into my circling thoughts and I glance up to find her knowing smile waiting, her tongue held between her teeth as she taps her own nails against her mug. "All a person needs is someone in their corner."

I breathe in her words and lean back, letting them settle around my busy mind. She doesn't know the full breadth of what happened. She would be deeply disappointed in her husband and son. I have a feeling she's heard enough of their bitching and complaining about what is and isn't fair to form a pretty solid picture, though. She's in Hollis's corner, and perhaps she's said things to Uncle Joel and to my cousin that can only truly be understood and relayed by a woman. I am in Hollis's corner, too. She *is* strong. And if the circumstances are right, she'll expose everyone for being who they are simply by being who she is. Maybe my job is to support her the way a man should. Lead by example, and let her shine.

I give my aunt a tight-lipped smile and stand from my seat, leaning forward to check the level of her coffee. I rinse my mug out and leave it on the counter, then grab the pot and top her off, kissing the top of her head while she gives my arm a squeeze.

I put the pot back and grab my keys from the counter, grabbing the hoodie I left hanging on the hook by the door.

"I got a corner to get to," I say over my shoulder. My aunt raises her cup and I smile. I text Hollis that I'm on my way to her house, and I tell her to bundle up. We've got some ziplines to explore.

20

HOLLIS

This abandoned park is definitely a different experience during the day. Unlike our trips across the canyon at dawn, this afternoon adventure offers clear views of exactly how far the drop is. I never thought I was afraid of heights, but maybe I just needed to meet the right circumstances.

I cling to Cannon for the first trip across, and barely loosen my grip on the way back. But now, on our fifth ride, I'm able to scope out everything below, including the icy stream that trickles across some gnarly logs and rocks.

"What's on this side?" I ask while Cannon unhooks us in preparation for our climb up the eastern pedestal.

He squints from the bright sun and clouds, scanning the thick woods, then shrugs.

"Don't know. Zack and I didn't explore this stuff."

"We should check it out." I clutch the front of his hoodie with my hand. I wore my knit gloves with the fingers cut out so I could grip better when I climbed.

The trip here was easier in Cannon's truck, and I haven't seen or heard a single vehicle in the area all morning, and we've been here an hour. While the young adventurer in my heart does like the idea of wandering around the woods to explore, the seventeen-year-old who has been holding on to Cannon's tight arms and broad chest wants to explore *other* things, maybe under a little extra cover of some wintered branches.

Cannon helps me out of my harness before kicking the straps away from his own legs. We climb down from the middle platform, jumping the last few feet onto the hard ground still dotted with blotches of ice and snow.

I can see my breath, but at this very moment, I am not cold. Not in the least.

"Come on," I say, grabbing his hand in mine and heading straight ahead through the thickest cluster of trees.

"Are you trying to get us lost?"

"Yes!" I reply.

He laughs as he tags along behind me, my pace rushed because all I can think about is how I'm going to feel when his hands are on me. I keep glancing backward, testing to see whether I can still spot the poles, the lines over the gulch, and Cannon's truck. I decide we're far enough when we get a quarter mile out and I spin on my heels, letting my body collide with his.

"Whoa!" He laughs, the fog from his mouth intermingling with mine.

I practically climb onto him, holding his sweatshirt in clutched fists while pulling him tight against me. Every first move is mine, the kiss hard and swift. My hands cover his and guide them under my three layers of shirts, up my sides and against my bare skin, letting go just below my breasts. My own hands roam across the ripples and valleys of his chest and sides, teasing the V that travels from his stomach into his joggers. Emboldened and heated to my core, I dip my hands lower, finding him hard and eager for my touch.

"Oh, fuck," he breathes out the moment my hand wraps fully around his erection.

I smile against his lips, loving the way I make them quiver. I love being in charge. I also am ready for him to take over.

"Just exploring the woods, huh?" Devilish laughter gurgles from his lips as he dips his chin and holds my gaze. His eyes are as hard as he is. His hood has slid from his head, and his mussy hair is soft and calling to me. I stroke him to encourage him and let him know I want this. I do it again, and he reacts, his fingers digging in more against my back, dropping lower until they slide under my waistband and grip my ass.

I let go of him and move my arms over his shoulders, my hands sliding into his thick hair just as he lifts me up; I wrap my legs around his body. In three steps, he has my back against a tree, and we are kissing so hard my lips feel raw from the friction and the cold. I don't care if I can't speak for a week. I need this, need him.

Now.

I tug at the bottom of his sweatshirt. In one fluid move-ment, I drop back to my feet and he lets go to free his arms and toss his shirts to the ground. His hard chest is smooth like a marble sculpture under my touch, his skin hot.

His eyes meet mine as his hands gather my sweatshirt

and the two long-sleeved tees I have layered underneath. I nod and lift my chin, giving permission, and he pulls the clothing up and over my head, taking my knit cap off with it. My hair falls around my bare shoulders, strands blowing across my face in the slight breeze. Light spills through the thick branches, dead leaves still plastered to the ground from the melted and dried snow. There's a hint of wood burning in the air, a scent from someone's cabin perhaps. The thought of being caught out here with him excites me.

Cannon pulls me to him, kissing me and letting his teeth drag against my lower lip as his thumbs slide the straps of my bra down my shoulders. I wore the only pretty undergarment I own just so he could see me in it. I unclasp the hooks at my back and let the garment fall to the ground with the rest of our clothing as he pushes his head against mine so he can take in my bare breasts. The freezing air tightens my nipples into hard buds that ache for his touch. I arch instinctively as his hand glides up my spine, lifting my tits to encourage his mouth to taste them. He takes the hint, suckling one into a raw peak, his tongue swirling around the tip while I moan and lift one of my legs to hook around his hip.

In a swift, smooth movement, Cannon lifts me against him again, supporting my legs while I steady myself with my arms around his neck. His tongue draws lines like a map around my neck and jaw as he circles us so we're positioned to fall on our pile of clothes on the ground. He lowers to one knee before breaking our kiss and resting me on my back atop our sweatshirts. I pant wildly as he stands, straddling me, his erection so strained that it peeks out of the top of his boxers and pants.

"I have condoms," I admit, biting my lip and reaching into the back pocket of my jeans. I pull out two and hold them up.

Cannon takes the packets in his hand and holds my stare with a crooked smile.

"You're the one who brought condoms. Goddamn," he says, shaking his head with a breathy laugh.

I shrug, shivering and wanting his warmth on top of me stat.

"I'm a modern woman. What can I say?"

Truth is, I have an honest relationship with my mom, and she knows I have been sexually active. I got the talk in sixth grade, even though I was a virgin until I was sixteen. Condoms are things that are just purchased along with the rest of my feminine stuff.

My body clenches as Cannon slides his pants down his hips and his very large penis springs free. While he tears the packet open and rolls on the condom, I unbutton and unzip my jeans, lifting my hips to prepare myself for sliding them down my legs. Cannon stops me before I can, parting my legs and dropping to his knees. He covers my hands with his and stares at my bare stomach with his mouth hung open, hungry.

"Please let me do this. It's part of the fantasy I have lived for the last two nights."

"Only two?" I tease.

He smirks and briefly meets my gaze.

"Fine, three," he jokes.

I bite at my lip, mostly because I'm nervous and want to look sexy. I'm not afraid of the act; I'm afraid of the change that follows sex. I more than like Cannon, and he

GINGER SCOTT

has the power to crush me if he wants to. All of the hazing and teasing in the world wouldn't compare to a broken heart from him.

As if he can hear my thoughts and worries, he bends down and draws my lips up with a soft kiss, whispering against them as he lifts my hips and drags my jeans and panties down my thighs.

"So, so beautiful," he says.

My eyelids flutter closed, the rush of cold mixing with my hot core as he says that tiny phrase over and over until I feel him push my pants completely free from my body. We're out here in nothing but thick socks, and it's oddly hot as fuck. Sitting back between my legs, Cannon brings my knees up, then runs his hand along my thighs until his thumbs press into my swollen center, sliding over the slick skin and sending shockwaves through my body that force me to rock uncontrollable with his touch.

"Oh, my God," I cry out, already feeling the threat of an orgasm.

I arch my back but open my eyes, wanting to see his face when he enters me. I feel his tip slide against my skin and both our mouths open in awe, our breaths held until he slowly pushes in, eyes locked on mine to make sure I'm okay, that I'm all in.

I stretch to fit him, the burn of his size subsiding into silk as he rocks into me. I cling to his back, my nails digging into his skin, leaving scratches along the hard surface of his thick muscles. We find our rhythm, his gentle movements growing faster and more urgent as he bends his head down, the tips of his hair tickling against my cheeks. I raise my chin until our lips meet, and we nibble at each other between pants and half-breaths.

My chest beads with moisture and I swear steam rises from our bodies. I lift my knees to hug him against me, wrapping my legs around him to hold him to me tight while he pushes into my very core, hitting places inside that threaten to break wide open with pleasure every time his hot skin passes against mine.

I let my arms fall above my head while he cradles me between his forearms and holds up his body weight to gaze into my eyes. The ground beneath my head is damp from the recent snow, and my hair sticks to sharp twigs poking out of the ground. But my body is protected, Cannon quick to shield my skin with his hands as we move together. He swells inside me when my own body climbs, and I encourage him by biting his earlobe, gently at first, then suckling it as his breathing becomes more feral, more urgent. Each rock of his hips gets hard, and his right hand sweeps behind my back to hold me up and protect me from the sharp ground as he slides me back an inch at a time with each pummel.

My own orgasm peaks and I grip him tightly, crying into his ear with a single word—*please!* It's enough to push him over the edge with me, and he pulses in me while my insides squeeze and shudder with pleasure.

He holds me close through every shiver, the nerves rolling from my shoulders down my chest and stomach and into my toes. I want to flatten our bodies together, to hold him here against me forever, to never let him leave the places where he is inside of me. And when the word slips out, I don't even care or feel vulnerable because it's mine to say when I feel like it, and I feel like it now.

"I love you," I breathe out, the sudden confession not jarring him visibly as his breathing slows to normal and he holds me close, rolling so I'm on top and his body takes the weight and the bluntness of the ground.

The chill hits my skin, but the harshness is erotic for now, my body still feeling satiated and teeming with excitement from what we did, where we are, and how I feel right this very moment. I lift my head enough to look him in the eyes and he tucks his chin into his chest as his gaze sweeps around my face, his hand pulling a leaf from my tangled hair as he laughs. The quake in his chest is like a warm fire on a winter day.

His fingers comb through my hair a few more times until the strands are smooth enough for him to curl around his fingers. His eyes follow the movement as my hair slips through his fingers like golden ribbons and he brings one curl to the tip of his nose, drawing in the scent as if he's trying to etch it into his memory. His focus slips from his own hands to my eyes as the strand slides free and falls back to the ground beside my face. His eyes soften and I tremble lightly, the breeze breaking through our lust and finally cutting into my skin. Sensing I'm cold, Cannon draws my arms into his protection, tucking most of my body within his before peppering my shoulder with kisses.

"There is not a single thing I don't love about you, Hollis. Not one single thing."

He rests his head flat against my chest, listening to my heart, maybe waiting for it to react. I'm glad he's there, because he can make sure I'm still alive. I'm pretty sure my heart stopped with his words. Stopped, then exploded. I will walk this world as a ghost from here on out, one who feels as though she can do anything. Reborn a little stronger, moving from warrior to queen. If I can own Cannon Jennings's heart, then there is nothing I can't claim. And I want it all.

21

CANNON

Tryouts are closed to parents, but that hasn't stopped my uncle from setting up in the parking lot. Everyone sees him. He's the only truck sitting so close to the field. From the outfield, I spot him holding binoculars to his eyes as we run by for our cool down. I bet he's proud and glowing right now. Zack had a decent day. He still wasn't as solid as Hollis behind the plate, though.

A week ago I might have let my uncle's presence change my mind from what I pledged to do today. But being with Hollis is a feeling I won't trade for all the family loyalty in the world, especially when I don't believe in the ideas my cousin and uncle preach.

Zack and I haven't spoken since Friday night at the bowling alley. He was conveniently gone for the weekend, probably spending the night at Jay's house. We both needed our space. It also let my parents arrive and get settled into the room I've been sleeping in while I slept alone in Zack's. I doubt I will be welcome in there after today, but I talked things out with my dad, and we agreed that a few days on the floor in their room was worth it while my parents nailed down a rental.

My dad went through the same emotions I did when I told him everything. We both believe that Uncle Joel would draw the line at what my cousin did, but while my dad wanted me to sit down and tell my uncle everything last night when we talked, I convinced him it would be better to give the power to Hollis. This is her story to control, and I will echo and preach her gospel all damn day, but only when she says so.

Giving things a little nudge, however, might be called for. I had a teacher in junior high who used this technique with us. She called it flushing out the bad seeds, which, upon reflection, was probably a harsh way to categorize thirteen-year-olds. But we had some real assholes in my school, including the Hayworth twins who ditched their last hour to steal bikes, then put them up for sale online the same day. She flushed them out by sitting everyone down and showing a slideshow of used bikes for sale, all posted within the last month. They needed a little extra heat, so she called the number posted on one of the ads. Lo and behold, Kale Hayworth's phone lit up like a restaurant buzzer. Their mini chop shop ended real fast.

I'm not going to put the screws on like Mrs. Reed did back then. But I am going to set up a community standard that won't tolerate the kinds of things Zack and Jay and Roland did on Friday. When that standard goes up, I have a feeling they'll out themselves.

"Alright, everyone, circle up!" Coach Taylor and his assistants stand around the mound while the sixty or so of us out here for tryouts all take a knee. I should probably listen harder than I am, but I can't stop mentally rehearsing everything I plan to say.

"We saw some good stuff out there today. Keep in mind, tomorrow is scrimmage day. You'll be broken up into six squads, and we'll be using all three fields. You'll get a text with your team tonight, and that's your only notification. You're all young adults now, so no excuses if you bring the wrong color shirt, don't have your cleats, forget your glove."

There's a murmur of laughter among us because we've all done at least one of those.

"Your moms and dads are not the ones trying out. *You* are. Which brings me to point number two. Please remind your parents, no matter who they are, that our tryouts are closed." Coach Taylor folds his arms around his clipboard and holds it to his chest, scanning the crowd but pausing pointedly on my cousin. Even his sunglasses can't mask that he's calling out my Uncle Joel.

"If anyone would like personal feedback about their performances today, please see me or any of the assistant coaches. Our ultimate goal is for you to achieve growth. We want to help you get better because we all can. Except me. I'm the best coach of all time." His joke gets bigger laughs this time. I'm mostly amused by the way his daughter rolls her eyes.

"Anything else?" He leans forward and looks down the line at his coaches, and I prepare myself. I get my hand in position to raise it high and clear my throat quietly so my words come out loud and clear.

"Gentlemen, any questions?"

I maybe should wait a beat before jetting my hand up in case anyone else has something to say, but it's too late now. My arm is already in the air.

"Jennings, shoot," Coach Taylor says.

I get to my feet and remind myself not to look at anyone in particular, especially not Hollis. I'm sure both she and my cousin are on high alert, though. Only one of them should be.

"I don't actually have a question, but more something I want to say, as a senior trying out this year, and as a new member of this school." My voice breaks a little and my heart pounds behind my ribs. I can throw fastballs in front of a crowd but I'm absolutely screwed when it comes to speaking in front of people. It's freaking cold out here, yet sweat is dripping down my spine.

"Go on." Coach shifts his posture, settling in with eager ears. Here goes nothing.

"Right, okay. Well, I'm a bit of a baseball nerd, I guess. My dad is always sending me these blog links to read about baseball psychology and team dynamics and all of that, and recently he sent me this story about character. It got me thinking about how important that is, maybe even more than skill, when it comes to a team's chemistry." I look down at some of the guys kneeling near me. Most of the faces are looking at me, and I'm relieved I haven't lost people yet.

"The article was about this team in Texas that had a serious problem with hazing." I haven't looked at Zack once, yet I know just from saying that word out loud— *hazing*—that his eyes are on me. I can feel the heat from them, and I welcome it.

"It got so bad that the rumors about players being pulled into bathrooms and pink bellied or held down and sprayed with water turned students off from playing any sport at that school, period. Colleges heard the stories and revoked scholarships. Finally, some of the star pitchers were expelled from the school because, and I'm quoting the reporter who spoke to law enforcement, 'Whether you call it hazing or not, at its core, the act is assault.' Basically, what the story says is it doesn't matter why it's done or when it's done or who you do it to. If you physically or mentally harm someone intentionally, you are an assailant. At that moment, you cease to be a ballplayer and you become a criminal.'"

I glance around the crowd and catch one or two yawns, but for the most part, eyes are wide and mouths shut.

"I heard something the other day that I didn't like. It made me feel ashamed to be here. And maybe it's only a rumor, but that's how things started at this other school too —with rumors. I decided I'd stand up today and pledge to act honorably, respectfully, and with character. I'd like to invite the rest of you to do the same. And not like in some ceremony or whatever, but maybe after Coach dismisses us. Let's shake on it. I'll promise you individually, and you do the same."

When I practiced this speech in the shower this morning, I kinda imagined the slow clap coming in right about now. My expectations probably make the silence feel more awkward than it is, but I'm still glad I said it all, every word.

"Thanks, Cannon. That displays leadership, and it's what I hope to see from all of you, especially the seniors,"

Coach says, nodding at me. Before he can continue his talk, though, my cousin's fragile ego takes over the space.

"Fucking bullshit," Zack utters. Whether it's poor timing that he said those words in a quiet lull or he just couldn't contain his aggression, all eyes are now on him. He's got the stage, but he is not the one I expected to stand up in this spotlight. I thought Hollis would call him out, but not until we are dismissed. Maybe he'll call himself out. He can make things right or he can drown—here and now—in his own bad choices. I kneel, letting him have his moment. I'd like to say I am rooting for him, but I'm not. I'm so damn ashamed of what he did and the person he's become that I'm not being the bigger person. I want him to fall apart. I want him to fail.

"What was that?" Coach Taylor's glasses are off, and there is no mistaking the direction of his stare.

"Nothing," Zack says, trying to erase the last ten seconds and literally eat his words.

"No, you had something to add, clearly. We all heard it. Go on." Coach takes a few steps and the freshmen on their knees in the front crawl out of his way. Nobody wants to get caught in crossfire.

A standoff is underway between Coach and my cousin, and for an uncomfortable and full minute, I worry neither will give in. Hollis's dad is clearly fine standing in that spot all night with his arms crossed and his heavy brow leveled at my cousin's head. Young and stupid, though, are two qualities that can be toxic when mixed, and my cousin is about to turn them into a back-firing grenade.

"I said it was bullshit," my cousin finally says.

"I believe you used the words *fucking* bullshit, in

response to a speech about character. Please, elaborate." A few noticeable mumbles simmer around us. A few "Oh, my God's" and "Oh shits."

"Fine. I will. That speech was all just more *fucking bullshit.* My cousin doesn't believe that crap. I've played ball with him before, for years."

"Maybe I've grown," I speak up. I'm a little surprised myself, but now that I'm in it, I realize exactly how much my speech and that made-up story about a school means to me—how much my own character means to me. I'm going to defend it.

"Ha, sure. Whatever. Or maybe you're just in love." There's a collective gasp.

"Maybe you're threatened by a girl." My heart stops at the sound of her voice. This was my end goal, but suddenly I'm surprised to hear Hollis assert herself. I turn to find her standing several feet away, her arms folded over her chest, like her father's.

"Sweetheart, I'm not—"

"Sexist? Is that what you were going to follow that up with? Or do you call everybody sweetheart?" Hollis steps over a few of the guys and brushes against my chest as she passes me and jets straight toward Zack. They're toe-to-toe, and Jay and Roland are staring at the grass, too chicken shit to look her in the eyes.

"I'll go head-to-head with you anytime and win." Nobody else would notice the slight grit to my cousin's voice, but I hear it. I also see the way his jaw is working. He knows he's lying, but he's paddling for air, frantic to save face with desperate words followed by *more* desperate words. What's worse is his father is taking long strides behind him, crossing the football field on his way to see what's going down.

"Ha! I wish that were the case, but you can't handle a fair fight with me. You're too afraid you'll lose. You're so afraid that—"

"Are you still bent over that little fun we had with the field hose on Friday?" His snarky laughter stands out in the sudden quiet. Even the breeze stops, and with darkness coming on quick, the air is cold and sound travels. My uncle is plenty close enough to hear that. Zack obviously has no idea he's there, standing with about four rows of players between them.

Hollis steps in closer, turning four feet into two, then one, and eventually pushing at Zack's chest with her finger. "You held me down," she growls. "You belittled me in front of my teammates. *You made them participate!* I'm working my ass off, trying to earn respect, and at every turn you're there, trying to strip it away. That story your cousin told isn't bullshit. It's true. Only that assault didn't happen in Texas, did it Zack?"

My cousin looks down and to the side, rolling his eyes as if she's crazy and making things up.

"Roland? Jay?" I call out their names to offer them a chance to stand up for her. They keep their eyes on the ground, but their silence is validation enough.

"Zachery!" My uncle's voice booms over everything else, and my cousin spins on his heels, coming face-to-face with the man who should have been a better role model.

My chest squeezes with guilt I haven't felt until now. What maybe should have been a private moment is now very public. I don't feel as right about any of it as I thought I would, but I don't feel wrong, either.

Hollis stands her ground, not giving my cousin a place to turn so he's forced to face his father. Her own dad calls everyone's attention back to him. I remain in this limbo where I'm paying attention to everything and nothing all at once.

"I think maybe we need to add something to our tryouts this year. An interview," he says, and as I turn to face him, our eyes meet. "One about your character."

I swallow, worried that he's questioning mine after all this. It's so hard to decide what's right, and maybe I was on a crusade. Maybe I was in more than her corner with this; maybe I took up her whole damn room, siphoning the air and taking all the credit.

"Bring it in," Coach says. Everyone scrambles to their feet and moves to form a tight circle around him. Everyone but the three of us.

Leaving Zack alone with his dad, Hollis turns until she faces me. I'm speechless, my face a blank slate, probably the same as hers. I don't know if I let her down or lifted her up, but I do know I want to be a better person. I know she's the reason. Because of her, I'm not as selfish, or I try not to be. I'm less closed off, and more open to criticism and coaching. I'm a better player for sure, but a better human too. I've still got work though.

"One, two, three—Eagles!"

"Hollis." I say her name just as the cheer breaks behind me. She blinks twice, her expression never changing, then moves her focus to the dugout where her gear sits in a pile.

"Hey." I reach out toward her as she moves toward her

things. When she brings her arms in close to avoid my touch, I feel a punch to my gut. I didn't do this right. I fucked this up.

I wallow in my own self-pity until my uncle marches back to his truck, leaving my cousin to swim in his alone. There won't be any lights coming on. Tryouts are done when the sun sets, and with the gray sky looming above, that's a little earlier tonight.

"Jennings." Both Zack and I turn at the sound of our name being called. Coach's form is barely visible in the dwindling light. He's alone, most of the players well on their way to the parking lot. His daughter is in the dugout under the yellow glow of lights that barely work. She looks furious, something I can read from her posture even this far away.

"Both of you," he begins, and we move closer to him.

My heart pounds in my chest, the rush of adrenaline from everything I've done and said, and the fear of being called out for something unexpected. Stronger than my fear of Coach, though, is my crushing dread that I messed things up with Hollis. That I broke her trust and told her secret. I'll run a thousand miles if that's what Coach asks me to do, if it means I might be able to make it up to her. My intent was good. She must know that.

"Sorry, Coach," I say right out of the gate. My cousin doesn't call me a kiss-up this time, and he's probably mad that I apologized first.

"Fix this." Coach wiggles his finger between us then points over his shoulder with his thumb toward Hollis.

"And you." He shifts his position, closing me off so he's

speaking only to Zack. "I want you to look deep inside tonight and assess yourself. You have decisions to make."

Zack swallows loud enough that I hear it.

"Yes, sir," he says.

His eyes shift to me briefly. I can't apologize for giving him his due. He did that all on his own.

"Come ready to throw tomorrow." Coach's eyes square with mine and I nod, uttering the same, "Yes, sir" that my cousin did.

Coach Taylor turns his back on us and heads toward the back of the gym where his office is, whistling toward the dugout to let Hollis know to follow. My cousin leaves me standing there alone, too caught up in his own drama and misplaced rage to stick this out. I take every bit of my punishment, though, from her first steps from the dugout when the lights inside go out to the point where she reaches the walkway that splits in two directions. Hollis will either head toward me or her father's office, and I can't help but feel that the direction she chooses is a commentary on who makes her feel the safest.

I'm not totally surprised when it isn't me. Still, it hurts like hell.

22

HOLLIS

I've already cried my cry. I'm not doing it again. I'm not living it again. I did it and it's done. Every time my dad asks if I have anything he needs to know, though, the damn tears threaten to show their ugly side in the corners of my eyes.

"I need to know if I have to report something." His face is stern, and it's hard not to feel attacked. It isn't fair; I'm not the person who should be getting grilled about this.

"It's handled," I say, leveling him with another blank stare. We take turns blinking at one another as if it's a contest.

I don't know why it's our method, but it is. When I was a kid and did something wrong, my father would look at me, wordlessly, and blink through a long hard stare until I broke under the pressure and admitted to everything. As I got older, I learned the same trick worked on him, only I used it when he told me no for no good reason. Throw in a "Please, Daddy," and the world was mine.

"I hate this world for you. You know that, right?" He finally gives in and doesn't force me to make this into something bigger. Maybe it should be. What Zack did isn't okay, but I don't want to be the poster child. I just want to play baseball. That's it. If my face shows up in the newspaper, I want it to be for an All-Star bid or for some college that's taking a chance on a girl who can catch.

"I'll change it. This world will be just fine when I'm done."

He laughs at my confident response, but it's a sad laugh. It breaks down some of my bravado.

"I might be a little late here, you know," he says, holding up his scoring book filled with charts and notes he made from today's tryout. He flops it down on top of the four others from his assistants.

"I'll help," I say, putting my finger on the spiral binding of one of them. He pulls them away and gives me a sideways glance.

"I know, I know. Coach's daughter can't be involved. No showing favoritism. Just . . . tell me. What did Coach Dixon think of my sixty time?"

My father smirks and a genuine laugh finally slips out from his wind-burned lips.

"I don't have to read it to tell you he said you got a slow jump and need to work on breaking faster."

I pull in my brow, scowling at him.

"*You* said that. And I know." I sigh.

I sit back in the chair on the opposite side of his desk and put a foot up on the corner, near his mug that reads World's Best Coach. I gave him that in Little League and we all signed it. Most of the signatures have worn off, but I love that he still drinks out of it every single day.

"Are you just gonna stare at me while I go through these?" He's slipped on his reading glasses and asks me while glaring over the rims. It's funny to see him old, though he'd be quick to put me in my place.

"Nah," I say, leaning to the side and pulling out my pack of gum. I unwrap a piece and pop it in my mouth, then hold the pack out for him. He shakes his head.

"Suit yourself," I say, pushing it back into my right back pocket then shifting my weight to pull my phone out of my left. I prop my device up on my knee and open the meme app that always makes me laugh. It starts off with a bang with a video of a kitten on top of a record player, spinning.

"I think I'd rather you stare at me than make that sound," my dad says.

I glance up at him and snap my gum.

"What sound?"

He flattens his pencil on his desk and drops his head into his hands, pulling his glasses away so he can pinch the bridge of his nose.

"Sorry." I shrink into my seat and turn the volume down on my phone, then spit my barely broken in gum into the wastebasket at my side.

My father continues to stare at me, and I know it's because he feels guilty that I was somebody's target again. This is exactly what I didn't want. I don't want sympathy, I want change, but that is going to be slow, and probably not fully happen in my lifetime. But if I start something, if I inspire someone—a little version of me? Maybe my great granddaughter will be able to go out for whatever sport she wants and get the respect she deserves.

"You know there's a pretty decent guy hovering outside my door waiting to take you home, right?" My mouth drops because no, I didn't.

I look over my shoulder at the closed door with nothing but a slit window that's dirty and impossible to see through.

"He's texted me twice," my dad admits. He twists his own phone around to show me, pushing it forward on his desk with one finger so I can read it. It feels a little intrusive, but it doesn't stop me.

Coach, I am sorry if I caused problems today. If Hollis is still here, can you tell her I'm outside?

Coach, I'm still outside. Does Hollis need a ride home?

I don't realize I'm grinning until my dad calls me on it, covering the screen with his palm until I look up and feel it sting my face.

"He was trying to do right by you," my father says. He shrugs, then adds, "Be part of that change you want, you know?"

I look down to my hands kneading in my lap and pick at the dry corners of my nails. I know he meant well, and the position I put him in, having to hold in a secret like that, was unfair. It's just that I'm so tired of the fight. Every time, with everything—*a fight.*

"Go on. If you stay here, you're going to get on my nerves."

I meet my dad's stare and it's earnest, and he isn't lying. I will drive him nuts for the next two hours. I'll also spend the time sitting here wondering if Cannon is going to text me, if he's still outside.

"See ya at home?" I lift my bag up over my shoulder.

My dad points at me.

"Promptly home. This is a school night." He puts his glasses back on but lets his glare linger for a second. I snort out a laugh, mostly because it gets under his skin. He just looks down at his work and waves me off.

All of the sureness in my decision fades away the second I step outside. I look to my left and my right, adjusting to the stark darkness outside.

"Cannon?" I whisper his name, testing the sound. The only response is a whistle of wind against my face. I drop my bag to pull out my heavy sweatshirt and pull it on, then tug my bag up on my arm and light my pathway with my phone.

"Cannon?" I call out louder this time, my chest tightening. I'm afraid. I'm scared because I'm a woman alone in the dark. I'm so mad that I have to feel this way, that I'm looking for someone I trust while fearing those I don't. Goddamn Zack for making me feel that way!

When my phone buzzes in my hand, I jump and flatten my back against the wall. I touch my screen to read the message, my pulse skipping for a good reason this time when I see Cannon's name.

Was that you? I'm still here.

I type back *Yes* and walk faster toward the parking lot.

"Hollis?" My name is called from around the building, so I rush toward the sound and round the corner, running into his chest, his arms swallowing me up. I'm crying on impact, and let it happen. It's not a bad cry this time. It's one born from relief, from happiness that he's still here.

"I'm so sorry. I only wanted to help, and—"

I shake my head and drop my bag at our feet, holding his face between my freezing palms so I can kiss him.

"Shut up," I demand. "I know. *I know.*"

As good as his kiss feels, it's his hug that makes a world of difference. Every misfire in my chest rights itself, my breaths even out, and my eyes focus on the soft sweatshirt and hard chest in front of me, around me, holding me.

Cannon is an ally. He is a voice different than mine but up for fighting my battles along with me. He's tender and honest and fearless. He gives me hope, and that's all I ask for. Hope, and the chance to catch for a pitcher like him.

"Let me take you home, Hollis Taylor from Indiana." His soft smile shines back at me. I rub my arm across my eyes to dry the tears and make room for the smile I mean with every bit of my soul.

There will be more to face tomorrow, questions from people who were there, accusations from Cannon's uncle, and poor excuses from Zack. It'll be ugly, and I wanted to spare everyone from that. But all I did was keep the negative for myself, take the abuse, and make myself small. I'm ready to live large again.

I thread my fingers through Cannon's while he hoists my bag up on his shoulder with a heavy groan. Catcher's gear is no joke, and he's used to nothing but a glove. It's about time I let someone else carry the load.

EPILOGUE
CANNON

When we first started this journey, there was snow on the ground. Never a lot, but it was there. Today, it's unseasonably warm—a balmy eighty-five with humidity crawling up and down my ass. How Hollis survives in that gear beats me, but we're literally one out away from going to state.

One.

I'm at eighty-one pitches. That means I can throw this guy eighteen and still be under my cap. God help me if I have to throw more than four, though. My arm is beat.

I'd like more than a one-run lead in my arsenal, especially now that the Henderson team seems to know what to do with my fastball, but I'm glad to have the edge. My dad has always told me that pressure is what makes the man on the mound. Well, if I'm not man enough after throwing up my orange Gatorade behind the dugout before this inning and still climbing back up on this rubber, I don't know what a man is.

"Come on, Can. You got this."

My dad's voice cuts through everyone else's and I manage to block the rest of the noise. We started this inning in the heart of their line-up, and the guy at the plate is the only one to have gotten a hit off me tonight. It was a dinger over the right field fence.

Breathe in through the nose, out through the mouth. Repeat.

My cousin taught me that trick when we were kids. I don't know if there's any truth to it, but he said it controls the heart rate and helps you clear your head. Maybe it's all voodoo bullshit he made up, but in baseball, whatever works is never considered weird. Hell, Hollis has worn the same socks for every game in the division playoffs— unwashed. If we make it to the state championship, her dad is going to make her ride on the roof of the bus, or at least put her socks in cargo.

"Hey!" Her muffled voice carries through her mask and she punches her mitt to get me focused. I wait for her sign, praying it isn't a fastball. My ego can't take another dinger. She gives me the slider sign, and I take another one of those deep breaths before bringing my glove in to my chest and winding up. I miss my mark, but Mr. Eager Homerun Hitter swings and misses.

"That's right, Can! Go right at him!"

This time, it's Zack's voice that breaks through. After all the shit we went through, somehow, we've mended a lot of broken trust. It took an entire season to get to where we are, and we still have a ways to go, but I credit Zack for making the first move. He marched into Coach's office the morning after he sent him home to think and told him to remove him from the potential roster for the season. In the back of his mind, maybe he thought Coach Taylor would go soft and tell him to stay, but he couldn't, not after everything he did. And not after a two-week suspension from school on top of it all.

At this point, baseball isn't healthy for Zack. At least, not competing. It's something he's slowly come to realize, thanks to therapy. That was his second move, an idea of his own. Being a fierce competitor who sometimes gets carried away isn't so bad when you're eight and weigh fifty-seven pounds. When you shave and weigh two-ten? Different story. Zack's anger issues were more than festering, they were exploding, and it'll take him a while to fully scratch the surface and see what's underneath. Competition, though, is a trigger. That much he's learned. But he seems to handle it all right when he's on the coaching side.

I went to Coach Taylor in mid-April, right before playoffs started, and with Hollis's blessing, asked if he could be team manager. Zack missed the comradery so much, and it never seemed fair that Jay and Roland got to skate by but he didn't. Hollis didn't call them out publicly, and neither did Zack. They accepted the free pass, and that's on their consciences. Every time they ask Hollis to forgive them, though, she says, "No." They get a taste of what they deserve.

Zack's worked his way back into some good grace, though I think he will always be held at arm's length by Hollis and her dad. My Uncle Joel was also pretty rocked by the realization that his son was willing to physically intimidate a girl just to get his way on the field. There was a lot of self-reckoning at the start of the season, and my uncle has learned enough over the last few months to know that he can't be here to watch while his son sits inside the dugout with a clipboard. This was never part of the dream.

Breathe in through the nose, out through the mouth. Repeat.

Hollis sets up for another slider and I take her sign, willing my arm to listen to her this time and throw the ball exactly where she wants it. I'm closer, but I still miss my location, and the little piece of the ball that the giant in the batter's box gets goes flying into the night sky and across the road that runs behind the clubhouse, slamming into the metal roof of someone's shed. I can't fathom the dents that must exist up there.

Eighty-three pitches thrown. One more, and I can be done. One more, and this guy goes home. *We* go home. I kiss Hollis. I get that offer from Vandy that I've been holding out for before committing to Cal Tech. Hollis is in Tennessee, at a small D-two that has no idea the bargain they got when they offered her a scholarship. I need to be in Tennessee so I can witness it happen—the moment she changes the world.

I'm no longer able to block out the noise. I can't focus on only my father, or coach, or Zack. It's all chaos ringing in my ears, my mental state too zapped to do more than focus on throwing a ball ninety feet right where Hollis wants it.

I shake my arms out at my sides and lean forward for her sign. She gives me a fastball and I shake her off. She looks down then over to her dad, and I take the time for one more round of voodoo.

Breathe in through the nose, out through the mouth. No time to repeat.

Hollis punches her mitt, and I read into the force she puts behind it. She's gonna call for a fastball, and if I shake her off, she'll call time and come talk to me. I just don't know if I can throw it to this guy.

She gives me the sign and I stare at it for a solid three seconds before giving in with a nod. I don't have faith in my arm, but for some reason, she does. If I've learned anything from four months of throwing to this woman, it's that she knows her shit, and when I don't listen, I get burned.

I bring the ball in and spare a glance at the hitter's eyes. He's squinting, and I'm not sure whether he can't see me or he's so amped with adrenaline that he's narrowed his vision down to nothing but the ball.

Hollis flashes her glove at the outside corner then sets up inside in an attempt to throw him off. I feel for the threads of the ball with my fingers, search for that perfect spot. There's one thread that's a millimeter thicker than the rest. I've located it before, and I swear it gives me an extra mile per hour on release. My index finger finds it and my lip ticks up.

Okay, buddy.

I wind up, trying hard to give nothing away, but grunt when I release the ball. I swear everything gets all movie magic-like the moment the ball leaves my hand. I hear music in my head and the ball seems to travel in slow-motion from my fingertips to Hollis's glove. The rotation is perfect, and my leg rotation is enough to send me down the mound and off to the left. I keep my glove up, ready for the big guy to zip the ball right back at me, and with the swing he's loading, if he does, it will knock out my teeth.

I flinch as his bat passes through the zone. When I hear the smack of the ball against Hollis's leather, I fall to the ground in exhausted disbelief.

The rush of cheering caves in on me as I blink up at the sky, letting my glove fall off my hand and the stupid grin eat up my face. Hollis falls on top of me first, her mask tossed off somewhere along the way.

"That's what I'm talking about!" She's screaming in my ear, and it's glorious. I poke at her sides and she pokes back until more of our teammates pile on. We're suddenly children, wallowing and kicking in the dirt and grass because we won a plastic trophy that will sit in a glass case for fifty years. It's a big-ass plastic trophy, though, and that's worth it.

I finally get to my feet and rush over to my cousin, lifting him in a bear hug as he pounds on my head with excitement.

"Yeah!" He growls as I set him down and we bump chests. Having him here for this, still, despite everything, hits me hard, and I hug him a second time. Tighter.

"I'm so proud of you," he says, his mouth at my ear. "So fucking proud."

And happy tears break free.

His heavy hand pats my back as we rock, and then he hands me off to Coach who is as big a cry baby about this as I am. In fact, a quick look around the celebration and I realize Hollis is the only one of us with dry eyes. So much for stereotypes.

When the division president walks out from the

dugout with our trophy in hand, we settle down, each of us taking a knee despite the fact we want to keep jumping and screaming until our voices are gone.

"Coach Travis Taylor," the man says, holding the trophy on one side while Coach holds the other. Flashes go off for the photo op while parents and students whistle and clap. "On behalf of District Twelve in the great state of Indiana, our congratulations to the Allensville Public Fighting Eagles for winning this season's district championship tournament. Represent us well at State."

Our roar breaks through before he can finish his words. He shakes our coach's hand, and takes a step back so Coach Taylor can hold that pretty award high above his head.

"You did this! Lady, gentlemen." We all laugh because it's maybe the first time he's gotten Hollis's request right.

The moment is amazing all on its own, and would be enough if it ended here. But then something unexpected trumps everything else.

"Hol-lis. Hol-lis. Hol-lis."

Zack starts the chant, clapping with her name, encouraging others to join in. That one-run lead we had came off her bat. She drove in two, and those runs were the only ones we scored all night. I may have thrown well, but even that is thanks to her. This game? This series? It's her win as much as it is ours.

"Hol-lis! Hol-lis! Hol-lis!"

We're all doing it now, clapping loudly and turning her cheeks cherry red. Her dad walks toward her with the trophy in hand and urges her to her feet. She's bashful about it, but I know at her core, she's also eating up the moment. Inside that body lives a tiger.

As soon as she takes the trophy from her dad, our howling becomes deafening. We're on our feet in a second, and Miguel, our shortstop, and I raise Hollis up on our shoulders. I watch his hands because as proud as I am of her, I'm also a jealous boyfriend. I'll take over her full weight and run her ass out into the parking lot if he makes a move.

Miguel keeps his hands in check, though, and Hollis wears a smile that dents her cheeks with dimples so deep I think they may never get erased. Her brother begs for the trophy at her father's side, so we finally let her down and Coach Taylor takes over possession, keeping guard on the prize while everyone alternates taking pictures with it.

The only prize I care about is still in my arms.

"You know the Vandy guy came, right?" She puckers her lips into a controlled smile while I nod, swaying her in my arms while we stand apart from the crowd.

"Uh huh." I'd actually managed to keep that thought under control for that last batter, and it's a good thing I did. If I let that thought enter my domain, I probably would have sailed my first pitch into the dugout.

"I have a good feeling," she says, leaning into me until our foreheads touch.

I let my hands fall to her hips and close my eyes to protect this moment and keep this small space between only us.

"I've had a good feeling since midnight on January first," I say.

"Oh, is that right?" she asks.

"*Mmm*. It is."

"Still, though. Vandy." She lets my dream linger in the air as a wish.

"I have a good feeling, too," I finally admit. "My gut instinct has very little to do with tonight's game, though."

She pulls back enough to show me her quirked brow.

I tuck her hair behind her ear, knowing she'll tie it in a knot the first chance she gets.

"There can be no Hollis Taylor of Tennessee without a Cannon Jennings in the same area code."

My stupid joke earns a beautiful smile, and we seal it with a kiss before joining our family and teammates and friends for what promises to be a long night of celebration. That wish will have to linger a little while longer, but I'm no longer worried about it coming true.

What Hollis says goes, and if it doesn't, she'll bend it to her will.

She's a game-changer.

SERIES EPILOGUE
LUCAS FULLER

Whoever thinks being smart must equate to being good at giving speeches clearly never heard my attempts.

Writing my graduation speech was easy. I knocked that sucker out in forty minutes. It's just one big trope when you think about it. *The future is waiting. It's yours to take. We all will change, yet stay the same . . . blah . . . blah . . . blah.* Saying it in front of six hundred people, however, is a whole different ball game.

And Tory will not quit bagging on me about it.

"Don't forget to take your change, I mean make change, I mean accept change, or I'm changing. I change, you change, we all change! *Weee!*" He's really latched on to the theme, which I blundered and completely blew, forgetting two lines then going back to them later, awkwardly.

I punch his arm hard enough to make him spill a little beer in his lap.

"Hey!"

"You done now?" I glare at him and he brings his mug close to his chest, hugging it with both hands.

"Ch-ch-ch-changes." He gets out one more, but thankfully Abby made it back in time for graduation and is there to smack him on the back of the neck for me.

"Thank you," I say to her, crossing behind her and kissing the top of her head.

It's after hours at Eight Lanes. Well, technically, it's closed. But June still has a key, and her former boss pretty much thinks she walks on water, so we moved the party here. We all chipped in forty bucks to pay for the beer we plan to drink tonight because we don't want to steal. But we do aim to get lit. Hayden and Lola volunteered to play sober, so we'll make it home in decent shape.

I can't believe after tonight, half our crew will be gone. It still doesn't feel real, even though in less than twelve hours, it's happening.

Cannon and Hollis are the first to go, and I think the only reason they're partying it up tonight is because they know they have a thirty-one-hour bus ride to look forward to when they wake up. I love football, but man, there's no sport on the planet I find important enough to ride on a bus for that long. They're going to Cali for a summer baseball league before making that same awful trip back in August so Cannon can report to fall camp for Vanderbilt. It's too bad that Central Metropolitan doesn't get to play Vandy just for one exhibition. I'd love to see those two go head-to-head on the field. June and I plan to go watch a few of their games in Cali, a last-hurrah trip before we pack up and move in together in Boston.

I'm surprised her mom went for it, but when June got accepted at the last minute to Boston College, one of the best ways to cut costs was for the both of us to split a bedroom in a two-bedroom apartment. Our roommates are a gay couple who have lived in the place for two years, and after a few video chats to make sure we all gel, June and I decided they are the same exact personalities as us. Conner is June, for sure, and Dax is me, to the point he and I have already made plans to host the fantasy football draft for the league we're starting in the fall.

I have a damn good feeling about life there—*life with June in general.* But one step at a time. We both come from broken marriages, so taking the long route to forever gets us there all the same.

Lola, Hayden and Naomi are leaving next week for Europe. I guess that's what I get for opting out of my last year of Spanish. They both stuck with it and get to go on an immersion trip to Spain for three weeks. It'll also cancel their language requirement for their undergrad without having to test out of it. I'm going to have to spend my summer on a refresher crash course so I pass when I get to MIT. My brain only has room for so much, and with the math I'm looking to face, language classes are out.

At least Tory and Abby will be around for most of the summer, though I can tell they're anxious to get to Chicago permanently. They've driven there at least six times in the last month for theater auditions, registration, and freaking deep-dish.

I'm a little lost in the nostalgia when June crawls into my lap, but she has a way of bringing me back to the present. She's home, and as I look around at my group of friends, I realize in so many senses of the word, we are all home to one another.

We've taken over one of the pool tables because lighting up the lanes makes this place look way too open. Tonight is all about us, our final time together, and we don't want outsiders busting in.

"Ladies and gents! A toast!" Tory announces.

June hands me a ten spot without looking over her shoulder because I won our bet for who would be the first person to stand on the table. It's always D'Angelo—always *this* D'Angelo.

Properly beered up, we each raise a glass, holding our amber-filled mugs high and proud.

"To ups and downs, and forever friends. Allensville will never look the same without us. In fact, someone might say that this place is going to *change*." I lean my head back and close my eyes while I groan. He is literally *never* going to stop making fun of me.

"Cheers!" June says, doing what she does best by putting the focus on the positive.

"Cheers!" The sound of our collective voices imprints in my mind and I immediately tell myself to hold on to it. To this moment.

We're scattering. It's inevitable. But we'll all still have this place in time. We'll always have *us,* and that was the point of my speech. Change happens regardless of how hard you hold on—to people, to places—and want to keep them the same. But life isn't about the place or the time— it's the friendships. And when you change together with those you love, you can always find your way back.

The End.

ACKNOWLEDGMENTS

It's always bittersweet coming to an end. I have loved every inch of this series. These characters have floated around my imagination, in some form or another, for quite a while. The series was born when I started to realize how these interesting people fit together. These are friends—lifelong-type of friends. I hope you have enjoyed spending time in their lives as much as I have.

These books have also been a wonderful escape for me. I think we can all agree that this year—the *Pandemic* one—has been a load of crap. I could not have gotten to this finish line without the help of a lot of people. This starts first and foremost with my boys. Tim and Carter, you are my air and life. I love you. Tina Scott, I love you and hit the lottery in the mom department. Mariah Dietz and Jennie Marts – thank you for the sprints! Alyson Santos, you genius with words you, thank you for being an amazing critique partner and for working with my weird-ass schedule and process this go-round. My betas, Jen,

TeriLyn and Shelley, you are the masters of my weird-ass process and the fact that you are still willing to open my emails means so much to me! Thank you for every ounce of your time. I'm so grateful. Autumn – you know you complete me. Sometimes, you complete me in places I didn't even realize I was missing things lol! (Autumn keeps me from being a mess.) Michelle Lancaster, my God, woman—you are a talent behind the lens. I have wanted to use one of your photos for a cover for a long time, and I feel like this was that perfect moment. Andy Murray, you were the perfect muse for Cannon's spirit. Thank you both for being YOU!

Lastly, and not even close to least, Brenda Letendre . . . you single-handedly carried my limping self across this finish line. You are more than an editor; you are a true friend. You helped me move life's mountains out of the way to get this book to you and to readers, and I will be forever grateful.

If you liked this book and/or series, please don't be shy about it. I wanna hear. More than that, I would be so grateful if you would tell others. Reviews are life for us authors, but so are things like recommendations in person or on websites, posts on social media, mentions and tags and creative awesome-sauce that readers come up with. The Varsity Series finds the readers it's meant to because of readers like you, because you are the most amazing readers in the entire world. I can't thank you enough for your support. We've come to this finish line, but that means I'm at the starting gates again, and I can't wait to give you more.

XO

Ginger Scott

ALSO BY GINGER SCOTT

The Varsity Series

Varsity Heartbreaker

Varsity Tiebreaker

Varsity Rulebreaker

The Waiting Series

Waiting on the Sidelines

Going Long

The Hail Mary

Like Us Duet

A Boy Like You

A Girl Like Me

The Falling Series

This Is Falling

You And Everything After

The Girl I Was Before

In Your Dreams

The Harper Boys

Wild Reckless

Wicked Restless

Standalone Reads

Cowboy Villain Damsel Duel

Drummer Girl

BRED

Cry Baby

The Hard Count

Memphis

Hold My Breath

Blindness

How We Deal With Gravity

ABOUT THE AUTHOR

Ginger Scott is an Amazon-bestselling and Goodreads Choice and Rita Award-nominated author from Peoria, Arizona. She is the author of several young and new adult romances, including bestsellers Cry Baby, The Hard Count, A Boy Like You, This Is Falling and Wild Reckless.

A sucker for a good romance, Ginger's other passion is sports, and she often blends the two in her stories. When she's not writing, the odds are high that she's somewhere near a baseball diamond, either watching her son swing for the fences or cheering on her favorite baseball team, the Arizona Diamondbacks. Ginger lives in Arizona and is married to her college sweetheart whom she met at ASU (fork 'em, Devils).

FIND GINGER ONLINE: www.littlemisswrite.com

facebook.com/GingerScottAuthor

twitter.com/TheGingerScott

instagram.com/authorgingerscott